For Lin

A RIDDLE of WIZARDS

Ravencroft Hall
Book #2

KAT ROSS

A Riddle of Wizards

ISBN-13: 978-1-957358-25-3 (ebook)
ISBN-13: 978-1-957358-26-0 (paperback)

CONTENTS

1

MIRROR, MIRROR

The secret library at Ravencroft Hall always smelled pleasantly of old parchment, beeswax candles, and hot chocolate. But today I caught a whiff of something sharper.

Something like the earthy, metallic zing of a thunderstorm.

Magic.

I used to like that word. It inspired feelings of wonder and possibility. Fae, of course, and the ancient power of the Wild Wood.

Now I associated it with things going suddenly, badly wrong. Forget an adorable bunny popping out of a hat. I'm talking about those snakes made of springs that fly into your face when you open a tin of mixed nuts.

Lord Ravencroft, the wizard in question, stood before an oval mirror. He held an open spell book and his brow was furrowed in concentration. My oldest friend Layla Deen hovered at his elbow, eyes shiny with hope behind her round glasses.

"Remember," she said, "the second word has a glottal stop. And the final phrase should rise in pitch."

"Understood." Richard's jaw tensed. He looked down at the spell book, then up at the mirror. It reflected a tall man in the prime of life with a shock of black hair, sharp features, and vampire-pale skin. His free hand came up to touch the moonstone amulet at his throat—a nervous habit.

I was nervous, too, though I hid it behind an encouraging smile. Richard was doing his best, and I loved him for it. The problem was that he had no tutor besides Layla (expert on the Fair Folk, yes; wizard, no) and thus was forced to learn magic from books, which is rather like trying to land a jumbo jet by skimming the manual.

Last week, he'd cast a calming spell on the topiary animals to keep them from roaming the estate. Instead, they doubled in size. The water buffalo bowled over the milkman when he delivered the brownies' cream, and the hedgehog—after rampaging merrily through the flowerbeds—curled up to nap on the bonnet of Richard's car, leaving a massive dent.

We'd yet to locate the lions, but there had been sightings, along with several flocks of emotionally traumatized sheep.

Then, just yesterday, during an attempt to repair the Hall's Victorian-era wiring, he'd turned the foyer chandelier into a wasp's nest. The less said about that one, the better.

This comedy of errors had been going on for months, but Richard refused to quit. Stubbornness was one of his best—and worst—qualities.

Now here we were, about to attempt a spell Layla had found in the advanced section of the library, where the books hissed at you and rattled their chains. She was convinced it might work if Richard could only pronounce the archaic pre-Roman dialect it was written in.

Outside the windows, illusory snow swirled through a

stand of fir trees. The fireplace crackled with blazing logs, and a trolley rattled about, offering hot drinks—or brandy if you needed something stronger. I eyed the decanter with longing, but needed to keep my wits in case we had to run for the door in . . . oh, the next thirty seconds or so.

Yet all the chaos would be worth it if the finding spell *did* work this time.

Layla had been a little girl when her father disappeared in the Wild Wood. Arush Deen set off to hunt mushrooms on a fine spring morning and never returned. Everyone assumed he'd been taken by the fae. The wood could be a dangerous place for mortals.

That was twenty-three years ago. I'd given up hope he would ever return, but with Richard's magic . . . Well, we finally had a chance to find out the truth.

Layla handed him her father's watch, a treasured personal item. "Ready?" she asked.

Richard gave a decisive nod. "Ready."

I crossed my fingers behind my back.

He drew a breath and began. The words came out low and measured, each syllable placed with the care of a man crossing a frozen pond. Layla claimed the language was older than Anglo-Saxon, older than Latin, possibly older than anything human. It echoed strangely, as if the room had to make space for it.

Midway through, the candles guttered. The drinks trolley halted abruptly with a rattle of glassware. I rubbed my arms as the air turned icy and the flames in the hearth shrank to blue pinpoints.

The mirror lost its silvery sheen, the glass rippling like water. It seemed to swallow all the light in the room. For a long moment, there was only darkness, and Richard's voice threading through it like a needle pulling silk. Then Layla inhaled sharply.

A face appeared . . . but it was not her father.

Instead, it was a creature with mismatched eyes and hair split down the middle: the left a frosty white, the right an inky black. I recognised him at once. We had met when Richard and I visited the Court of Silver Shadows. The faerie's name was Halfglint, and he was the chamberlain to Lord and Lady Vael.

The view was odd—we were looking up from beneath as he appeared to study his own reflection, one hand raised to touch the lock of silver hair. His knuckles bore scars I hadn't noticed before, a webbing of fine white lines.

Halfglint suddenly stiffened. "Ravencroft?" he demanded, his voice rippling through the glass like a warped LP record. "What the devil are you doing in my washbasin?"

I bit my cheek to stifle a laugh. Richard shot me a brief, worried glance. Halfglint was the last person he wanted to find by accident. If Lord and Lady Vael knew about his lack of control, they might take his power away. And they could do it on a whim, since all mortal magic stemmed from pacts with the fae courts.

The thought sobered me, but Richard came from a long line of dark wizards and quickly found his feet.

"Master Halfglint," he said smoothly. "I apologize if this is an inconvenient time. I wished only to affirm that I will attend the Court of Silver Shadows on the Frost Moon, to dance with the Princess Maeryn until the stars fade, as promised."

Halfglint's eyes—one light, one dark—narrowed to slits. "That you will attend the court is assumed, Ravencroft," he said irritably. "There was no need to affirm it." The faerie's gaze shifted to me. "Katherine Boot," he added with a sly grin that revealed pointy teeth. "The forfeit prize."

A reptilian slither of fear crawled down my back.

"Kitty is no one's *prize*," Richard said coldly.

"Not yet," Halfglint agreed. "Not as long as you keep the bargain. But if you fail to appear at the scheduled hour . . ."

Layla's elbow dug into my ribs. "What's he talking about?" she hissed.

"Later," I whispered back. Halfglint had not taken his eyes off me, and beneath the smirk, I sensed something else. Something serious, though I could not for the life of me say what it was.

"I will appear before Lord and Lady Vael," Richard snapped, "of that you can be certain."

Halfglint inclined his head. He leaned forward, his foxlike face filling the mirror's frame. "I will relay your message, Lord Ravencroft," he said in a faintly mocking tone. "Is there anything else?"

"No," Richard ground out. "That is all." The image faded to his own reflection, dark hair rumpled into a crest from his habit of dragging his hands through it.

The instant Halfglint was gone, Layla rounded on us. "What was that talk of a forfeit?"

"Now, don't get angry." I tried for a placating tone. "I didn't tell you the full story of our excursion to Faerie last year—"

"Well, that's obvious!" She pushed her glasses up on her nose.

"Because I knew you'd be worried," I finished.

"And now I'm *more* worried," Layla shot back. "I suppose you two thought I'd never find out."

Richard and I exchanged a guilty look.

"Out with it," she said. "What exactly did you promise?"

"The bargain itself is fair," I protested. "Richard must appear—"

"On November's Frost Moon and dance with this fae princess," Layla interrupted. "I know *that* part. Tell me about this *forfeit.*"

Richard loosened his collar with a grimace. "I opposed it, Layla, I want you to know that."

"Kitty?" Her fierce gaze swiveled my way. "I suppose you have to be their servant. Just tell me it's not forever."

"It's not forever," I said.

She sniffed. "Thank God for that."

"It's for as long as I live."

Layla threw her hands up. "Did you listen to *anything* I told you? How could you make such a stupid bargain?"

"We had no choice," I retorted. "You weren't there. Lord and Lady Vael refused Richard's first offer to get his magic back." I gently took her slender shoulders. "Everything will be fine as long as Richard keeps to the pact. One dance, once a year. That's all."

"That's all," she muttered. "Next time, tell me the full truth."

"I promise," I said, chastened. "And I'm sorry."

She grunted.

"I'm sorry, too," Richard said. "For not telling you before, and also for the spell. I'm not sure what went wrong."

Layla's expression was neutral, though I could see the disappointment etched around her eyes. "Perhaps nothing went wrong," she said after a moment. "Maybe the spell showed us Halfglint because my father is at the Court of Silver Shadows."

Of course, this had occurred to us already. "I didn't see him among the courtiers," I reminded her, "but perhaps they're holding him elsewhere."

It was possible. The fae were fond of keeping mortals—as servants, as entertainment, as lovers. They bent time strangely, too. A day in their realm might be years in ours, or the reverse.

"I'll try the spell again tomorrow," Richard offered. "I'm not sure I got the pronunciation right. Let me study it some more."

Layla sighed. "It's not your fault." She laid a hand on his arm and added softly, "Thank you for trying."

"Of course," he replied, covering her hand in his own larger one. "And I won't quit until . . . well, until we know one way or another where your father is."

Richard returned the spell book to its shelf and locked it to its neighbors with a delicate silver chain (we had discovered the hard way that unlike regular books, magical books seldom remained where you left them). Layla tossed a black cloth over the mirror, and I tossed back a dram of brandy from the cart. Truth be told, I was still unnerved by Halfglint and the almost covetous way he'd looked at me.

Not that I would mention it to Richard. He had enough on his mind, and I knew he felt responsible for the admittedly terrible bargain we'd struck. Layla was right. We'd made a mess of things.

I consoled myself with the thought that at least we'd managed to save the village and the Wild Wood, and restore Richard's magic. No price was too high for that.

The three of us left the library the way we'd come in, through a tunnel that led to a false fireplace in the billiards room. The hearth swung shut behind us with a gentle click, and we were back in an ordinary world of green baize and rain streaking the windows.

It was October the 9th, but despite the leaden skies, the land did not seem to realise that winter would soon be upon its doorstep. The gardens were still a riot of colour, and the trees held their leaves, without a hint of autumn's gaudy red or gold. Oh, the season would turn eventually, but Little Groating was always a month or two behind the rest of the country.

It was the natural magic of the Wild Wood. A different sort of magic from Richard's spellcraft—old and deep and uncaring of the ways of mortals.

Layla gathered her coat and said goodbye at the front door, heading down the drive toward the village. I watched her go—small, straight-backed, determined—and felt the familiar ache of wanting to fix something that might not be fixable.

I reminded myself that Layla had a good life. She and her wife Briar owned a popular shop called Sugar & Sprites, selling baked goods, books, and faerie-themed souvenirs to the tourists who came to the village on the weekends. Layla's mum owned the local inn—The Dancing Toadstool. I lived there with my Nan, and also worked there as a waitress.

Until last year, I'd made extra money leading faerie walking tours. In fact, that's how I met Richard. We were tramping around his estate and he came running out of Ravencroft Hall with pixies in his hair.

The house had sat empty for two decades so you can imagine my surprise—and the awkwardness that ensued when I was forced to explain what we were doing there. Richard's parents were notorious dark wizards, now banished to Romania, and it was a highlight of my tour to take selfies in front of Ravencroft Hall.

Needless to say, now that there was a wizard in residence again, I no longer brought tourists here. The village had other points of interest—a ruined abbey, an orchard, and the barrows where ancient kings lay buried—but lately, Layla and I had been spending our free time combing through the library for spells to find her father.

"That was nearly a disaster," Richard muttered. "Halfglint! Of all creatures."

"You handled it perfectly. I'm sure he didn't suspect a thing."

I laced my fingers in his as we stood on the front steps under the dripping eaves. After hours cocooned in the library, with its fake snowfall, it was disorienting to see the real world again, warm and smelling of fresh-mown grass. Speaking of which . . .

Across the vast emerald lawn, two shapes bounded toward us with the joy of dogs who'd been let off their leads. I inched closer to Richard as the topiary beasts reached us in a thunder of rustling leaves. The water buffalo skidded to a halt and shook its curling horns. The dragon reared up on its hind legs and pawed the air.

Richard gave a sharp whistle. "Down! Sit!" he laughed, good-naturedly fending them off.

I tried not to flinch as the buffalo snuffled my shoulder. It smelled of boxwood and damp earth.

Richard awkwardly patted the dragon's long snout. "Good lads. Go on, then."

They bounded away, racing each other down the drive.

"At least they seem happy," I remarked.

God only knew where the lions had gone off to. But the hedgehog was back on the bonnet of Richard's Mini, dozing in the massive dent like a cat curled in a basket. He gazed at it and sighed.

"They're protective of this place," he said. "I suppose they'll come in handy if Montfort ever returns."

Ambrose Montfort was a vile man who had tried to buy Ravencroft Hall and convert it into a faerie theme park and zoo. The sale was averted at the last moment—but not before a great deal of trouble that I will not recount in these pages.

"Or his cronies, Blight and Penhaligon," I added. "I doubt they will, though. Not after you turned them into swine."

Richard perked up. "At least that spell went right."

I was about to suggest we go inside for a midafternoon snack—watching him do magic always made me hungry—when I saw a peculiar thing, even for Ravencroft Hall.

A man was galloping up the drive. On an actual white horse. He wore a cloak the colour of midsummer twilight that billowed cinematically behind him. I glanced around to see if there might be a princess nearby who needed saving. Richard uttered a groan—but it was too late to ask why. Sir Lancelot was upon us.

He dismounted gracefully, bent a knee, and clasped my hand in his gloved one. His hood fell back, revealing tanned skin and hair the dark gold of an ancient coin.

"Enchanté," he murmured, brushing his lips against my wrist. "You must be Katherine Boot."

I blinked. "I'm afraid you have me at a disadvantage, good sir."

His smile was dazzling. "I am Adrien Christophe de Questel." He straightened and beamed his goodwill at a stunned-looking Richard. "Greetings, cousin! Are you not glad to see me?"

2

AN UNEXPECTED VISITOR

The Hall's formal drawing room was decorated in silver and black, the Ravencroft colours. Deep armchairs in charcoal damask had been arranged before a fireplace big enough to warm a small cathedral.

I sat across from Adrien, who sprawled in his seat with the casual ease of a man who'd grown up in rooms exactly like this one. Richard's cousin resembled a stained-glass angel—flaxen hair pulled into a ponytail, wide blue eyes, Gallic nose, and an athletic physique. Under the cloak, he wore a dove-grey morning suit that looked quietly expensive.

Next to Adrien, Richard was funereal, all in black with only the glimmer of his moonstone amulet.

Adrien Questel was a wizard, too, and clearly one of accomplishment. I had been wondering what to do with the white horse (the stables hadn't been used in forever, and there certainly was no longer a groom on call) when Adrien murmured some words and the beast vanished, leaving a heap of luggage on the front steps.

Richard looked none too happy at that.

But my curiosity was piqued. He seldom talked about his family, and he'd never mentioned cousins, though I knew his mother's maiden name was Questel, and that she was from France.

The silence had just turned awkward when Nettle bustled in carrying a silver tray. The house brownie's button eyes flicked between Richard and Adrien as she laid out the tea things on the table between us.

"Master Adrien," she said, her scratchy voice conveying fondness. "We are so pleased that you've come to call. It's been an age. I made your favourite—lemon curd tarts with blackberry jam."

"Nettle, you magnificent creature!" Adrien exclaimed. "Your memory is as impeccable as your pastry."

The brownie ducked her head, grey-tufted brows lifting with pleasure. "Will there be anything else?"

"No, thank you, Nettle," Richard replied stiffly.

Adrien watched her retreat, then turned his high-beam smile on us.

"The last time I saw you," Adrien said to Richard, helping himself to a tart, "you dared me to a race down to the pond. Somehow, you neglected to mention the child-eating hag that dwelt there. If my reflexes were not so quick, I wouldn't be sitting here today." He took a bite of the tart and sighed in contentment.

"Bah, Nelly is harmless," Richard declared, which we both knew to be patently untrue. "Besides, I let you win, didn't I?"

Adrien laughed. There was warmth in it, but something else too—a glint, like light off a blade. These two had history, and it was the kind that involved both affection and score-keeping. "You were a ruthless eight-year-old," he said, devouring the rest of the tart.

"And you were an insufferable six-year-old," Richard replied.

"Tea, Miss Boot?" Adrien inquired, lifting the pot.

"Call me Kitty. And yes, thank you. Milk, please." I leaned forward to snag a tart before Adrien ate them all, then accepted the cup.

"Tea, cousin?"

"No," Richard said. "Thank you."

"Do you remember that Christmas at Villa du Soleil?" Adrien asked, eyes twinkling. "We were playing hide and seek in the wine cellar, and I found that bottle of crème de cassis."

"And you convinced me to open it," Richard shook his head, smiling a bit despite himself. "It was a Mouton Rothschild. Worth what? Six hundred pounds?"

"Uncle Ransom turned the most terrifying shade of puce when he found us drunk," Adrien agreed cheerfully. "Worth every moment of the punishment." He grinned at me. "You should have seen my cousin as a boy, Kitty. Just as terribly serious as his father."

I'm sure Adrien meant it as gentle ribbing, but any mention of Richard's parents tended to throw a damper on things. Richard's smile faded.

"So," he said with a touch of impatience. "To what do I owe this unexpected visit?"

Adrien's smile didn't waver. "As your closest relations, we have certain obligations regarding your welfare. And your responsibilities," he added pointedly.

I winced. It was precisely the wrong approach.

Richard's expression grew cool. "I'm thirty. Don't you think it's a bit late to turn up and poke into my affairs?"

Adrien held his palms up. "That's not what I'm trying to do—"

"Isn't it? I might ask why, as *my closest relations*, you never intervened when my parents were exiled? When I was sent off to live with the Earl of Kilmarnock, and then to boarding school in Scotland? It's been twenty years!" Richard leaned forward. "Where were you, Adrien?" he asked in a low voice that couldn't mask the pain.

Adrien's sunny facade collapsed. He looked remorseful. "My parents tried," he said after a moment, bitterness edging his tone. "Repeatedly. They petitioned the English authorities, argued that blood should remain with blood. But the queen was insistent. She wanted you far from your family's influence, raised by someone loyal to the crown. That earl was chosen precisely because he despised magic."

"I'm well aware," Richard said tightly. He vented a breath. "Though not about the first part."

Adrien looked puzzled. "We all wrote you letters. Dozens. Did you not get them?"

Richard shook his head. "I thought you'd forgotten about me."

Adrien tossed the remains of his tart aside in disgust. "Mon dieu. The man probably burned them."

There was a pause, but it wasn't quite so brittle.

"How did you know I'd returned to Ravencroft Hall?" Richard asked at last.

"Word spreads," Adrien replied. He sprang to his feet and paced to the fireplace. "I am here because the Riddle approaches. You must prepare for it, cousin, and I will help you do so."

Richard merely stared at him, aloof and inscrutable once more. I got the impression that he knew what this Riddle was, but the prospect wasn't appealing.

"What's a Riddle?" I asked. "Some new test by the fae?"

Adrien shook his head. "It is the annual gathering of all

the wizards in Western Europe. Every house and bloodline all under the roof of one grand castle in the Alps."

"Ah." I glanced warily at Richard, whose arms were folded in a protective gesture. "And what happens at this Riddle?"

"It's part ceremony, part—how would you say?—diplomatic summit." Adrien turned back to Richard. "Now that you've claimed the Ravencroft magic, you must attend."

"I'm afraid I'm far too busy," Richard said flatly. "Please convey my regrets."

Adrien's brows lifted. "It's not an invitation, cousin. To refuse would be taken as an insult at best. At worst . . ." He paused. "Well, the other families will assume you're plotting against them."

"That's absurd."

"Is it? Your parents have been gone for twenty years, but many still believe them guilty of scheming against the Crown—"

"Don't you?" Richard interrupted. Beneath his reserve, I sensed a desperate hope.

"Of course not!" Adrien exclaimed, outrage in his voice. "They would never have done such a thing willingly. My father is certain they were framed, though he does not know who was behind it."

A muscle ticked in Richard's jaw. I knew how it troubled him to have the Ravencroft name stained with treason. At boarding school, he'd been ruthlessly bullied by the other boys. And his parents had never answered any of his letters—although now I wondered if the horrible earl hadn't intercepted those too.

"Have you heard from them?" Richard asked quietly.

"No." Adrien frowned. "Haven't you?"

"We are estranged."

Adrien's face fell. "I'm sorry, I didn't realise."

"It's fine." Richard sat back and crossed his long legs. "It's true that I have claimed my magic." He glanced at me. "But I plan to lead a peaceful life in the country. I want nothing to do with wizard intrigues." His tone hardened. "And I am not a curiosity to be gawked at."

"Certainly not," Adrien replied reasonably. "But you *are* one of us. The other families will not let you hide in your manor forever."

"Let me?" He bristled. "They have no say in the matter."

Adrien sighed. "I'm not here to command you. My parents are delighted you claimed your inheritance, and we all care deeply about your future. It's only a few days, cousin. You will shake some hands, attend the sessions. *C'est du gâteau*. A piece of cake, as you English say. But they must see your face. Know that you are a force to be reckoned with. Every prominent wizard in Western Europe will be at the Riddle."

"I don't care what they think of me," Richard said dismissively.

"And he has responsibilities here," I added, hurrying to defend him. "Richard is our village doctor."

Adrien barked a laugh. "A wizard with a medical practice? I have not heard of such a thing before, although . . . why not? Our great-uncle Bertrand owned a racecourse." His voice lowered. "Though I think he cheated on the bets."

Richard's brows drew down. "I'm serious about the patients under my care, and I don't care to discuss the matter further."

Oh, how well I knew that tone! Once his mind was set, you'd have better luck convincing the topiary dragon to take up knitting than changing his opinion.

Adrien seemed to recognise this. He shrugged, helping

himself to another pastry. "Very well. I delivered the message."

The abrupt forfeit struck me as suspicious. Silence settled over the room. Richard appeared fascinated by the rain pelting the windows.

"I don't suppose," Adrien added casually, "that I might impose on your hospitality for a while? I can hardly return home and tell my mother I've failed to convince you. She'll have me translating ancient grimoires for a month as punishment."

Richard's gaze narrowed, but then he sighed. "Of course you can stay. The Hall has more bedrooms than I know what to do with."

"Excellent!" Adrien slapped his thigh. "I've missed this draughty old pile."

"Nettle will see to your needs," Richard said, standing. "But you'll have to excuse me. I have patient rounds to make in the village."

"Of course, of course." He winked. "Don't let me keep you from your duties."

I stood as well. "It's been lovely to meet you, but I'll catch a ride with Richard. I'm helping out with dinner at the Dancing Toadstool."

Adrien's face lit up. "Ah, the local inn! I look forward to visiting. We were never allowed as children."

"You'd be welcome anytime," I said, meaning it despite the complications his arrival seemed to herald.

Adrien pressed my hand between both of his. "Kitty, you have brought light to this dark and dreary place." He cast a mischievous glance at Richard. "Not to mention its dour master."

We left him in Nettle's capable hands, the brownie chattering about which rooms would suit him best. Richard grabbed his black doctor's bag and we walked to his car in the drizzle.

"Shoo," he told the hedgehog, giving it a prod. "Go nap in the kennels."

It was curled into a ball and looked like a large shrub that had been inexplicably dropped on the car's bonnet. With a creak of branches, the hedgehog untucked its pointy snout, gave a small squeak of protest, and ambled away.

Richard eyed the dent. "I suppose I ought to do something about that."

"Why bother? It'll just make another one."

"I suppose you're right. At least the engine still runs." He went around to open my door. They had old-fashioned manners, these wizards, which I didn't mind at all.

"You needn't explain yourself," I said as Richard slid behind the wheel.

His dark eyes searched my face. "I don't, eh?"

"You care for Adrien," I said. "He's family. But you don't want to face the other wizards until you've mastered your power."

He stared through the windscreen. "I'm thirty years old, yet I barely have the control of a child."

"It will come in time. But you were brave enough to start over. Most people never do that once in their lives, let alone twice."

Richard turned to me, then leaned over and gave me a soft, lingering kiss that sent warmth down to my toes. "How do you always know just what to say, Kitty?"

"It's a gift." I smiled. "Now we'd best be off, Dr. Ravencroft, or I'll be late for my shift."

He started the engine, and we drove in silence down the beech-lined drive to Little Groating. I knew he was mulling over everything Adrien had said. Richard might be stubborn, but he wasn't a fool, and this Riddle was no trifling matter. If only Adrien had waited to come until next year! This life was still very new to Richard, and pressure was the last thing he needed.

The sight of the Dancing Toadstool, with smoke drifting from its crooked chimney and mullioned windows spilling yellow light, lifted my spirits. Richard stopped the car in front.

"Do as you please," I told him firmly. "I'm proud of you. You have nothing to prove to anyone."

He looked grave. "I fear that isn't entirely true, but I love you for saying it."

I watched him drive away, the car disappearing around the bend toward the surgery he had taken over from Dr. Singer. We both knew cousin Adrien would not be put off so easily. The Riddle, whatever it meant, was coming for Richard whether he was ready or not.

But that was a worry for tomorrow. Tonight, there were pies to plate and pints to pull, and in the snug kitchen behind the bar, friends who would listen to my stories, no matter how strange they got.

3

THE OAK AND THE DRYAD

After Richard drove away, I stood for a moment, breathing in the familiar scents of home—woodsmoke, primroses, and the sweet aroma of curry wafting from an open window.

The incessant rain had paused and I still had a few minutes before supper, so I headed around the side of the inn, past the herb garden with its rows of thyme and rosemary, toward the meadow where a special oak tree had taken root.

The path behind the inn wound through tall grass and wildflowers. Butterflies drifted between purple thistles, and somewhere nearby, a thrush was singing its heart out. My leggings quickly turned damp.

The oak stood alone in the centre of the meadow. Last winter, it had been nothing but an acorn in my palm—a gift from my friend Nyx, a dryad who lived in the Wild Wood. Now, it stood ten feet high, thick with luxurious growth. A red squirrel darted along one of the branches, scolding me with a rapid-fire series of chirps.

"I'm only visiting," I assured it, which did nothing to soothe its temper.

I pressed my palm against the oak's trunk. The bark felt warm and alive under my hand. This was no ordinary tree. It was the offspring of an ancient faerie oak, planted in soil that lay on the boundary between our world and the Otherworld. I'd felt its magic growing stronger each time I visited.

A breeze stirred the oak's leaves and something flickered at the corner of my vision. The brief impression of a small, dark face peering from behind the trunk.

"Hello," I said softly.

No response came. The young dryad who had claimed this tree was shy—more so than Nyx, who had become a friend. I never caught more than an occasional glimpse. Some things needed time and patience.

"You're doing a fine job," I said. "Your tree is very strong and straight."

The squirrel scolded again, more insistently.

"Yes, I'm leaving now," I conceded, backing away. "Some creatures have no manners," I added in a stage whisper. This time, a tiny, bell-like laugh answered me.

Satisfied that the child of Nyx's oak was flourishing, I hurried to the inn. Dark clouds mounded over the wood, and I quickened my pace, slipping through the door as the first raindrops dashed against the flagstone walk.

The Dancing Toadstool's common room was quiet in the lull before the dinner hour. It was midweek in the off-season and we only had a few guests staying anyway—an older couple celebrating their anniversary and three Finnish backpackers in their twenties who were tall, blond, and very polite.

A fire crackled in the hearth, casting a glow over worn flagstones and age-dark beams that had sheltered travelers since the inn had been a hostel for the nearby monastery. We had our own house brownie, Quince, but he only came out at night.

In a pair of armchairs drawn close to the flames sat my Nan and Dr. Singer, their heads tilted toward each other, both dozing. Barbarossa, the inn's aged black cat, curled at their feet. Nan looked happy, her ninety-two years softened by the firelight. Dr. Singer's hand rested near hers on the arm of his chair, their fingers not quite touching but existing in each other's orbit.

They'd been married less than a year, but had settled into each other's lives with the comfortable ease of old books finding their places on a familiar shelf.

Not wanting to disturb them, I tiptoed past toward the kitchen, where the clatter of pots and the murmur of voices promised more active company.

Mrs. Deen stood at the stove, stirring a pot of something that smelled of cinnamon and cardamom. Layla sat at the scrubbed wooden table, her laptop open before her, while Briar piled steaming circles of naan bread into cloth-wrapped baskets. They closed Sugar & Sprites at four on weekdays and came over to the inn to help with supper.

"There you are," Briar said with a smile, glancing at the drops pattering against the window. "And you just beat the rain." She was a sturdy woman with strong arms from kneading and stirring, lots of freckles, and red-gold hair that made her look like a Highlands lass, though she was actually an American from Vermont.

"I checked on our baby oak," I said, hanging my wet macintosh on a peg by the door. "It's thriving—already looks a decade old."

Mrs. Deen smiled. She wore her thick dark hair pulled into a bun and looked like an older version of Layla, with large eyes and an elfin chin. "Magic follows its own time," she said, her voice carrying the musical lilt of her Sri Lankan homeland. "Here, taste." She held out a spoon of amber liquid, which I sipped.

"Perfect," I said, the spices blooming on my tongue. "Ceylon cinnamon?"

She nodded, pleased. "For the rain. It warms the spirit."

"Speaking of spirits," I said, pulling up a stool beside Layla, "we had a visitor after you left."

Layla's fingers paused over her laptop. "Oh?"

"Richard's cousin from France—Adrien Questel. Rode in on a white steed like something from a storybook, all golden hair and charm."

Briar's ginger eyebrows rose. "Sounds dashing."

I laughed and began to gather cutlery for the sideboard. "Yes, and he plays the role for all its worth."

"A friendly visit, then?" Mrs. Deen asked.

I wiggled a hand to convey complications. "He's come to deliver a summons to something called a Riddle. A gathering of wizard families that happens every year."

Layla perked up. "I've heard of it, but almost nothing is known about it. Wizards are so secretive. Is Richard going?"

"He refused, but his cousin is determined to change his mind. He claims the other wizards would take it as a threat if he stays away."

Layla snorted. "Everything's political with them, isn't it?"

"Poor Lord Ravencroft," Mrs. Deen said, adding a pinch of salt to the pot. "Why can't they just let him be?"

"That's exactly what I said!" I exclaimed, grabbing a pile of cloth napkins. "Well, I didn't actually say it. Adrien was trying to be charming, and I didn't want to seem rude, but—"

"Rude and impertinent!" a voice screeched from behind me. "Cap'n said thirty lashes for the lot of ye!"

Sir Francis Drake, Nan's outspoken grey parrot, sailed through the kitchen door and alit on the windowsill. He was followed by Nan herself, Dr. Singer at her elbow. She was still spry, and looked dashing in her red velvet smoking jacket, her white hair arranged in perfect finger waves.

"Who is charming?" she demanded. "And why didn't you invite them for supper, Kitty?"

"Richard's cousin just arrived from France," I explained. "A wizard named Adrien de Questel."

"Ah, the Questels." She nodded sagely. "That would be Desdemona Ravencroft's kin. From somewhere near Cannes, I believe." Her eyes misted as they did so often these days. "I spent a summer on the Riviera with a Bohemian count once. Handsome but boring. He knew seventeen ways to prepare escarole."

Dr. Singer chuckled. "Now, love, you promised not to make me jealous of your former admirers."

"Pish," she waved a hand, setting her bracelets to jangling "You're the only dandy for me now."

Mrs. Deen smiled at their banter. "Dinner is almost ready. Kitty, would you take this out?"

She handed me tureens of rice and curry, which I carried to the common room. The Finns were already hovering at the buffet and thanked me in perfect English as they heaped their plates high. I made sure the pitcher of ice water was full, pulled them a couple of pints, and added Briar's naan to the table and an arrangement of fresh fruit.

Once the guests were settled with their meals, I joined my own family—blood and found—in the inn's small private dining room. Barbarossa commanded his usual position under the table, tail curled around Mrs. Deen's ankle.

Layla lit candles in silver holders while Briar passed around Nan's mismatched china, collected during her sailing adventures. Soon we were all digging into Mrs. Deen's incomparable cooking and a fresh salad from the garden. Damp fog pressed against the windows, making the room feel even cozier.

"So, this Riddle business," Nan said, gesturing with a fork. "What exactly is it?"

I tried to recall the exact words. "Adrien said it was both ceremonial and some kind of diplomatic summit." I helped myself to tamarind chutney. "But he was rather vague. Layla?"

She was the resident expert on all things magical. But Layla only shook her head. "Like I said, wizards are secretive, and almost nothing has been published about it."

For the rest of the meal, they speculated about what might await Richard if he were roped into it. Layla suggested magical duels, while Briar bet it would involve silly hats and odd rituals, like a Freemasons' convention.

It was all lighthearted. They cared for Richard, too, and had welcomed him like a long-lost son. Yet they didn't know him as I did, or understand how deep the scars of his parents' abandonment ran. Not to mention that he was a man accustomed to being highly competent in his chosen profession of medicine, and did not take well to being a novice again.

I felt a bit guilty gossiping behind his back and was relieved when the topic changed and Layla made a toast to Briar, whose new savoury samosas had sold out at Sugar & Sprites in one hour that morning. We all raised our glasses, at which point Sir Francis Drake woke up from his perch and screamed hoarsely, "For God's sake, don't trust the cup!"

In addition to anarchist pirates, Sir Francis had been owned by a German countess accused—although never convicted—of poisoning her lovers.

"Poor dear, he has trust issues about beverages," Briar said, offering the bird a grape.

Sir Francis eyed the grape, then muttered, "Test it on the valet," before swallowing it whole.

"I think Richard should go," Layla said, as she gathered up the dirty plates. "He needs to connect with his heritage, doesn't he? Learn more about his powers?"

Mrs. Deen nodded. "Sometimes we must look back to move forward. My father always said this."

"And what if the other wizards are plotting against him?" I countered, voicing a concern that had been nagging at me. "Richard's parents were accused of treason, after all. Adrien implied there was bad blood."

"All the more reason for him to face them directly," Nan said. "Hiding never solved anything."

"Um, he doesn't want to go," Briar reminded her. "And maybe he's right. He's not ready."

I shot her a grateful look, and she squeezed my hand.

"Speaking of Richard," Mrs. Deen said, "Layla told me you tried another finding spell today." Her dark eyes held disappointment, and my heart twisted.

"It didn't work as we hoped," I agreed. "Instead of showing us Mr. Deen, it connected to someone at the Court of Silver Shadows—Halfglint."

"Through his washbasin," Layla added, which earned a surprised laugh from Dr. Singer.

"Richard thinks he mispronounced part of the spell," Layla said. "He's going to try again."

"There's no rush, dears," Mrs. Deen said firmly. "It's been more than twenty years."

The conversation drifted to other topics—the summer fae festival that needed volunteers, Mrs. Greenwald's prize-winning roses that had mysteriously changed colour overnight (suspected gnome mischief), and Briar's plans to add a new line of sourdough.

Yet as I returned to the common room and cleared away the buffet, my thoughts kept returning to Layla's father. Even if we found him alive, would he recognise his wife and daughter? I had never heard of a mortal coming back from Faerie after so long—not with their mind intact.

A chill crept over me, but I decided that I would believe in miracles until proven otherwise. Nan always said it was better to face disappointment, no matter how bitter it might be, than never to have hope at all.

4

THIS DREARY ENGLISH GLOOM

Morning arrived with the ever-present rain drumming on the roof of my garret room on the inn's top floor. Downstairs, the warm smell of Mrs. Deen's cardamom porridge drifted through the common room.

I was wiping down tables when Richard ducked through the door, wearing a harried expression.

"Coffee?" I offered.

"God, yes, please." He set his black doctor's bag by the door and shrugged out of his overcoat. "Strong, if you have it."

I fetched a cup from the kitchen and a bowl of porridge studded with dates and honey. He took a table near the window, shoulders hunched, and wrapped both hands around the cup as though it were a lifeline. Droplets streaked the glass, transforming the village green into an impressionist painting.

"Rough night?" I asked.

He gave a mirthless chuckle. "I don't suppose you have an extra room to let?"

"That bad?"

Richard raked a hand through his damp hair. "Adrien has made himself entirely at home. I don't think he ever intends to leave! He has the kitchen staff churning out a steady stream of crepes. And he's rearranged all my closets 'for better feng shui.'"

I laughed. "Your cousin is amusing, you must admit."

"Exhausting, more like it," Richard countered. A faint Scottish burr clipped the words. He'd acquired it at boarding school, and it only came out when he was in a foul humour. "Hasn't changed since we were children. He keeps badgering me about the blasted Riddle and I have rounds to make. Mr. Hargreaves is having another gout attack, and the Finch twins are covered in a mysterious rash."

He gulped the coffee and brightened as caffeine worked its modest magic. "I was hoping to try the finding spell again this afternoon. But what are we to do about Adrien? You can be sure he'll poke his nose in."

An idea struck me. "I'll bring Layla and Briar up to the Hall to keep him occupied. They're both dying to meet him."

Hope kindled in Richard's eyes. "Would you? That would be . . . God, that would be perfect."

"Consider it managed," I said. "Though I should warn you, Briar will definitely ask embarrassing questions about your childhood."

Richard laughed. "I can live with that." He lowered his voice, though the common room was empty except for Barbarossa, who watched us with slitted yellow eyes. "There's just one thing—please don't let on to Adrien that I'm struggling. It's hard enough without him knowing I can barely manage an elementary finding spell."

The vulnerability in his voice tugged at my heart. I remembered how hard it had been for Richard to accept his heritage, how long he'd fought against it. Now he was trying to master magic Adrien had probably learned when he was a teenager.

"I won't breathe a word," I promised. "And I'll swear Layla and Briar to secrecy too."

Relief softened his sharp features. He stood, bending to kiss me. "You're a lifesaver, Kitty."

After Richard left, I finished up a few chores around the inn. Then I pulled on my macintosh and grabbed an umbrella. The rain had settled into a steady, soaking downpour, transforming the High Street into a network of puddles and rivulets. I splashed up the hill to Sugar & Sprites, the bell above the door jingling merrily as I entered.

The shop was toasty and smelled divine, with Briar's pastries displayed on one side and Layla's carefully curated selection of books—fiction and non-fiction—and faerie-themed souvenirs on the other.

Sean Davies manned the register, his broad chest filling out his apron as he wrapped a parcel for Mrs. Greenwald. Layla had hired him to help out since she was spending so much time researching spells. I really liked Sean. We'd all gone to school together, and he could be relied on in a pinch.

"Morning, Kitty." He gave me a gap-toothed smile. "Filthy weather, innit?"

"Biblical," I agreed, shaking water from my umbrella.

Mrs. Greenwald tucked her package under her arm. We exchanged a friendly nod as I pushed through the swinging door into the kitchen, where Briar was sliding a tray of golden eclairs onto a cooling rack.

"Perfect timing," she said. "Try one." An éclair was thrust into my hand before I could protest. "A hint of orange blossom water in the filling."

I had vowed to cut back on Briar's treats after the waistband of my favourite leggings became uncomfortably tight, but . . . just this once.

"It's divine," I said, licking chocolate from my fingers. "Is Layla around? I have a proposition for you both."

"Tell me it's something fun," Layla called, emerging from the storeroom with a clipboard. "I desperately need a break from inventory."

"Richard's cousin is up at the Hall, and Richard needed to make his rounds in the village. I offered to bring you both up to keep Adrien entertained for a few hours."

Briar's blue eyes lit up. "The mysterious French cousin? I'm in."

"Me too," Layla said. "I have a thousand questions about this Riddle. Sean can mind the shop."

"Brilliant," I said. "But there's one condition—Richard asked that we not mention he's having trouble mastering his magic."

"Mum's the word," Briar promised, untying her flour-dusted apron.

Layla nodded agreement and we armed ourselves with umbrellas—hers had faeries, of course, Briar's was bright yellow with red polka dots, mine was black and bent from the wind into a bat-like shape.

We soon left the village behind and took a path that wound through the fields toward Ravencroft Hall. The Wild Wood rose dense and green to our right. From somewhere in its depths came a low, guttural cough that made my neck prickle.

Briar clutched my sleeve. "What was that?"

"Just the lions," I said.

She stared at me for a long moment, blue eyes wide. "Did you say *lions*?"

"Not real ones. Hedge ones. They like to roam."

She scanned the edge of the forest. Mist drifted low through the trees. "Is that all they do? Roam?"

"She's asking if they eat people, like Nelly Longarms," Layla said.

"Certainly not!" I replied. "And besides which, even if they tried—which I doubt they would, mind you—but even if they did, they don't have stomachs."

"No digestive systems," Layla mused. "That's reassuring."

"Or teeth," I added. "Just . . . sort of twiggy things."

Briar splashed through a puddle. "I guess it would be like getting stuck in a hedgerow. And then you could claw your way out." She mimed this with her free hand.

"Exactly right," I said heartily. "None the worse for wear!"

She seemed satisfied with this answer, but the truth is that I had never encountered the lions without Richard. The topiary beasts regarded him as their master, and they'd never harmed anyone. Not even those sheep I mentioned earlier, though the poor things had gotten quite a scare.

But I was still relieved when we topped a rise and saw Ravencroft Hall, a grand brick manor with towers and gables and a grey slate roof. We reached the boundary of the estate a few minutes later, collectively shuddering as we passed the pair of stone gargoyles who guarded the entrance—a mild curse cast by some Ravencroft ancestor to discourage trespassers.

"Can't Richard do something about that?" Briar wondered. "I almost wet my pants every time."

"*Almost* is better than the alternative," I said. "Which I've witnessed on occasion."

Layla snickered. She knew all my walking tour stories.

"You're right though," I told Briar. "Richard's working up to it. But if he got the counter-spell wrong . . ."

Briar nodded sagely. "The curse might get even worse.

Like the gargoyles might flap around snatching infants from cradles."

"Or small dogs," Layla put in. "Like the flying monkeys from *The Wizard of Oz.*"

"Those terrified me as a kid," I admitted.

"You and everyone else," Briar said.

Nettle opened the heavy oak door before we could knock. The brownie wrung her small hands, button eyes shiny with distress as she ushered us inside.

"Oh, Miss Boot, thank goodness you've come," she whispered, taking our dripping umbrellas. "Master Questel has been locked in the music room since last night. Won't touch a morsel of food or drink."

"Is he ill?" Layla asked, peeling off her wet coat.

"I do not know." Nettle grey brows drooped. "He will not speak to me."

"I'm sure he's simply bored," I assured her. "We've come to keep him company until Richard returns."

"Very good." Nettle sighed. "This way."

We followed her up the grand staircase. The music room was in the east wing, its double doors inlaid with mother-of-pearl patterns in the shape of musical notes. As we approached, I heard a violin playing something mournful in a minor key.

Nettle knocked. There was no answer. She pushed the doors open and sweat instantly coated my face. The fireplace was heaped with logs, flames roaring up the chimney with such ferocity I half expected to see the stones glowing red. The violin hovered in midair, bow moving across the strings with no hand to guide it.

Adrien lay stretched out on the Persian carpet, one arm flung across his face in a pose of exquisite suffering. His white linen shirt was open at the collar, his golden hair fanned out on the rug. He looked cool and elegant, as though he'd found the one comfortable spot in purgatory.

"Leave me, Nettle," he muttered in desolate tones. "I told you, I do not wish to be disturbed."

"Er, hullo, Adrien," I ventured.

He cracked an eye, saw us standing there, and leapt to his feet. "Demoiselles!" he said, sketching a bow. "Please forgive me, but I am frozen to my very marrow in this gloomy realm." He gave a dramatic shudder. "At my family's villa on the Côte d'Azur, the sun actually shows his face for more than three minutes."

"You seem to be making do." I glanced at the raging inferno and blotted sweat from my brow.

Adrien gestured at the violin and the melancholy air cut off with a squeak. "I've cast a cantrip to improve the weather, but these things take time. Until then, we must endure." He crossed the room with a bouncy energy. Adrien reminded me of a bizarre cross between Eeyore and Tigger. "You must be Miss Deen and Miss Godwin," he exclaimed, blue eyes crinkling at the corners. "My cousin mentioned a bookshop with fairy lore."

"It's half bakery, half bookshop," Briar clarified. "I handle the baking, Layla handles the books."

"A marriage of both mind and spirit. How perfect!" He gestured for us to sit and, with a casual flick of his wrist, sent the hovering violin to its stand in the corner. "I fear I am accustomed to the Mediterranean sunshine. Like a hothouse flower, I wither in this dreary English gloom. But I cannot return until I've convinced my cousin to attend the Riddle."

I shared a glance with Layla. "It sounds fascinating," she said in a conspiratorial tone. "What happens at this Riddle?"

Adrien leaned against the mantel, heedless of the roaring flames at his rear. "We all affirm an ancient pact that none of us shall meddle in each other's affairs—particularly the fae courts we are bound to."

"Well, that sounds admirable," Layla said. "But surely there's more to it than that."

"Indeed. The Riddle is a place to settle old grudges—and nurse new ones. To share information about spellcraft and forge alliances through marriage. There are nine Venerable Bloodlines and countless cadet branches. They intermingle to a shocking degree. Wizards are obsessed with blood, Layla, since that is what keeps their magic strong. It is quite tedious, if I'm being honest."

She opened her mouth—no doubt to ask another question—but Adrien neatly headed her off. "You must tell me everything about Little Groating. Richard is hopeless at gossip." He pronounced it *Ree-shard*. "I know nothing except that the village has an inn, a bakery, and a doctor who works too hard."

Briar laughed. "That's about the size of it. Little Groating is a quiet place, which is why we like it."

"You are an American, yes?"

She nodded. "I came to visit a few years ago and never left."

He smiled. "True love. You know, I have fond memories of coming to the Hall for weekend parties. On rainy days, we would play cards. What do you say?"

"Layla is a shark," I warned him. "She beats me at everything."

Briar cast me a sympathetic look. She knew this was true.

"Are we playing for money?" Layla asked, removing her glasses to defog the lenses. Behind her squint, I could see steel traps being carefully baited.

"I wish!" Adrien turned out the pockets of his trousers

and made a sad face. "But alas, I have not a farthing to my name. For the fun of it?"

Layla gave a disgruntled nod. He produced a beautiful vintage deck with peacocks and attempted to teach us a game called Barbu that involved insanely complicated rules. Of course, Layla grasped them immediately. Briar, good-natured as she was, muddled along, as did I.

Surprise, surprise, cousin Adrien turned out to be a shark, too. Unlike Layla, though, who could have held her own with the high-rollers of Monte Carlo, he was exuberant when he won, gracious when he lost, and inclined to tell stories about his family's estate on the French Riviera.

"The Villa du Soleil has been in the Questel family for four hundred years," he said, discarding a queen. "It is on the Île Sainte-Marguerite."

Layla played a heart and Adrien murmured approval. I hadn't a clue what was going on and threw down cards at random.

"Sainte-Marguerite," she repeated. "I've heard that name."

He grinned. "It's near Cannes. But the island is most famous for Fort Royal—the prison where they held the Man in the Iron Mask."

"Oh!" I said. "Like the Dumas novel."

"Precisely." Adrien took a trick and winced. Apparently, taking tricks was bad. "The prisoner's name remains unknown to this day."

"Someone who offended the French king," Layla said dryly.

"Or threatened his rule," Briar added. "I was a history minor in college. Louis the fourteenth, right? I seem to remember someone saying it might have been his illegitimate older brother."

"That is one theory," Adrien agreed. "But at least the part

about the iron mask was exaggerated. It was made of black velvet, and they did not make him wear it all the time. Mon dieu, that iron mask gave me nightmares as a child, until my mother told me it was make-believe."

Briar tried to play a jack of spades. Layla shot her a look and gave a tiny shake of the head.

"Ooooh, you're cheating!" I cried. "They're cheating, Adrien!"

Layla regarded me with pity. "Kitty has these strange fancies sometimes. Did you take your pills this morning, darling?"

"I think we should send you to the Fort Royal. That's where cheaters go to serve hard time!"

She made a *pfffft* sound and threw down the last card. "All yours, Kitty."

I stared at the pile. "Did I win?"

Layla patted my hand and turned to Adrien. "Poor dear. She's a little slow, too."

I threw a cushion at her and Layla ducked, laughing.

Adrien gathered the cards and began to shuffle. "My family's estate is far more pleasant than Fort Royal, I can promise you. Gardens that lead down to the sea, and many orange trees. When the sun sets, the walls turn gold. Hence the name House of the Sun."

"It does sound lovely," Briar said wistfully.

"You must visit." Adrien glanced at me. "All of you. Richard included, if I can ever convince him to take a holiday."

Nettle brought tea. We built card houses and Adrien regaled us with stories about Ravencroft Hall in the old days. Balls and Christmas parties and family get-togethers. It gave me a bittersweet feeling. How different Richard's life must have been before his parents were sent away.

The afternoon passed pleasantly, the rain continuing its steady drumbeat against the windows. At four-thirty, *Reeshard* himself appeared, looking more relaxed than when I'd seen him that morning.

"You seem to have hit it off," he said, surveying the cards strewn about. He unbuttoned his collar. "Christ, it's hot in here."

"You get used to it," Briar said. She'd tied her hair up in a messy bun, and we'd all stripped down to t-shirts.

"I cast a spell to banish the clouds that insist on hovering over this island," Adrien said. "Perhaps by tomorrow afternoon we'll see sunshine."

"You can't just alter the weather to suit your own whims," Richard protested. "Er, can you?"

Adrien winked. "Cousin, there is very little I cannot do when properly motivated. And I am extremely motivated to see the sun before I develop moss on my northern side, like one of your garden statues."

We stayed for dinner, and then retired to the drawing room for charades—a game at which Adrien, with his natural theatrics, excelled. When the grandfather clock in the hall struck eleven, Layla stifled a yawn.

"We should head back to the village," she said. "The shop opens early tomorrow."

"I'll drive you," Richard offered, but Briar shook her head.

"The rain's stopped, and it's a nice walk. The moon's out."

Indeed, when we looked outside, the clouds had parted to reveal a nearly full moon floating in a star-scattered sky.

Since the Court of Silver Shadows, I could not look at a full moon without thinking of Lord and Lady Vael, and Richard's bargain. But the Frost Moon did not arrive until November—several weeks away.

"What did I tell you?" Adrien remarked with a hint of smugness. "My weather charm is working."

After Layla and Briar departed, he declared his intention to "soak the English chill from my bones" in a hot bath. He bade us goodnight and disappeared up the grand staircase, humming the same melancholy tune the violin had played earlier.

Richard and I found ourselves alone in the drawing room, the fire now burned down to toasty coals. He sank onto the sofa beside me. "Thank you," he said, taking my hand. "I don't think I could have managed on my own."

I leaned my head against his shoulder. "How are the Finch twins?"

"Turned out to be hives. They ate an entire sack of oranges and had an allergic reaction."

"To *oranges*? Never heard of that one."

He chuckled. "It was a first. I gave them an antihistamine."

"I don't suppose you had time to try the finding spell again?"

Richard sighed. "I'm sorry. I had a few other calls, and the day ran later than I expected. But I will try again. You know that, Kitty."

"Of course." I gathered my courage. "Don't take this the wrong way, but have you considered asking Adrien? He might have advice."

Richard was silent for a moment. "I know. And I will, if need be. Just let me try again on my own. If I can't manage it this time . . ."

"It's not a failure to accept help," I told him gently. "Especially from family."

"You don't know Adrien. He'll gloat for days."

I laughed. "Yes, I believe he would. You'll just have to soldier on, Dr. Ravencroft."

"Oh, will I, Miss Boot?" he replied in a severe tone that got my blood racing.

Something electric passed between us and we both leaned in. Richard brushed my lips. Then he pulled me close, his hands sliding down my back. My breath caught as he scooped me into his arms and carried me up the grand staircase to his bedchamber.

It was a lovely room—high ceilings, ornate plasterwork, and a four-poster bed piled with quilts. Moonlight streamed through the casement windows, casting silver diamonds across the carpet as Richard kicked the door shut with one foot.

He kissed me again, and this time there was nothing tentative about it. His hands found the buttons of my cardigan. My fingers worked at his shirt. We tumbled to the bed, shedding clothes and reservations in equal measure. The fire burned low and the world outside faded to nothing but the sound of our breath in the dark.

5

JUST A GAME

I woke the next morning to dazzling sunlight. Richard stood at the window, staring at a cloudless blue sky. He wore nothing but the moonstone amulet on its silver chain, which he never removed, not even to bathe. I gave a contented sigh and took a moment to enjoy the view.

"Are you ogling me?" he demanded without turning around.

I laughed and propped myself up on my elbows. "How did you know I was awake?"

He glanced over his shoulder and arched a black brow. "Wizards have their ways."

"I might have been," I admitted, "but that's your fault for having such a magnificent bottom."

Richard threw me a mock scowl, then turned to gaze out the window. "I hate to admit it, but Adrien's weather spell worked. It's like summer again."

"Ha!" I gave a luxurious stretch. "Now we'll never hear the end of it."

"Yes, but at least he'll cease his endless carping about the dreadful rain." Richard came over and sat on the edge of the bed, the frame creaking under his weight. "Ready for one of Nettle's hearty breakfasts, cariad?"

"Oh, yes, I'm starved."

He leaned down to give me a kiss, my arms twined around his neck, and it turned into a rather long delay. But by ten-thirty, we were showered and dressed and came down to find Layla in the breakfast room. She was with Adrien, who wore a white polo, a cardigan tied across his shoulders, and crisply ironed white shorts.

"You look like an advert for a cruise holiday," Richard remarked.

"We're going to play tennis," Layla exclaimed. "Doubles!"

Richard frowned. I could tell he was about to refuse—until he noted Adrien's challenging smirk.

"Tennis? I'd love nothing more," Richard said, holding his cousin's gaze. "It's been far too long since we had a match."

"Splendid!" Adrien rubbed his hands together. "I shall dig out the equipment. Attic?"

Richard gave a brusque nod. Twenty minutes later, after a hasty brunch, the four of us trooped out to the lawn. I'd donned my usual jumper and leggings. Richard wore slacks —I could not picture him in shorts and doubted he even owned a pair—and a black button-up shirt. His only concession to sport was a white sweatband that made him look like the world's most dangerous squash coach.

Layla wore jeans, a hoodie that declared: *This Is My Resting Witch Face,* and a moth-eaten terrycloth visor she'd found in the attic. She was animated in a way I seldom saw, bouncing in her trainers as Adrien handed out the racquets. They were the vintage wooden kind and smelled faintly of mildew.

"I've read about wizard tennis," Layla said, pulling the

visor down and performing a series of squats. "The historical accounts are fascinating. A viscount once fell into a coma for three years after a particularly nasty match."

Adrien nodded. "*Oui,* a Questel ancestor. He tried to cheat. The balls knew it and took revenge. They pummeled him into pudding."

I stared at Layla. "No one said anything about wizard tennis. I thought . . . To be honest, I'm not even good at regular tennis. Maybe I should sit this out."

"Ah, you'll be fine." She patted my cheek. "Just do your best. We need four for doubles."

Richard swished his racquet vigorously through the air. "I haven't played since I was nine."

"It's like riding a bicycle," Adrien assured him. "A bicycle that tries to throw you off and insult your mother, but the principle is the same."

He muttered an incantation and sketched a rectangle in the air. Layla gave a hoot as a court appeared. The grass was trimmed ruler-straight, the boxes laid out in perfect white lines. It all looked standard. The only off-putting part was the net, which sprouted shaggy hair like an angora goat.

"Right then," Layla said, her jaw firming. "I should warn you, I was Little Groating's junior badminton champion three years running."

Adrien laughed. "I knew I liked you. We shall make mincemeat of them. Now, let me introduce our balls."

He fished in the pocket of his skin-tight shorts and somehow extracted a cylinder, which held three tennis balls covered in lime-green fur. One of them yawned, revealing tiny teeth.

"They're alive," I said, taking a startled step back.

"Quasi-sentient," Adrien corrected. "And opinionated about technique."

As if to prove his point, one of the balls piped up in a high, angry voice, "Get on with it, you French fop! I'm itching for a volley."

"You might want these," Adrien said, fishing in the other pocket of his very tight shorts and producing four pairs of heavy, padded gloves like you'd wear to prune rosebushes.

"Why?" I asked, not wanting to know the answer.

"Sometimes the balls . . . they nip," Adrien admitted.

"Nip?" Richard pulled up his trouser leg to reveal a circular white scar about an inch wide on his calf. "Little bastards take a chunk of you."

"Like piranha!" Layla said.

I grimly tugged my gloves on. We took our positions on the court, Richard and I on one side, Adrien and Layla on the other. The topiary beasts paced the sidelines, the dragon puffing trails of steam from its leafy snout.

Richard laughed. "I just remembered—they like to retrieve the balls. Though sometimes they decide to keep them."

I smiled nervously, then squinted. The court lines looked different, as if they'd moved a few feet since I last checked.

Adrien served first, tossing a ball into the air and striking it with a hollow thunk. It let out a whoop as it sailed over the net, directly toward me. I swung awkwardly and managed to connect, sending it hurtling back.

"I've got it!" Layla shouted.

She dived for it, arm outstretched. The return shot whizzed past Richard's ear. He swung and missed.

"Too slow, Ravencroft!" the ball taunted, earning a muttered curse from my partner.

"Fifteen-love," Adrien called. He pointed at the ball, beckoning impatiently. It made a rude noise and bounced into Adrien's hand.

Richard adjusted his grip on the racquet. I recognised the gleam in his eye—the same one he'd had when facing down Lord and Lady Vael. A commitment to winning, whatever it took.

What followed was the strangest game I have ever played. The court lines changed without warning, sometimes receding so far that we had to sprint across half the lawn, other times shrinking until we were practically on top of the net. Meanwhile, the balls scoffed, jeered, and catcalled in tiny, piercing voices.

"That was clearly out!" one shrieked after Richard returned a vicious serve from Adrien that glanced off the baseline.

"In what dimension?" Richard snarled back, dark hair tumbling across his sweatband as he lunged for the next serve.

The topiary animals bounded around the edges of the court in chaotic glee. In the fourth game, the hedgehog snapped up the ball mid-flight and swallowed it, leading to a ten-minute delay while Adrien coaxed the creature to spit the furious ball back out.

I had to concede that he and Layla made a good team. Her obsessive, ruthless focus complemented his flamboyant style, and they high-fived each other after each point. I got in a few decent shots myself, but mostly I tried not to end up like that unlucky viscount. Richard's scowl grew deeper with every point lost.

"It's only a game, love," I reminded him after he threw his racquet at the net for the third time.

"That's what the vanquished always say," he muttered darkly.

Layla and Adrien won the last set by a narrow margin, though the exact score was disputed by both the balls and

Richard. Afterwards, we collapsed on the terrace, where Nettle had left a pitcher of gin-spiked lemonade. Layla stretched out on a chaise lounge, her face tipped to the sun.

"That was brilliant," she said, accepting a tall glass beaded with icy moisture from Adrien. "We should turn pro. Is there a Wimbledon for wizard tennis?"

"There is," he replied. "But be warned: the court has sink-holes that spit you out two kilometers away into a briar patch." He dug through the pocket of his white shorts and took out a pair of mirrored sunglasses, then lay back on the adjacent lounge chair. "Ah, this is the life."

"I should have brought mine," Layla said, shading her eyes with one hand.

The visor, I am sad to report, had been yanked off her head by a passing ball and then chewed to shreds by the dragon.

"Not to worry, I have just your style." Again, Adrien fished through the pocket that, quite honestly, looked as though it would barely accommodate a pack of chewing gum. "Here you are. They're the same brand worn by Princess Maria-Olympia of Greece."

Layla slipped on the enormous pitch-black glasses and sipped her gin lemonade with a happy sigh. Neither of them looked like they had any plans to leave the terrace for a while. I shot a meaningful look at Richard and mouthed the word "spell."

He stood abruptly. "Kitty, shall we go change?"

"Oh, yes," I said, "I'm all sweaty."

"If you see Nettle," Adrien called as we entered the house, "do ask her to please bring some of those *galettes*. The ones with spinach and gruyere—"

His voice cut off as Richard slammed the terrace door.

We hurried to the billiards room. Richard twisted the beak of the stone griffin perched on the mantel, giving it a half-turn clockwise, then a full turn counterclockwise. With a grating rumble, the firebox swung forward, revealing the passage to the secret library.

His moonstone amulet cast a pale light on narrow stone walls. The way was tight and dark—but mercifully short, leading to a spiral staircase and in turn, a wooden door with a brass knob.

We stepped into the library, with its four tiered galleries and sliding ladders at each level. As always, snow fell beyond the windows and a fire burned in the grate. The moment we entered, the drinks trolley made an aggressive bid to dispense refreshments, lurching over with a clatter of wheels. Richard waved a hand and it backed off.

"I think the trolley is starting to respect you," I said. "Good job!"

He arched a brow and moved to the central reading table. "Maybe we should send it to the Riddle in my place."

"Sorry, did that sound patronizing?" I added. "I only meant—"

He grinned at me. "I was joking, Kitty. But look here." He held up a small leather-bound book. "Between rounds, I managed to drop by the shop yesterday and borrow this from Layla. It's her father's field journal."

"A fresh approach to the finding spell?"

"Exactly. The spell requires an anchor. An object that held deep meaning for the person. Last time, we used Arush Deen's pocket watch. It was a birthday gift from his wife. But the journal might be even more powerful. He wrote in it nearly every day."

I frowned. "He didn't have it with him?"

"No, he left it behind on the breakfast table the morning he disappeared."

The journal's red cover was faded from years of being slipped in and out of pockets. "A. DEEN" was stamped on the front.

"It's filled with his observations," Richard said. "Drawings of plants and fungi, notes about weather patterns. According to Layla, he was studying mushrooms that only grow on the boundaries between our world and Faerie."

A slight chill rippled through me as I picked up the journal. It was one of the last things he had touched before vanishing. Mr. Deen was a good man. A man who loved his family and loved nature, too. He respected the fae, and would never have knowingly given offense or caused harm to any living thing.

I carefully turned the pages. There were sketches of mushrooms—some familiar, others fantastical—alongside neat handwriting. Notations in the margins detailed locations, dates, and conditions: "North edge of Wild Wood, dawn after new moon. Ground frost. Spores luminescent."

"This was his passion," Richard said. "The journal should provide a powerful anchor for the spell."

He lifted the black cloth covering the mirror. It had a silver frame carved with runes. I laid the journal on a small table before the mirror as Richard retrieved the spell book from its shelf.

"I've been practicing," he said. "There's a subtle inflection in the third phrase that I missed."

"When did you find time for that?" I wondered.

"Last night," he said absently, scanning the text. "After you fell asleep."

I studied his face in the lamplight. Noticed the dark smudges beneath his eyes. He was trying so hard. Surely, this time we would find answers.

"I believe in you," I said. "And so does Layla."

He briefly looked up. "Thank you. It means a great deal."

That faint smell of ozone tickled my nose as Richard gazed into the mirror, journal in one hand, spell book in the other.

He began the incantation. It sounded the same to me, but I knew that even a tiny change in the pronunciation could have a large effect.

As before, the temperature in the room dropped. The illusory snowflakes in the windows froze in mid-fall, suspended like tiny stars. The mirror's surface darkened, swirling with shadows that coalesced and then parted like curtains being drawn back.

An image appeared—but not of a faerie realm or a lost mushroom-hunter. Instead, it was a perfectly ordinary sight. One I knew as well as my own face.

The common room of the Dancing Toadstool.

Afternoon sun streamed through the windows. There were Nan and Dr. Singer in their usual chairs, conversing quietly. Barbarossa dozed in a basket, ragged black tail curled across his nose.

"That can't be right," Richard muttered. "Bloody hell, I was sure I had it this time."

The image lingered for a few seconds, then faded. Richard flipped through the spell book, scanning the pages with mounting agitation.

"I don't understand. My focus was clear. I'm certain the pronunciation was correct. I spent hours on it . . . " He trailed off, slamming the book shut. "Something is wrong with my magic. *Again*." A storm brewed behind his black eyes. "It's the Vaels. Or Halfglint! They've sabotaged me—"

I laid a hand on his arm. "Don't leap to conclusions. Perhaps it's something else—something we don't understand yet."

He looked down at me, troubled. "Like what?"

"I have no idea," I admitted. "But I think it's time to consult your cousin."

Richard hesitated. I could see the battle waging inside him—pride and stubbornness versus the desire to help Layla. I let it play out in silence, already knowing which side would win.

"You're right," he said decisively after a moment. "We'll fetch him now."

"It doesn't mean you've failed," I said, squeezing his hand. "It means you're being smart enough to use all available resources."

Richard barked a laugh. "You ought to go into politics, Kitty. You have a gift for making defeat sound like strategy."

We found our tennis champions sunbathing on the terrace, munching on savoury crepes with an array of dipping sauces.

"—and that's how my grandmother ended up dueling her own sister at a wedding breakfast," Adrien was saying as we approached.

Layla noticed us first. "Still licking your wounds? We can always have a rematch."

I sat down on the edge of her lounge chair. "It's not that. Richard tried the finding spell again, but something is off."

She sobered immediately. "So the journal didn't work either?"

Adrien lifted his mirrored sunglasses. "Did you say spell?"

I nodded at Layla and she spilled the beans. "We're trying to find my father," she explained. "He disappeared when I was a child. Taken by the fae, I think."

Adrien's blue eyes were grave. "I'm sorry. This is terrible."

"We hoped a finding spell would locate him, but it's not working," I added.

"I just tried again," Richard admitted. "The mirror showed the common room at the Dancing Toadstool. The one place we can be certain her father is *not*."

Adrien mulled this over. "That's unusual. Finding spells typically locate the subject or nothing at all."

"What if he's dead?" Layla asked tightly.

"You would see only darkness in the mirror," Adrien replied.

She swallowed hard and nodded.

"Will you help us?" Richard asked. "Your experience with this type of magic is . . . more extensive than mine."

Adrien leapt to his feet. "But of course! Do you have an anchor for the spell?"

BACK IN THE SECRET LIBRARY, RICHARD GAVE HIS COUSIN MR. Deen's journal. Adrien repeated the spell. I listened closely and felt certain there was no difference to how Richard had done it.

The mirror's surface clouded, then cleared—to reveal the exact same image. The common room of the Dancing Toadstool, with Nan and Dr. Singer by the fire, Barbarossa in his basket.

Adrien closed the book with a puzzled expression. "I've performed hundreds of finding spells. They always worked."

"Could the spell be blocked by other magic?" Layla asked.

Adrien shook his head. "Finding spells are basic—they locate the essence of a person. Only the most powerful enchantments could redirect or block them, and even then . . ." He trailed off. "This is all most unusual."

"It did show the same image both times," I pointed out.

"Yes," Adrien mused. "Which suggests . . . Perhaps we are overthinking this. Maybe the spell *is* working."

"How?" Layla demanded.

"The spell shows us where Arush Deen is," Adrien said, "or rather, where his essence is most strongly present at this very moment. If that is the Dancing Toadstool . . ."

Layla shook her head. "No, it's impossible. We would have seen him."

"Not necessarily," Adrien replied, his expression thoughtful. "Not if he's changed."

"Changed *how*?" Layla asked, her voice fracturing.

"We'd better go to the inn," I said. "It's the only way to find out for sure."

Five minutes later, the four of us were piling into Richard's Mini. He threw it into gear and sped maniacally down the road (which was his normal mode of driving). Layla clutched the journal, her face a mix of hope and anxiety. The mystery of Arush Deen had taken a peculiar turn, leading us not to the Otherworld but to the very heart of Little Groating.

6

HIDING IN PLAIN SIGHT

We burst through the door of the Dancing Toadstool, Layla leading the charge with Richard and Adrien close behind. I brought up the rear, colliding with Richard when he stopped abruptly in the common room.

The scene looked just as it had in the mirror—boringly normal. And yet, according to the finding spell cast by two different wizards, Mr. Deen was here somewhere.

"Has anything unusual happened here in the last hour?" Layla demanded.

Nan looked up from her knitting with mild surprise. Her bracelets jangled as she set her needles down. "My dear, this is the faerie capital of England. You'll have to be more specific."

"Any visitors, strange sounds, objects moving on their own?" I asked.

Dr. Singer looked bewildered. "Only the usual creaks of an old building settling its bones." He patted the arm of his chair affectionately, as if it were a faithful old dog.

I scanned the room. Madame de Berry occupied a table

with four of her elderly boarders, their Sunday ritual of beer and mince pies as predictable as the tides.

"Charlotte," I called over, "have you noticed anything odd today?"

Madame de Berry looked up from her mug with a smile. "Only that the sun has remembered its duties after weeks of sulking," she said. "Though Mr. Pembroke here claims his joints always ache before faerie mischief."

The elderly man beside her harrumphed. "Reliable as a barometer, my knee is. No trouble today."

The other boarders nodded agreement.

Layla's face fell. "I don't understand. The spell showed us this room. Twice!"

At the sound of her daughter's voice, Mrs. Deen emerged from the kitchen. Adrien stepped forward with a courtly bow. "Madame Deen, I presume? I am Adrien Questel. Your establishment is as charming as I've been told."

Mrs. Deen smoothed her sari. "You're very kind. Any relation of Richard's is welcome here."

Adrien didn't reply. He had turned to stare at Barbarossa, who stared back. The cat's tail began to lash. With a sudden burst of energy, he sprang from his basket and bolted for the stairs.

"Le chat!" Adrien cried. "Mon dieu, it's been the cat all along!"

"What?" Layla demanded wildly. "What?"

Adrien slapped his thigh. "The spell worked perfectly. It showed us your father. Do you not see? He is the cat!"

Stunned silence followed this pronouncement. Then everyone began speaking at once.

"Don't be ridiculous—"

"How is that possible—"

"Are you bloody saying—"

Richard held up his hands. "This had better not be some sort of bad joke," he told his cousin sternly.

Adrien looked wounded. "What do you take me for? Now that I am close, I can plainly sense the enchantment. As you would, too, cousin, if only you . . ." He trailed off at Richard's expression.

Layla crossed her arms. "Let me get this straight. You're saying *my father is Barbarossa?*"

Mrs. Deen drew a sharp breath and covered her mouth with one hand.

"I fear so," Adrien said.

"We need to find him," I said.

We spread out, poking into closets and behind furniture. I called his name even though I knew it was useless. Cats never come unless you're banging a tin with a spoon. I was about to try that when I found him crouched under a four-poster bed in one of the empty guest rooms.

"In here!" I shouted.

I lay on my stomach, groping through the dust. After a brief tussle, I managed to drag him out just as Layla came in. When he saw her, the fight left him and he sagged in my arms.

"I think Adrien might be right," I panted. "There's something . . . different about him, now that I'm looking."

"I need Briar," Layla said faintly.

"I'll get her," I offered. "You take . . . Barbarossa."

For all his fussing, the cat didn't resist the handover. I dashed next door to Sugar & Sprites, the bell jangling as I burst in. Briar was arranging a tray of miniature quiches in the display case.

"You need to come to the inn," I gasped. "Right now."

She straightened and wiped her hands on her apron. "What's happened? Oh gosh, it isn't Nan—"

"No, no."

She laid a hand on her chest. "Thank God."

I hesitated, realising how insane it sounded. "We think . . . well, that Barbarossa is Layla's father."

Briar blinked twice. "Come again?"

I gabbled some half-coherent explanation. She untied her apron. "Never mind, explain while we walk," she said, flipping the sign on the door to *CLOSED* as we left.

I gave Briar a summary as we ran back to the Dancing Toadstool. By the time I returned, a small crowd had gathered in the kitchen. Barbarossa sat on the butcher block counter, looking disdainful as Adrien examined him from all angles. Richard stood beside his cousin, his expression thoughtful. Layla and her mother flanked the cat protectively, while Nan and Dr. Singer whispered together at the stove.

"I'm here, darling. What's happening?" Briar asked, moving to Layla's side.

"Adrien believes that *he*—" Layla pointed at the cat, "is my father."

Briar blinked. "Kitty told me. Is it really . . ."

Adrien straightened, tucking a strand of golden hair behind his ear. "The enchantment is complex, but I can say with certainty that this is no ordinary cat."

Mrs. Deen's hand trembled as she reached out to stroke his head. "How?" she demanded. "How could he have been with us all these years?" She shook her head. "And no one . . . not a suspicion . . ."

"How long has Barbarossa lived at the inn?" Richard asked.

She frowned. "Well, he just turned up on the doorstep one rainy morning. Soaking wet, meowing to be let in. So I did."

"When exactly?" Adrien pressed.

Nan spoke up. "About a month after Arush disappeared. I remember because Sanaja was beside herself, and the cat comforted her. He would sit in her lap for hours."

"Twenty-three years," Layla muttered. "It seemed like an awfully long life for a cat, but I was just grateful . . . I mean, we all love him so much . . ." She trailed off, wiping her eyes.

Barbarossa began to wash his paws, extending the claws to lick each one. For a moment, I thought Adrien must be wrong. It was madness! But then Barbarossa stood up and meowed softly, butting his head against her hand. His eyes were rheumy and his fur was scruffy. When he walked, it was with the stiff dignity of a very old cat.

Except when he'd rocketed out of his basket and up the stairs.

Not, I decided, *not normal.*

"I shall speak to Quince," Mrs. Deen said in a steely tone. "He knows everything that happens in this inn." She moved to the cupboard at the back of the pantry where the brownie made his home and rapped on the door three times. "Quince! Come out this instant."

Silence.

"Quince!" Her voice grew sharper. "I know you can hear me."

Still nothing.

"Please, Quince," Layla added, shooting her mother a quelling look. "We're not angry. We just need your help."

There was a long pause, then a tiny cough. The cupboard door creaked open. A small, hazelnut-brown face peered out, guilt written across his features. "I know nothing," the brownie mumbled, staring at the floor. "Nothing at all."

"Quince," Mrs. Deen said, in the tone mothers everywhere use when patience has worn thin. "We've been friends for a long time. I have always dealt fairly with you. Now you owe me the truth."

The brownie crept with obvious reluctance from his cupboard. He wore a waistcoat fashioned from a potholder and carried a silver toothpick rapier at his hip. He looked from face to face, then at the cat, who blinked slowly, as if bored by the entire proceeding.

"Very well," Quince said, his shoulders slumping. "Yes, Barbarossa is Master Deen. I saw through the enchantment immediately."

Layla made a pained sound. "You knew? All this time?"

Quince twisted his small hands together. "Master Deen ordered me not to tell. He was ashamed of his plight, and did not want to distress his family further." He looked up at Layla with remorse. "He believed you would be better off thinking him dead than knowing he was trapped in this form."

"But why didn't he ever try to communicate with us?" Mrs. Deen asked, her voice breaking. "We could have found a way to help him."

I studied Barbarossa with new eyes, thinking of all the times I'd rubbed his belly, fed him scraps, tried to rescue the mice he chased—or more accurately hobbled after—around the inn.

Well, all that was fine.

But once, when he was sitting in my lap, I'd picked chocolate chip cookie crumbs out of my bra, believing I was alone. It was a scoop-neck shirt and they went down the cleavage. I might have eaten them afterwards.

I talked out loud to myself, too, all the time. Sometimes I called him Barbie Doll. Or Mister Plumps. He didn't seem to mind. Maybe (*please, Lord*) he didn't understand—

"You must change him back at once," Layla said, her fierce gaze swinging to the two wizards.

Adrien raised his palms. "Of course we will find a way." His brow furrowed. "But I must warn you, this enchantment is sophisticated. Whoever cast it was very powerful."

"Can't you just reverse it?" Briar asked. She slipped an arm around Layla's waist and gave her a comforting squeeze.

Adrien shook his head. "I fear it is not so simple. The spell is bound up with traps. If I make a mistake, it could kill your father."

"No," Mrs. Deen said quietly. "We can't risk that."

"So we're back where we started?" Layla demanded. "Knowing he's alive but unable to help him?"

"Not necessarily," Adrien said. "There might be another way." He turned to Richard, his expression grave. "The Chalet where the Riddle is held has a fae archivist—a keeper of ancient knowledge who knows every spell ever devised."

Richard opened his mouth, no doubt to argue, but Adrien rode straight over him. "Hear me out. This is not a cheap attempt to force you to attend the Riddle. I would never barter a man's life in such a fashion. But the fae are the only ones powerful enough to safely break this enchantment."

Richard vented a short breath. "When is it held again?"

"At the end of October before Feenacht—Faerie Night," Adrien said. "An ancient wizard holiday that coincides with All Hallow's Eve."

"When the doors to the Otherworld stand open," Layla said softly.

"That's barely a week from now," Richard said.

Layla laid her hand on his arm. "Don't feel pressured. We can find another way."

Richard glanced at Barbarossa, who had dozed off. He

was an old cat. "There is no other way," Richard said. "I will go to the Riddle."

Sometimes . . . *often,* Richard had to be dragged into the right decision kicking and screaming. But once his mind was set, nothing could stop him from seeing it through. I loved him for that.

"What about your bargain with the Court of Silver Shadows?" Layla asked. "Dancing with the Princess Maeryn until the stars fade? You can't miss it or they'll take Kitty away as a forfeit."

A brief shadow crossed Richard's face. "The Frost Moon isn't until November fifteenth. Nearly a month away. There's plenty of time to save your father *and* fulfill my bargain to the Vaels."

Adrien clapped him on the back. "We'll leave as soon as possible. The journey itself is part of the fun. One does not simply arrive at the Chalet." He winked. "One must travel the old ways."

7

THE STARS NEVER LIE

I saw little of Richard for the next few days. He set up camp in the secret library, devouring intermediate spell books as if cramming for his A levels. From the glimpses I caught when I stuck my head in, he and Adrien had turned the reading room into a sea of precariously heaped tomes, balled-up notes, and dirty coffee cups.

I just hoped he learned enough to fool the other wizards. From the way Adrien described it, this Riddle sounded like a cross between a papal conclave and the court at Versailles.

Two days before they planned to leave, I finished my breakfast shift at the Dancing Toadstool and headed over to Sugar & Sprites. A wave of vanilla and cinnamon greeted me as I pushed open the door. Layla stood behind the counter, sorting through a box of new faerie-themed bookmarks. She wore a t-shirt with a baby dragon and the motto, *I Read Because Roasting People Is Frowned Upon.*

"Oh, hello, Kitty!" she said brightly. "I feel like I've gone mental! How about you?"

"Ah, love." I went over and hugged her. She felt thin.

Layla cleared her throat. "There's so many things . . . I've been wondering . . . when they change him back, will he look the way he did? Like a man in his late twenties? Or will he have aged like the cat?"

I shook my head. "Who can say? I mean, he is going a little grey around the whiskers . . ."

"Christ," Layla muttered. "To be honest, if it weren't for old photos, I'd barely remember what he looked like. I was so little when he disappeared." She began folding one of the bookmarks into smaller and smaller squares. "I keep thinking . . . has he been eavesdropping on our conversations all this time?"

"I know! I keep thinking the same thing."

She bit her lip. "I called him Old Bones sometimes. Because he's bony. I didn't mean it in an *insulting* way."

"Trust me," I said, "mine are worse. Mr. Plumps. Because he *is* bony, but he also has that gut that swings when he walks . . ."

She briefly shut her eyes. "Maybe he doesn't understand human speech."

"I think he does," Briar said, emerging from kitchen. "Sometimes I felt sure Barbarossa was listening. Remember when you were revising your guidebook last winter? He sat on your desk for hours, watching you write."

"And he always seemed to know when someone was upset," I added. "He'd jump into your lap, purring, like he knew you needed comfort."

A faint smile touched Layla's lips. "When I was sixteen and had that horrible row with Mum about not going away to university, Barbarossa followed me to my room and wouldn't leave. Not for days. I had to bring the litter box in there so he didn't pee on the rug." She blinked rapidly.

"Here's another question. What do I call him? Until he's changed back, I mean."

Briar and I exchanged a glance. "What do you prefer, darling?" she asked.

"I don't know." Layla tossed the mangled bookmark into a bin and started on another one. "I can't call him Dad. It's too bloody weird."

"Then let's stick with Barbarossa," I suggested. "For now. Until he's . . . fixed."

"No pun intended," Briar said.

Layla barked a manic laugh, but she looked relieved. "Yes, that's best." Then her expression darkened. "I've also been wondering who enchanted him. Dad was always kind. Mum says he knew the rules about dealing with faeries."

"The fae often punish mortals based on caprice," I reminded her. "You of all people know that."

"He might have violated some etiquette he didn't know existed," Briar put in.

"True," Layla sighed. "Unless he remembers who did it, we'll never find out."

We fell silent. Outside, Adrien's weather spell held firm and sunlight bathed the High Street. A pair of house sparrows chirped beneath the window.

"I want to go to the Riddle," Layla announced suddenly. "I need to be there when they break the enchantment." She turned to Briar. "What do you say, love?"

Briar looked surprised—but not *that* surprised. We both knew Layla. "Are you asking if I'll go? Then the answer is yes, of course, but—"

"Someone needs to mind the shop and keep Mum from losing her mind," Layla finished. "You stay. I just wanted to . . . to ask first."

"And I love you for it." She smiled. "But don't worry, I'll keep an eye on things here."

"I'll go with you," I said. "But there's one problem. Are non-wizards allowed to attend? It sounds like an exclusive affair."

A slow smile spread across Layla's face. "Actually, I have an idea about that."

The bell above the door jingled as a customer entered. Briar rose to greet them, but not before giving Layla a quick kiss. "Go plan your adventure," she said. "I'll hold down the fort."

LAYLA AND I FOUND THE COUSINS EXACTLY WHERE I'D LEFT them the night before—practicing basic spells in the secret library. Richard slumped in an armchair, his sharp nose buried in a book. A teetering stack stood at his elbow. His shirt was rumpled, his sleeves rolled up, and his dark hair stood on end.

But there were no swarms of purple bees or singularities bending space and time, so I figured he was getting better at it.

Adrien lounged nearby, one leg thrown over the arm of a settee, a slender volume balanced on his knee. His golden locks looked as if they'd just been professionally styled, though he hadn't bothered to dress and wore a pair of silk pyjamas.

"Ladies!" Adrien said, straightening. "Please tell me you've brought food."

I tossed him a paper bag from the shop and he made a noise of gratitude.

"We have a proposition," Layla said.

Richard looked up from his book.

"We want to come with you to the Riddle," I said, deciding that directness was the best approach.

Richard did not object nor did he ask why, which made me love him all the more. Instead, he turned to Adrien and asked, "Is that allowed?"

Adrien bit into a cheddar and chive biscuit. "No, but I'm listening."

I exchanged a glance with Layla, who nodded for me to continue. We'd rehearsed our arguments on the walk over, dividing the points between us.

"First, someone has to care for Barbarossa," I began. "He'll need to be brought along so this faerie can break the enchantment. You'll both be too busy to deal with a cat. Litter box, feeding, all that. He's on a special digestive diet because he's always sicking up."

We'd invented that part, but Adrien grimaced. "Very well, go on."

Layla stepped forward. "Second, you'll both be busy attending the Riddle. If Richard disappears, it will cause gossip—or worse."

"You make valid points," Adrien conceded, "but the gathering is restricted to the Venerable Bloodlines and their retainers."

"That's where my next idea comes in," Layla said. "Wizards have astrologers, alchemists, and other specialists in their employ, correct?"

Adrien arched a brow. "Sometimes."

"I propose that I attend as Richard's personal astrologer," Layla said.

Richard looked skeptical. "It's not just a matter of memorizing the daily horoscope."

Layla rolled her eyes. "I'm the founding president of the Little Groating Amateur Drama Club." She removed her glasses, undid her braid, and tossed her glossy chestnut hair back. "Lord Ravencroft," she intoned in a vaguely continental accent. "The alignment of Saturn with Venus in your third house suggests you must exercise extreme caution in matters of magic this cycle."

She gestured with a flourish toward the ceiling. "I see a great confluence of energies surrounding you—dark forces, but also unexpected allies." She fixed Richard with an unsettling stare. "The stars do not lie, my lord, and they speak to me of your triumph—if you heed my counsel."

Adrien burst into delighted laughter, clapping his hands. "Brava!"

Layla bowed. "Mrs. Voss, widow with clairvoyant powers, at your service."

Richard couldn't suppress a smile. "All right, Mrs. Voss. If my cousin agrees, I welcome your counsel."

Adrien beckoned to the trolley, which came hurtling over in a rattle of glassware. "For all their power, most wizards see what they expect to," he remarked. "I predict Mrs. Voss will have them falling over themselves to steal her away from you, Richard." He poured himself coffee and saluted Layla with the cup. "Besides which, it will be the most fun I've had at a Riddle in years. "

"Brilliant," Layla said. "And you can bring Kitty as your partner," she added to Richard.

Adrien's expression clouded. "That would be a mistake."

"Why?" I asked. "I want to come."

"It would put a target on your back to be presented as Richard's paramour," he replied. "The Ravencrofts have enemies who would not hesitate to strike at him through those he loves."

Richard scowled. "I can protect her."

"At the Chalet?" Adrien asked quietly. "Where your magic will be dimmed so far from your own estate?"

Richard's gaze narrowed. "What do you suggest?"

"I will bring Kitty as a guest of the Questels. A relation from one of the cadet branches. There are always dozens of young observers wandering about. One more distant cousin will hardly raise an eyebrow."

Richard clearly disliked this arrangement. "I don't want us separated."

"You won't be," Adrien said. "Our families are intertwined by marriage. We shall be seated together for dinners. And you can see her anytime you like in the Questel tower."

I looked at Richard. "It doesn't sound so bad. And it's only for, what . . . three days?"

"Very well." His dark eyes turned to Adrien. "But I hold you responsible for her welfare. If anything happens—"

"It shall not," Adrien replied firmly. "She will be surrounded by family."

"Are there no other Ravencrofts?" Layla wondered.

Richard shook his head. "A few by marriage, but most of them moved away after the scandal. The name was too notorious and the press wouldn't stop hounding them." He sighed. "My father's line has dwindled over the years. Other than some second cousins in America, it ends with me."

Adrien regarded us both with a twinkle in his eye. "Perhaps in time there shall be more," he said.

My face warmed. We had not discussed children yet . . . though I wouldn't mind—as long as we put up a fence around Nelly's Pond. The hag did fancy plump bairns.

Richard cleared his throat. "Erm . . ."

"Then it's settled," Layla said, gallantly coming to our

rescue. "Mrs. Voss and Miss Questel will accompany you both to the Riddle."

I felt a surge of excitement. But most of all, I hoped for a happy outcome for the Deens.

"We leave in two days," Adrien said. "The journey must begin under the waxing moon." He tossed back the dregs of his coffee. "I suggest you pack for alpine chill. My magical sunshine, regrettably, does not travel well."

WITH THAT SETTLED, LAYLA AND I GOT CRACKING. SHE needed a costume that telegraphed "clairvoyant astrologer," Richard needed a cloak in the Ravencroft colours, and I needed something nicer than leggings and Nan's handmade jumpers. That meant a visit to Charlotte de Berry's boarding house.

Richard made weak protests, but I think he was secretly desperate to escape the increasingly aggressive trolley. Adrien required no persuading. He was eager to meet the elegant Frenchwoman who had made Little Groating her home.

As we approached the white-painted porch with its gingerbread trim, laughter drifted from the open windows, along with the wavering notes of an old gramophone playing something jazzy.

We found Madame de Berry in the parlor, presiding over afternoon tea. The room was a temple to cozy clutter—antimacassars on every armchair, old photographs in silver frames, and overgrown spider plants dangling from the shelves. Madame de Berry herself was resplendent in a flowing caftan of peacock blue, her silver afro floating around her head.

"What a marvelous surprise!" she said. "We were just discussing Mr. Pembroke's latest crossword victory."

"Three minutes and forty-two seconds," said the gentleman in question, his mustache quivering. "A personal best."

We all murmured congratulations.

"I've come to ask a favour," I said, after declining an offer of lemon cake. I planned to suck my gut in for the fitting and every bit helped. "We need costumes for, er, a gala."

"Then you've come to the right place." Madame de Berry clapped her hands. "Mrs. Cavendish, fetch my measuring tape, would you, cherie? Miss Haddock, my fabric samples. And Mr. Pembroke, kindly move the tea things—we'll need the table."

Within moments, the parlor transformed into a hive of activity. The elderly residents bustled about, pulling out drawers and fetching sewing baskets. Layla drew Madame de Berry aside and explained the situation. She gave a decisive nod.

"Hop up here, Kitty," she commanded, nudging me onto a footstool. She circled me, muttering to herself, the measuring tape dancing between her nimble fingers. "Stand up straight, child! Aristocrats do not *slouch*."

I made a face at Layla, who ignored me. She was fingering the pile of fabrics. "Something striking for Mrs. Voss. But not too garish—I'm aiming for class."

"Midnight blue with gold embroidery," suggested one of the white-haired sisters. "Stars and moons and such."

"And a crystal pendant," added the other. "I have just the thing upstairs—belonged to my great-aunt Hester. Supposedly showed her visions, though honestly, I think that was the sherry talking."

When Charlotte had finished with me and Layla, she descended upon Richard. "The silver and black will be striking against your pale complexion," she said patting his cheek.

Richard submitted to her attentions with good grace, standing patiently as she fluttered around him with her measuring tape. "I do appreciate your help, Madame," he said.

"Nonsense," she replied firmly. "We can't have you anything short of magnificent." She turned to Adrien, looking him up and down appreciatively. "And you, Monsieur Questel? Shall I measure you as well?"

Adrien gave her a flirty grin. "You're most kind, but I've brought my formal attire from France. Though perhaps a small accent piece in the Questel colours would not go amiss?"

"A cravat in blue and green." She nodded. "I have the perfect silk."

The next hour passed in a whirl of swatches, sketches, and heated debates about the appropriate accessories for wizard gatherings. Mr. Pembroke insisted that I needed a handbag with a concealed compartment ("For messages, my dear, or a small dagger"), while Mrs. Weatherby expounded at length upon the merits of various glove styles.

Throughout it all, Adrien charmed the elderly boarders with outlandish stories of previous Riddles, including one about a Welsh wizard who had accidentally transformed himself into a salt cellar and spent three days in a cupboard before anyone noticed.

"Everything will be ready by tomorrow afternoon,"

Madame de Berry promised as we prepared to leave. "Come for a last fitting at four o'clock."

"You're a wonder," I told her, kissing her cheek. "Thank you."

She squeezed my hand. "Adventures are for the young," she said. "But the old can still participate in our own way." A glint appeared in her eye. "Besides, I haven't had this much fun since I disguised my second husband as a flamenco dancer to infiltrate the Spanish king's ball in '67."

THE NEXT DAY PASSED IN A WHIRL OF FINAL ARRANGEMENTS. With our new garments packed in boxes, we made our way to the Dancing Toadstool. Mrs. Deen had prepared a farewell feast and the inn glowed with candlelight and fellowship. As I expected, Adrien hit it off with Nan like a barn on fire. They sat together, heads bent close, laughing and trading fish tales.

I kept glancing at Barbarossa. He occupied his usual basket, tail curled over his nose. Poor old boy. In human years, he was 108 (I did the math). He was clinging on, but I feared his feline body was not meant to live so long.

If Richard had not come to Little Groating, and if Adrien had not arrived in his wake . . . well, we might never have known before it was too late.

As the evening drew to a close, Briar pulled Layla into a tight embrace, whispering something that made her eyes go shiny. Mrs. Deen packed a picnic hamper with leftovers, a fixed smile on her face. I could hardly imagine what she was thinking.

Sir Francis Drake picked up on the mood, growing so

agitated he refused the offer of a grape. He and Barbarossa didn't care for each other, mainly because Sir Francis enjoyed teasing the cat. Now, he fluttered over to the basket, hopping from one foot to the other.

"Heehaw!" the parrot screamed. "Heehaw heehaw!"

His donkey impression never failed to rouse Barbarossa's wrath. But this time, the cat merely cracked an eye and went back to sleep.

"Heehaw?" Sir Francis repeated, a bit dejectedly.

"Come here, you silly thing," Nan called, holding out her wrist, and he dutifully soared over to his mistress.

I petted Barbarossa's bony back for a while, and even got him to purr. Richard came and sat next to me. He said nothing at all, which was just right.

Later, after he and Adrien had driven back to the Hall and the inn had grown quiet, I stood at the window of my garret room, gazing up at the stars. My trunk was packed, sitting ready by the door—readier than I was. But whatever challenges waited in the Alps, at least we would all face them together.

8

A MOST WICKED SPELL

"Are you certain this will work?" Richard asked nervously.

Adrien clapped a hand on his shoulder. "I have every confidence in you. Do it just as we practiced."

Layla and I sat on the front steps of Ravencroft Hall surrounded by steamer trunks, suitcases, cat accessories, and various odds and ends. The two cousins had dragged Richard's old rocking horse down from the nursery, along with three My Little Ponies that Layla donated from her childhood collection. Their names were Twilight Sparkle, Rainbow Dash, and Applejack.

"This must be what it feels like to drop acid," Layla said, her face inscrutable behind huge black sunglasses.

The My Little Ponies were arranged on the gravel drive next to the rocking horse. If you grew up on the Moon and don't remember those toys, they're made of brightly coloured plastic with flowing manes and enormous pleading eyes.

"Come on," I said. "Didn't you secretly wish they were big enough to ride?"

"No. And my brothers played with them far more than I did."

Next to the rocking horse sat a large pumpkin from Mrs. Greenwald's garden—we'll get to that in a minute.

Richard cleared his throat. The moonstone amulet at his throat glowed with a soft pearlescent light. He began to chant the spell. Layla leaned forward and pushed the sunglasses up to her forehead. I had a sudden vision of rampaging pastel ponies.

"You can do it," I whispered. "I know you can—"

The pumpkin began to quiver and rock. I gripped Layla's arm. Richard's incantation grew stronger, more commanding. The coach solidified gradually. First the gleaming chassis, then the satiny black passenger compartment, and finally the harness and wheels.

I caught a whiff of burning plastic. *Goodbye Twilight Sparkle, Rainbow Dash, and Applejack.* With a loud pop, a team of stallions materialized in their place.

"Bloo-dy *hell*," Layla said.

Richard looked gobsmacked. "It worked!"

"Of course it did." Adrien beamed at him. "You are a Ravencroft wizard."

Three of the mounts looked startlingly real except for their forelocks—lavender, rainbow, and hot pink.

"Those have to be the gayest horses ever," I said admiringly.

"We should ride them up the High Street at next year's Little Groating Pride Parade," Layla said.

The last—formerly Richard's rocking horse—had a painted wooden head, but the others didn't seem to care. They nuzzled it in a friendly way.

"See how nice the gay horses are?" Layla said. "No judgment."

"Isn't Twilight Sparkle nonbinary?"

She dropped her sunglasses back down. "That's Dust Devil."

Richard squinted at the wooden-headed horse. "Perhaps I should try again—"

"No!" Layla and I said in unison.

"Er, it's perfectly fine," I added. "See, the body works!"

The rocking horse pawed the gravel, eager to be off.

Layla gave Richard a thumbs-up, and he tucked the spell book in his pocket.

Gilcarren—who along with Nettle was the most senior house brownie at the Hall—appeared in black and silver livery. He snapped his fingers and the luggage sailed onto the baggage boot.

"All is stowed away, my lord," Gilcarren called, climbing up to the driver's bench.

We bid goodbye to the topiary beasts, who ran a few excited circles around the coach and then tore away across the lawn. Nettle and the other house brownies stood on the steps, waving.

One by one, we climbed inside. The interior was roomy and plush, with a carpet underfoot, velvet cushions, and gauzy curtains covering the windows. I settled in next to Layla, who cradled a carrier from which occasional disgruntled meows emerged.

Richard and Adrien sat across from us. The journey would take a few days, so we all wore comfortable traveling clothes.

"Ready?" Richard asked with a smile. He seemed relaxed and I knew this minor victory had bolstered his confidence.

I slipped my hand into Layla's and we both nodded. He

tapped on the roof to signal Gilcarren and the coach lurched into motion down the beech-lined drive. But when we reached the gargoyles, we did not continue onward to Little Groating.

Instead, the coach veered across a meadow—straight toward the Wild Wood.

Adrien had already warned us that the Chalet could only be reached by faerie roads. Yet as we approached the dark trees, unease prickled along my skin. The wood was lovely but treacherous, home to both gentle and malicious fae. I'd walked there many times, but always during daylight—and never into the deepest places.

The first faerie road appeared when we were nearly upon it, a winding byway sunk several feet below the land's natural gradient. Branches creaked and parted to let us pass, and then we were picking up speed on packed earth.

It was dimmer beneath the canopy, with dappled glades here and there. Wildflowers scented the air, along with rich loam. There were the usual majestic oaks draped in moss and circles of red-speckled mushrooms that made me think of Mr. Deen.

The moment we entered the wood, the cat fell silent. I wondered if he had fallen asleep, but when I peeked into the carrier, he was awake and vigilant, whiskers twitching as he sniffed the air.

Adrien stretched his legs out and promptly started snoring. Richard gazed out the window, lost in his own thoughts. Layla took out a book on the northern Germanic fae authored by someone named Professor Greta Zickfoose. I found myself getting drowsy—the Wild Wood often had that effect—and slipped into an uneasy slumber.

When I awoke, dusk was falling and the moon rode high above us. Tiny lights flickered in the distance—will o' the wisps. The faerie road emerged from dense thickets on either side to a wide meadow. A brook babbled along one edge, its water so clear I glimpsed smooth stones at the bottom, even in the fading light.

"You may stop here, my good fellow!" Adrien called through the window.

Gilcarren shook the reins and our mismatched horses drew the coach to a halt.

Adrien hopped down and stretched. "This is one of my favourite spots to camp."

Barbarossa gave a plaintive wail from the carrier.

"He needs his food and litter box," Layla said.

"And did anyone remember to bring a tent?" I asked, somewhat belatedly.

Layla and I used to "camp" when we were kids, but we'd just drag blankets outside and build a pillow fort. If it started pouring—as happened more than once—we'd run shrieking back into the Dancing Toadstool.

Now she dug her sharp elbow into my ribs. "We haven't roughed it in years."

Adrien looked horrified. "My darling, I am a hearth wizard. I do not 'rough it.'"

"What's a hearth wizard?" I asked.

He rolled up his sleeves. "Observe."

With a series of flourishes and muttered cantrips, Adrien conjured a pavilion with blue and green stripes in the centre of the meadow. Its sides were open to the evening breeze, revealing a dining table set with silver and fine china.

Next, three even bigger tents took shape, each with a pennant fluttering at the peak. One had a black cat, one a raven, and the third a skylark, which I guessed was the Questel mascot.

"Shall we inspect our quarters?" he suggested, a bit smugly.

"Now that," Layla said, "is some cracking magic."

She strode off with the carrier for the nearest tent—yellow with the cat pennant—as Gilcarren sent the various items of luggage whizzing through the air to their proper tents.

Mine and Richard's featured a soft canopy bed, armchairs, oil lamps, and a copper bathtub steaming with hot water.

"My cousin cannot endure even minor discomfort," Richard observed dryly.

I grinned. "I hope you're not complaining about that. Who gets the first bath?"

He arched a brow. "Can't we share?"

When we all reconvened at the smaller pavilion, I pestered Adrien about this "hearth wizard" business over a cold but delicious meal from Mrs. Deen's hamper.

"We have a special mastery over warmth and cheer," he said, biting into an apple. "And we can wield fire when threatened, though I am far stronger within the boundaries of my own estate."

"That explains a good deal," I said, thinking of the blazing inferno he'd lit in the music room. "So is Richard a hearth wizard too? I mean, does it run in families?"

The cousins exchanged a look as if they'd discussed this already.

"Such talents do often run in families," Richard answered.

"Both my parents were storm summoners. But I don't know yet what my path will be."

"And what are the others?" Layla asked. "Besides hearth wizard and storm summoner."

Barbarossa sat in her lap like an aged king, accepting small bites of Whiskas Purrfectly Chicken pate.

"There are three," Adrien replied. "Tree wizard. Stone wizard. And Faun-tongue. They converse with animals."

Layla glanced at the cat. "I wish I were a Faun-tongue."

"It is the rarest path," Adrien said, "but yes, if I had been able to choose, I might have picked that one."

"So this talent . . . it isn't learned?" I asked.

"The path chooses the wizard," Richard said. "Not the other way around."

"But then the true studying begins," Adrien added. "It takes years to master any of them."

I wondered what sort of wizard Richard would turn out to be. It seemed no great mystery—both his parents were storm summoners, and he'd inherited the mercurial Ravencroft temper. Richard could shift from gentle to fierce in an eye-blink, but I had learned to weather his outbursts. They were seldom directed at me, rather frustration at his slow progress.

We finished our cheese and watercress sandwiches. Layla had brought Barbarossa's basket, hoping the familiar bit of home would comfort him. He sniffed the cushion, turned around three times, and curled up. I sat back, listening to the nearby brook and a tawny owl cry *too-wit too-woo!* in the dusk.

"Tell us more about the Chalet," Layla said. "I found nothing in my usual sources."

Adrien lit the candelabra with a flick of his finger. "It is neutral ground, maintained by an ancient fae clan called the Tempestarii."

"Sky faeries." She nodded. "Those I do know of. They control weather patterns and seldom interact with mortals."

"*Oui, c'est ça,*" Adrien agreed. "They care only for keeping the peace between wizard houses—and between mortals and Faerie."

"Why is it called the Chalet?" I asked.

Adrien leaned forward, his face grave. "It was once the house of a great Swiss wizard. Some say the strongest who ever lived. His name was Hans von Winteregg."

"What happened to him?" Layla wondered.

"He was cast out for practicing dark magic," Adrien replied. "The kind that seeks to sow chaos. The kind my aunt and uncle were falsely accused of attempting." He gazed at Richard. "But they are innocent—and someday we will prove it."

Richard stared into the candle flames, his expression stony. Yet I could imagine his hunger for this to be true. After twenty years of living in the shadow of his parents' treason, the possibility of their innocence would be alluring. Yet it would also reopen old wounds if Adrien were wrong.

I reached under the table and squeezed Richard's hand, feeling the tension in his fingers.

"You said my parents were framed," he said in a low voice. "But how am I to discover who did it?"

"Whoever it was," Layla said, "they're probably another wizard, don't you think? Which means they might be at the Riddle."

"I have always believed the same," Adrien said quietly. "But this villain cannot hide forever."

The conversation faltered after that. We all retired early,

and despite my misgivings, I slept well in Adrien's enchanted tent, untroubled by dreams.

I WOKE TO THE TRILL OF A WOOD THRUSH. SUNLIGHT FILTERED through the flap, and I heard Adrien singing in his tent next door, along with a great deal of splashing.

Richard rolled over. "We should join the others," he murmured, his voice still rough with sleep. "Get an early start." Then he promptly dozed off again.

I smoothed a lock of dark hair from his brow and pulled on my jumper and leggings. The smell of coffee was too good to resist.

Layla sat under the pavilion in her giant sunglasses, feet propped on a cushioned ottoman. "I'm ready to judge the jousting competition," she said.

I cut a thick slice of Briar's sourdough and slathered it with strawberry preserves.

"Did you know," I said, "that there used to be tournaments where instead of horses, the knights would stand in boats rowing quickly towards each other?"

She snorted. "You just made that up."

"I didn't."

"It sounds like a Monty Python sketch."

"It's not." I took a bite of bread and jam. "There are paintings of it."

She shook her head in amazement. "How do you know these things, Kitty?"

"I'm a tour guide. I memorise all sorts of ridiculous trivia."

"Give me another one."

I poured some coffee. "People used to pay for things with eels."

"Pffft. I already knew that."

I laughed. "You did not. But I'll give it to you anyway."

Layla smiled. "I'll give you six eels if you butter me a piece of that bread, darling."

The sun crept higher, the day grew warmer, and the men finally emerged from their tents. Adrien looked freshly scrubbed and radiant, his flaxen hair arrayed across his shoulders like a Renaissance prince. Or maybe Apollo. If they were to be gods, Richard would definitely be Hades, I decided, the darkly handsome Lord of the Underworld.

Once the luggage was stowed on the coach, Adrien reversed his glamping spell with a few words. Our fancy tents folded in upon themselves, shrinking until they disappeared entirely, leaving the meadow as we had found it save for a few bent grasses.

We resumed our journey along the faerie roads, Gilcarren on the driver's bench. Today's path led through deep green valleys dotted with lakes. Stands of evergreens lined the hillsides and the air tasted of cedar. Adrien said the region was called the Borderlands. It lay between two rival fae courts, and marked the halfway point to the Chalet.

When dusk fell, Gilcarren guided the coach to a sheltered hollow. Once again, Adrien conjured our camp. As Richard and Layla washed up for dinner, the brownie approached me with a worried expression.

"Miss Boot," he said, "I fear we are being followed."

I scanned the dark woods. "By what, Gilcarren?"

The brownie's pointed ears twitched nervously. "I cannot say. But I have felt . . . a lurking presence. It comes and goes. At first, I thought little of it. My kind are often curious. But it has been trailing us since we entered the forest."

I thanked him for the warning and relayed the information to the others. Richard's hand went to the moonstone amulet at his throat, while Adrien's usual good humour vanished, replaced by a sharp, assessing gaze as he scanned our surroundings.

"I'll set wards," he said. "We'll take watches tonight."

As darkness fell, Adrien walked the edges of camp, murmuring incantations. A misty shimmer rose from the ground, forming a dome of light that enclosed our tents and pavilion.

"I will know if anything approaches," he said, returning to the table. "And it may discourage whatever it is from trying."

Dinner was a subdued affair. We ate quickly and spoke little, alert to every sound from the darkness. Before retiring, we each took a two-hour watch, just in case Adrien's wards failed.

Gilcarren stayed with the coach. There was a large compartment beneath the driver's seat that he said was very cozy. Last I saw of him, he had donned a red sleeping cap and dressing gown and was carrying a candle into his quarters.

My turn came in the deepest part of the night. I pulled a chair to the tent flap and wrapped myself in a blanket, peering into the darkness. Twilight Sparkle, Rainbow Dash, and Applejack cropped at the grass. The horse with the wooden head—called Pip—stood companionably with the others, gazing into the distance. I walked over and gave them all a pat on the muzzle. Then I shared a few apples from the hamper.

Nothing approached during my watch. The wards remained undisturbed. Yet an uneasy mood lay over the journey now, and we broke camp at first light.

"If we make haste, we will reach the Chalet by nightfall," Adrien said.

"Then we'll push hard," Richard said. "No stopping."

After a few hours, the road left the forest and crossed a rolling prairie covered with high grass that rippled in purple waves and seemed as wide as an ocean. Low hills rose in the distance, grey against the blue sky.

We shared out the last of the food in the hamper. I amused myself watching long-necked herd animals with curling silver horns munch on the grass. They regarded the coach with disinterest.

"How much farther?" Richard asked.

"We should reach the next crossroads by evening," Adrien replied. "From there, we take the northern road—"

He broke off, frowning at the horizon. Where moments before there had been clear sky, a bank of dark clouds was spreading like spilled ink.

"That's not a natural storm," Richard said, his voice tight.

"No," Adrien agreed. He swore softly and rapped on the roof of the coach. "Gilcarren! Make for those hills with all speed!"

"Leave the road, Master Questel?" the brownie called down.

"Yes! Go cross country."

The horses veered off the track and broke into a gallop. The coach bounced over the uneven ground. I gripped the edge of my seat and watched the storm grow larger in the window. The herd of giraffe-like animals was now fleeing in the opposite direction.

"What on earth *is* that?" Layla asked, hugging Barbarossa's carrier to her chest. The jostling had woken him and low, apprehensive moans drifted through the mesh opening. I knew how he felt.

"A most wicked spell," Adrien replied, his blue eyes hard. "Someone does not want us to reach the Chalet."

The storm raced toward us with daunting speed. I watched as the last slice of blue sky was swallowed by darkness. A cold wind slithered through gaps in the doors and frost crept across the windows.

"There!" Adrien pointed toward a cleft in the hills ahead.

The storm growled as if in answer. Purple-white lightning forked down from its underbelly. Worse, fell voices rode the wind—hissing words I couldn't make out but which filled me with dread.

"It knows its quarry is fleeing," Adrien muttered. "Faster, Gilcarren!"

The horses strained against their traces, bright manes flowing in the wind. They were the only flashes of colour in a shadowy, monochromatic landscape.

Go, Pip! I urged silently. *Go Twilight Sparkle, Rainbow Dash, and Applejack!*

Layla turned to me, eyes magnified behind her round reading glasses. "It has to be a storm summoner. Or the Tempestarii—"

We both yelped as a sudden vicious gust shattered the window on my side. Snow flurries blew inside the compartment, stinging my cheeks. Richard pulled me away from the broken glass.

"Are you all right?"

I quickly checked myself. "Fine."

The coach careened toward the hills. We were getting close when a sideways gust batted the coach onto two wheels. I felt like one of the poor mice Barbarossa used to play hockey with. For a heart-stopping moment, it seemed certain we would tip over—and whatever rode the storm would catch us in its jaws.

Richard held me tight, shielding me with his body. Adrien shouted something in French. From beneath his shirt, he withdrew an amulet. A flash of lightning revealed a sapphire set in rose gold, surrounded by six emeralds. The stones flared—so bright I turned away and pressed my face into Richard's coat.

With a creaking shudder, the coach bounced down onto four wheels again. The wind died as we entered the narrow defile, rock walls racing past on either side.

My shoulders relaxed as the gloomy twilight faded. Warm sun streamed into the coach. The horses' frantic gallop slowed to a trot. I stared out the window in wonder. We had emerged into a fairytale landscape of pink flowers and azure sky. Barbarossa's ear-splitting howls shifted to nervous purring.

"Are we in Oz?" Layla asked.

"This is the Vale of Cherry Blossoms," Adrien replied with an odd, bittersweet smile. "The allied fae court of the Questels."

9

GUARDIANS OF THE EAST

The coach rolled along a wide track bordered by cherry trees at the peak of bloom, their petals floating on the breeze like snow. We were near the sea. I could hear the rhythmic crash of waves through the broken window, and the air smelled of brine.

"Whatever summoned that storm won't dare follow us here," Adrien said. "The Questels and the Vale have maintained an alliance for six centuries."

"Will they be angry that you turned up uninvited?" I asked.

"The Vale is not the Court of Silver Shadows," Adrien said. "And now that we're here, I cannot pass by without paying my respects." He looked at us each in turn. "I must reveal your names. To do otherwise would give offence. But the Fair Folk here will not use them against you, that I can promise. And their food and drink will have no ill effects."

Richard and I exchanged a wary look. I still dreamt about Lady Seraphine Vael, whose feral smile never reached her eyes. Yet what choice did we have? I might demand that

Gilcarren turn the coach around, but the magical storm would be waiting for us on the other side of that narrow defile.

I thought of the voices on the wind. The bone-chilling cold of them.

The Vale couldn't be worse, could it?

"Very well," Richard said, after Layla and I nodded agreement. "I trust *you*, cousin."

The emphasis was not lost on Adrien, but he didn't dispute the point. He turned to gaze out the window, lost in dark musings.

"I've read about the Vale of Cherry Blossoms," Layla said. "Seafaring Folk. Known to treat mortals fairly and with unusual kindness. Their realm is a place of eternal spring. I must say that out of all the known courts, I would choose this one if I were to be whisked away to live in Faerie."

I couldn't fault her eagerness—Layla had a scholar's curiosity—and the Vale *sounded* nice. But I recalled Adrien's bitter smile and knew that appearances were often deceiving.

"Tell us about the court," I said lightly. He seemed not to hear me, so I leaned over and tugged his coat sleeve.

Adrien blinked. "What?"

"The court," I repeated. "What is it like?"

He managed a smile, though it was a pale imitation of his usual amiable charm. "Two sisters rule here," he replied. "They guard the eastern shore of the realm while their parents pass the time sailing between islands. Like your grandmother, they have a passion for adventure."

"And the sisters?" I pressed. An uneasy feeling was worming into my gut. This place seemed too good to be true.

Again, his gaze darkened. "You shall meet them shortly."

"What about Barbarossa?" Layla unzipped the carrier just

enough to stick in a hand and scratch him under the chin. "Will you tell them about him?"

Adrien paused. "They will know whether I do or not," he said. "And they have some . . . experience with enchantments. Perhaps they can aid us."

The road sloped down, then up again, and the water came into view, clear aquamarine like an advert in a glossy travel magazine. On a bluff above the sandy shore stood a modest palace of pale pink stone, its balconies crowded with fruit trees.

"Well, I suppose that's rather nice," I said grudgingly.

"Is it not up to your standards, Kitty?" Layla arched a brow. "Not quite five-star?"

I stared at her. "Do you see a hot tub? Or a plunge pool?"

Richard gave a grim laugh. "Ask the mortal slaves. I mean, *servants*. Perhaps you can wrangle a massage."

Adrien ignored us. And I will admit, there were no abducted mortals to be seen. We were met in the courtyard by a group of lesser fae. Like Gilcarren, they stood no higher than my waist, with skin the bleached white of driftwood and shiny black kelp for hair.

One stepped forward. "Master Questel, the Guardians of the East welcome your party. The hospitality of the Vale is freely offered."

"My thanks, Pithwit," Adrien replied with a formal bow. "I accept the offer with gratitude."

The faerie's lips quirked in an almost-smile. "Come."

We left Gilcarren with the coach and followed our escort into the palace. It was open and bright, with high ceilings and lustrous floors that gleamed like the inside of an oyster shell. Layla had draped the carrier with one of Madame de Berry's shawls. Barbarossa stayed quiet, and I wondered if he felt the same unease I did.

Our hostesses waited in a breezy chamber overlooking the sea. To my surprise, they were alone, with no retainers or courtiers in attendance. They were also quite young-looking, though I reminded myself that this meant little among the fae.

The sisters shared the same medium-brown complexion and coral-pink hair. Only the style was different—the taller one wore hers in a crown of braids, while the shorter one had loose waves that rippled to her waist. Their eyes mirrored the ocean beyond, blue flecked with green—like Adrien's amulet.

As for their clothing, my expectations were confounded again. Instead of lavish gowns, they wore plain white tunics over knee-length white breeches. Their only ornament was a pair of gold-handled daggers in sheaths, thrust through their belts.

"Lady Clove." Adrien swept a deep bow to each in turn. "Lady Elowyn."

Elowyn gave a reserved nod, but Clove–the taller one—came forward to clasp his hands. "It has been long since you came to the Vale," she said warmly. "And you've brought friends."

"My cousin, Lord Ravencroft," Adrien said. "Miss Kitty Boot and Miss Layla Deen."

Elowyn's gaze lingered on Richard. "I knew your mother, Desdemona. She visited here once, many years ago. You have her eyes."

Richard looked surprised. "You knew her?"

"Not well, but I liked her. We were sorry to hear of her troubles. Sorry, too, that we could offer no aid. Our influence does not extend to mortal politics."

"It's all right," Richard said, his voice rough. "Thank you for the kind words."

Layla gave a graceful curtsy and set down Barbarossa's carrier. Elowyn stiffened, staring intently as though she could see straight through the shawl. Her expression was controlled, but I sensed some strong emotion running beneath the surface.

"Why have you brought him here?" she demanded.

"I . . . I'm sorry," Layla stammered. "Er, how did you know it's a *him*?"

"The fault is mine," Adrien said quickly. "I meant no offence. If it troubles you, we shall leave at once."

Clove glided to her sister's side and whispered in her ear. Elowyn's face softened a fraction. "Forgive my rudeness," she said. "It's just . . . I am sensitive to cruel magic. There is an enchantment involved, is there not?"

Layla nodded and glanced at the carrier. "He's . . . well, I'm pretty sure he's my father."

"We're taking him to the Riddle," Adrien added. "To the Tempestarii."

"Ah," Clove said. "You believe they can help?"

"From what I can tell," Adrien said, "this enchantment will be difficult to unravel but not impossible."

He did not look at Elowyn as he spoke, nor she at him. Yet an electric current ran between them.

Clove crouched beside the carrier. "May I?"

Layla unzipped the opening. Barbarossa refused to come out, retreating with one of his plaintive moans. But Clove knew the ways of cats. She did not try to force him. She allowed him to sniff her hand, and he finally emerged to sit on his haunches, whiskers twitching. Elowyn joined her sister, and the two of them examined the cat for a long moment.

"Oh," Elowyn said softly. "You poor man."

Barbarossa made a small sound, not quite a meow. More like a sigh.

The two sisters looked at each other. Some wordless communication passed between them. Then Elowyn stood. "We would break the enchantment if we could," she said, "but it is old and cunningly made. It is well you are taking him to the Tempestarii. They are more skilled at such magic."

Layla's face crumpled, just for a moment. Then she pulled herself together. "Adrien told me the same."

Clove smiled. "Do not lose hope." She turned to Adrien. "Is that why you came?"

"Not exactly. We were attacked on the road," he admitted. "Someone sent a storm to waylay us."

Both sisters frowned. "You do not know who?" Elowyn asked.

He shook his head. "But I fear Richard was the target. Someone doesn't want him to attend the Riddle."

Clove looked thoughtful. "All the more reason that he must. You will be safe here for the night. Pithwit will show you to your rooms."

Richard cleared his throat. "I fear we cannot stay—"

"But you cannot leave so soon!" Elowyn burst out, stricken. "You just arrived." She turned to Adrien. "Please," she added softly. "If you depart at first light, you will still arrive at the Riddle on time. But I . . . We so seldom have visitors. I would enjoy the company."

"My lady." He swept a bow, but not before I saw the painful hope in his eyes.

I revised my opinion. The sisters did not strike me as dangerous—not for me, Richard, and Layla. But some sadness cast a shadow over the Vale. I also got the impression that Adrien would like very much to stay, even though his feelings were ambivalent.

"One night is all right," I whispered to Richard. "Don't you think?"

He hesitated, then nodded. "One night."

THE LARGEST OF THE HOUSE'S VARIOUS TERRACES JUTTED OUT over the gardens like the prow of a ship. After freshening up in our rooms, we met there for supper, arrayed at a long stone table. From where I sat, I could see the water, going pink and gold in the last of the daylight. Glass lamps hung from thick rope knotted in elaborate patterns—sailor's knots, the kind that told stories about the seafaring Folk who'd tied them. The fireflies were just beginning their shift, winking on and off in the flowering shrubs below.

The fish had been caught that morning. I could tell by the way it tasted—briny and bright, with a sweetness that no fish ever kept past the first day. The vegetables were roasted with herbs I didn't recognise, and were so good I kept eating past the point of hunger. The wine was pale gold and tasted of sun-warmed afternoons, and made the world feel pleasantly soft around the edges.

Adrien sat between the two sisters, which struck me as either very fortunate or very cruel, depending on how you looked at it.

With Clove, he was himself—the version of himself I'd come to know, all charm and self-mockery and easy laughter. Where Elowyn was still and watchful, Clove sparred with him the way old friends do, trading jabs and stories. She threw a piece of bread at him at one point and he caught it without looking up from his wine, which made her groan with theatrical despair.

With Elowyn, he was different.

I noticed it the way you notice a change in temperature—not all at once, but gradually, as the evening wore on. He lowered his voice when he turned to her. They spoke seriously of names and places I'd never heard of, their heads angled toward each other, their voices almost inaudible beneath the sound of the sea below.

At one point, they both reached for the wine at the same moment. Their hands touched—barely, just fingertips—and they both pulled back as though the bottle had bitten them. Then they were both absorbed in their plates, and the conversation turned general again.

Layla, who missed nothing, caught my eye from across the table. I gave her a small shrug. She slipped Barbarossa a piece of fish. He sat in her lap, purring and more at ease than I'd seen since we left Little Groating.

After the dishes were cleared, Clove and Layla began discussing the seafaring customs of the Folk. She asked about the elaborate knotwork on display throughout the palace, and I drifted off to bed before the conversation ended, pleasantly full of fish and wine. I fell asleep almost immediately in a bed made from driftwood polished to silky smoothness.

I woke in what felt like the wee hours of the night. The wine, probably. Or the faint sound of the sea working itself into my dreams. I lay still for a while, staring at the ceiling, then gave up and pulled on my cardigan and went out.

The gardens were even more fragrant in the dark, with sight dimmed and other senses filling the void. Paths of crushed shells wound between orange and lemon trees, and, of course, more of the cherry blossoms for which the Vale was named. I walked aimlessly, following the meandering paths wherever they led, listening to the distant hiss and gurgle of the sea.

I heard them before I saw them. Adrien's voice, holding the frustrated edge of someone making an argument he'd made many times before. "I would rather spend one year with you," he said, "than a hundred with any other woman—"

"Don't." Elowyn's voice was quiet but heated. "It does no good for either of us."

He gave a mirthless laugh. "It does me no good to see you and know I cannot touch you, cannot—"

"I will not watch you die! *I will not.*"

She was breathing hard. Adrien fell silent.

"I have endured this once before. It was agony and I did not love Cael half as much as I love you. If I lost you, I would not survive it!"

"Elowyn . . ." He sounded shaken. Pleading.

I felt suddenly ashamed for eavesdropping—though I had not meant to—and backed away. They seemed too preoccupied with each other to hear the faint sound of my retreating footsteps. When their voices had faded away, I paused to catch my breath.

"A most tragic tale."

I spun around. Clove sat on a bench, scarcely visible in the meager starlight. A length of thick rope was coiled in her lap, and her fingers moved swiftly, tying knots.

"I wasn't trying to listen," I said quickly.

"I know. Join me." She patted the bench next to her. "Please."

I sat.

She worked the rope for a moment without speaking. The knot taking shape in her hands was a bulging thing made of dozens of smaller knots. A diabolically complex work of art.

"If you wish to understand, I will tell you about our parents, and why they sail from island to island, leaving us to govern their realm."

"I don't wish to pry—"

"I tell it freely. And then, if you wish, you may do something for me. But it is not a bargain. I make no demands on you."

That was stated plainly. I studied it from all angles and could find no loophole. And I will admit, I was curious.

"I would like to hear the story, Clove," I said.

She began working on another knot. "Our father, Lir, is very handsome. A long time ago, before we were born, he met Morana. My mother's older sister. They fell in love and planned to marry. But then our mother, Tarawyn, returned from a long sea voyage and stole his heart. Morana pretended to forgive this betrayal. She smiled at the wedding, gave them her blessing, and said not a harsh word."

I could guess where this was going. "But she didn't forgive them," I said.

"No," Clove agreed. "Morana waited, patient as the tides, until they had consummated the union and Tarawyn grew heavy with her first-born daughter."

"Elowyn."

"Yes. As our mother suckled the newborn at her breast, Morana entered her bedchamber. She laid a curse upon the child. A cruel, unbreakable curse. Elowyn would spend eternity alone. Any lover she took would die within a year. Then Morana left and none have seen her since." Clove's fingers stilled on the rope, then resumed knotting.

"Our mother kept the curse a secret. She tried to shield Elowyn from suitors. I was born two years later, and she hid us both away in this castle. But one day, a half-drowned prince washed up on the shore. His ship had foundered in a storm. There are treacherous reefs in the Amberjack Ocean.

"Elowyn nursed him back to health and he fell in love with her. When Tarawyn found out, she told Prince Cael the truth. He kissed Elowyn anyway because he was a lovesick fool. My sister forced him to leave, but it was too late. He drowned eleven months and three weeks later." Clove looked down at her hands. "Adrien would make the same sacrifice if she allowed him to." When she looked up, her face was more weary than angry. "He is like a brother to me. So the boon I ask of you is to convince him not to return to the Vale. It will end poorly."

With his death, I thought, sickened. "I have little sway over Adrien," I said gently. "I doubt he will listen."

"Once more cannot hurt."

"If I may . . . why is the curse unbreakable?"

"Because only Morana can take it back. Such is the nature of certain faerie curses. The worst ones." Clove sighed. "Morana has hidden herself away and no one can find her. Our parents have been searching since the day Elowyn was born."

What a great and terrible revenge to inflict the curse on the daughter and not the mother, yet it made sense. The infant was the living embodiment of Tarawyn's betrayal. If I were Morana, I would probably have hated her, too.

"Perhaps they will find her someday and convince her to reverse it," I said. "My friend Layla . . . she never gave up hope that her father would be found."

"I hope the Tempestarii help him," Clove said quietly.

We said goodnight, and I managed a few hours of sleep. The next morning, we gathered in the courtyard. Elowyn's eyes were red and puffy. I suspected she had been crying, or had been awake all night—perhaps both. As Clove said goodbye to Adrien and Richard, Elowyn surprised me by embracing Layla, then me, and saying something gracious about our visit that I suspect cost her some effort.

Adrien bowed to the sisters. His gaze lingered on Elowyn, but she pretended not to see until he turned away. Then she watched him climb into the coach as though no one else existed in the world. My heart swelled with pity for them both.

The coach jolted into motion along the road of cherry blossoms. Our pink and purple horses matched the colour scheme perfectly, and I expected Layla to crack a joke, but she looked preoccupied.

"We'll arrive at the Chalet by nightfall," Adrien said quietly. "Time to put on your masks, my friends."

The broken window had been repaired, and he stared through it with a distant expression. I thought of the storm that had pursued us. Of the mysterious Tempestarii, and whether they would help us or turn us away. Not to mention all those wily wizards gathered in one place, watching Richard for any sign of weakness.

As I took in the rugged but tranquil landscape, I found myself longing to stay in this safe haven. To sink my bare toes in the sand and listen to the eternal song of the sea. It might be Elowyn's prison, but at least she had her sister for company.

Then it occurred to me that the curse had ensnared Clove just as surely as Elowyn. She stayed here out of loyalty.

Somehow, I had come to believe that all fae were like Lady Seraphine Vael, cold and aloof and caring only for their own manipulative games. But I was wrong.

I glanced at Adrien and he managed one of his impudent grins. I grinned back.

Not all wizards were the same either.

10

THE CHALET

The Chalet clung to the spine of the mountains, a sprawling colossus of grey stone with snow-clad peaks looming on all sides. I counted a dozen turrets capped with sharp spires and narrow windows glowing amber against the blue-grey twilight.

As the horses trotted across a stone bridge to the gates, I was struck by the Chalet's beauty—and isolation. There were no villages for miles. Not a single smudge of chimney smoke or flock of sheep grazing in the green valleys.

Adrien leaned back against the velvet cushions with the ease of someone returning to a familiar haunt. "Wait until you see the interior," he said. "The ceiling of the great hall is painted with constellations that change with the seasons."

Richard said nothing. He looked tense, understandably. But Layla grinned at me, and I could tell she was just as excited and nervous as I was. She was already disguised as Mrs. Voss, in a floaty purple caftan and matching turban. The only thing still Layla-like was her glasses, which had fogged up in the stuffy confines of the coach.

The wheels bumped over cobblestones and we passed through an arched gatehouse into a courtyard. The coach came to a halt and small figures materialized. Their grey clothing blended with the stone of the Chalet, and each wore a jaunty pointed red hat. In moments, they were unloading the luggage from the rear.

"Kobolds," Adrien explained. "Germanic cousins to your brownies. Excellent housekeepers but equally prone to mischief if offended, so watch what you say."

Bells began to chime from high above, marking the hour with bright, crystalline notes. I climbed down from the coach, glad to stretch my legs after the long journey, and drew a breath of icy air.

"I will see to the horses, Lord Ravencroft," Gilcarren called down from the driver's bench. Then he added, in a low voice, "Good luck, sir. I will see you in your quarters."

Richard smiled faintly. "Thank you, Gilcarren."

With that, Gilcarren shook the reins and guided the coach away to the stables.

"The stars have aligned most favourably for our arrival," Layla announced in a vaguely Eastern European accent. "I sense powerful convergences, Lord Ravencroft. Yet the constellation of the Serpent warns: trust not the easy path."

"Thank you, Mrs. Voss," Richard replied dryly. "Your insights are, as always, invaluable."

A kobold approached, bowing to Richard. "If the Lord Ravencroft would follow me? Your suite has been prepared."

Another kobold appeared at Adrien's elbow. "Master Questel, your family awaits in the east tower."

We exchanged glances, the moment of separation upon us sooner than I'd expected. Richard stepped close to me, his voice low. "Be careful. And if anything feels wrong—"

"I'll find you," I promised, squeezing his hand. "Don't

worry. I'm a Questel cousin, remember? No one will pay me any mind."

Layla adjusted her turban and gave me a quick wink. "I predict we will meet again at dinner."

With that, she hefted the cat carrier and they followed their kobold across the courtyard. I watched until they disappeared through an arched doorway.

"Ready to meet the family?" Adrien asked, offering his arm.

I took it, grateful for his steadying presence. "As ready as I'll ever be."

The kobold led us in the opposite direction, toward a tower with blue and green pennants fluttering from its spire. The courtyard was quiet, with none of the commotion I'd expected.

"Where is everyone?" I asked.

"Already inside," Adrien explained. "Most wizards arrive well before sunset on the first day. They're settling into their quarters, renewing old acquaintances . . . or engaging in a bit of scheming before dinner."

We ascended a spiral staircase that seemed to go on forever, the steps worn smooth by centuries of use. Just when my legs began to protest, we emerged into a circular chamber.

The Questel suite occupied an entire floor of the tower, with windows on all sides offering spectacular views of the surrounding mountains. Unlike the austere stone corridors we'd passed through, this space was a haven of comfort. Plush blue carpets covered the floors, fires blazed in multiple hearths, and the air smelled of cinnamon and cloves. Delicate magical lights—like captured fireflies—hovered near the ceiling, casting a warm golden glow over everything.

The room buzzed with conversation in rapid French,

punctuated by shouts of laughter and the clinking of glasses. Perhaps a dozen people were scattered across the space in comfortable groupings, all of them with the same air of casual elegance.

"Adrien!" A tall man with silver-streaked golden hair detached himself from a nearby group, arms outstretched in welcome. "We were beginning to worry."

Adrien embraced him. "You know I must be fashionably late."

"And you must be Kitty Boot." The man turned to me, his dark blue eyes—so like Adrien's—twinkling with interest.

I held out my hand. "A pleasure to meet you."

He took my hand, bowing over it with courtly grace. "Any relation of ours is welcome, my dear. And please, call me Jean-Marie."

His English was perfect, though his Gallic accent was stronger than Adrien's. I could see echoes of Richard in his features—the same bold nose and proud bearing, though softened by an easy charm.

"Brother, you didn't tell me you were bringing such charming company." A younger man approached, bearing a striking resemblance to Adrien though perhaps five years his junior. He wore his golden hair shorter, though his smile was equally mischievous.

"Because I knew you'd try to monopolize her, Théo," Adrien replied with a laugh. "Kitty, my younger brother, Théodore. Feel free to ignore him entirely."

Théodore took my hand and kissed it with a flourish. "But I am by far the more amusing brother. Welcome to our humble accommodations, Miss Boot."

"Thank you," I said, finding myself smiling despite the nervous flutter in my stomach. There was something infectious about the Questels' warmth and vitality.

Over the next half hour, I was introduced to a bewildering array of cousins, aunts, and uncles, all of whom greeted me with the same easy familiarity. Names blurred together—François, Marguerite, Henri, Camille—their faces all bearing a family resemblance to Adrien, their English varying from fluent to charmingly broken.

"Your mother couldn't attend?" I asked Adrien during a brief lull.

His shrugged regretfully. "She's down with a cold. Father nearly stayed home to care for her, but she insisted he represent the family." He brightened. "She sent Ginger, though."

He whistled and a brown dog with floppy ears and soulful eyes trotted over, pressing against my legs.

"Hello there," I said, bending to pet the silky head. The dog responded with enthusiastic tail-wagging.

"She likes you," Théodore observed, joining us with glasses of something amber and effervescent. "Ginger is an excellent judge of character. She growled at the Austrian ambassador for twenty minutes last Midsummer—two weeks later we discovered he was embezzling from his country's treasury."

I accepted the drink, finding it spiced and warming. Ginger stayed pressed against me as I settled onto a cushioned window seat, content to observe. There was an easy affection among them, casual touches and inside jokes, debates that flared and subsided without lingering tension.

The contrast with Richard's solitary upbringing couldn't have been more stark. While the Questels moved around each other like planets in a familiar orbit, Richard had grown up alone, shuttled between boarding schools and the cold discipline of the Earl of Kilmarnock.

"It's a shame Richard wasn't sent to live with your family,"

I said quietly to Adrien, who had settled beside me. "He would have been much happier."

Adrien's smile faded. "Yes," he agreed. "He would have."

His smile returned, though it didn't reach his eyes. "The past is the past. Richard has found his way back to his heritage despite all attempts to sever him from it." He raised his glass. "And everyone in the family is looking forward to seeing him at dinner." His expression brightened. "Speaking of which, we should get ready. It's nearly time."

I glanced out the window to find that darkness had fallen, the mountains black silhouettes against a star-scattered sky. Ginger whined as I stood.

"I'll see you soon," I promised, giving her a scratch behind the ears before following Adrien's directions to my room—a smaller chamber off the main suite, but no less luxurious.

A kobold had unpacked my things, and laid out the dress Madame de Berry had made for my first night at the Riddle. The dark blue silk shimmered in the lamplight. It had a high collar and lace-trimmed sleeves, lending it an elegant, old-fashioned air.

I pinned my chin-length brown hair in the simple but elegant style Nan had taught me for special occasions. The blue of the dress matched the Questel colours—a not-so-subtle hint at our supposed family connection.

When I emerged, the suite had transformed. Gone were the casual—yet very expensive—clothes and relaxed postures. The men had changed into bespoke suits, the women into gowns that shimmered with subtle enchantments. Adrien looked quite handsome in his cloak of deep blue lined with forest green, fastened at the shoulder with a silver brooch in the shape of a hearth flame.

"You look magnificent," he said to me, offering his arm.

"Ready to meet the most powerful, dangerous, and insufferable wizards of Western Europe?"

"It's not funny," I chastised him. "One of them tried to kill us."

Adrien sobered. "I know. But you will be safe with me." He glanced around. "And my family. You are one of us now."

His eyes held kindness, and I knew he meant that seriously—not just as part of the ruse.

"Thank you," I said, taking his arm. *"Je . . . je suis honoré."*

He gave a theatrical wince, laying a hand on his chest. "I am touched that you are honored, Kitty. You may thank me by not mangling my beloved language again."

I elbowed him and we descended the tower stairs en masse, the Questels talking amongst themselves in French. Through arched corridors and down grand staircases we went, until we reached a pair of massive doors carved with scenes of a hunt. Kobolds stood on either side, their red caps the only spots of colour against their grey uniforms.

The doors swung open and we entered the great hall as a unified front, the Questel family a blue-and-green tide that swept me along in its wake. Massive hearths blazed at either end, and chandeliers hung from a ceiling with constellations that, true to Adrien's word, twinkled with real starlight. Long tables stretched in parallel rows, filled with wizards in their finery.

"The opening dinner," Adrien murmured in my ear, "where old alliances are affirmed, new ones are tested, and everyone pretends not to be assessing each other's power and status."

His arm was steady beneath my hand as we stepped forward into the light, the first move in a game whose rules I was barely beginning to understand.

11

VENERABLE BLOODLINES

Three massive hearths pushed back the alpine chill of the vast room. It buzzed with conversation, the sound rising to the vaulted ceiling and returning as a genteel murmur. Wizards in formal attire stood in groups, exchanging greetings that ranged from warm embraces to stiff nods.

I followed the Questels toward a long table covered in snowy linen and set with crystal goblets, gilded plates, and a bewildering array of cutlery.

"The Nine Venerable Bloodlines," Adrien said, his hand light at my elbow as he guided me forward. "Ravencroft and Questel you already know, of course. Those are the Ab Owains over there. Welsh and longtime allies of the Ravencrofts. Their patriarch is Merwyn, he's wearing the emerald cloak with an oak leaf."

I took it all in as we crossed the room. A few younger wizards eyed us curiously, but we weren't the centre of attention—just as I'd hoped.

"Those are the Footes of Ireland," Adrien continued, "and

the MacLeods from the Isle of Skye." He indicated a table dominated by broad-shouldered wizards in navy and copper. "And those are the Drexlers. Germanic efficiency in human form. They're master metallurgists—any magical item requiring precision work passes through their hands."

"What about the wizards in light blue?' I asked.

"The Montabas from Spain," he replied. "They fought a secret war against the Inquisition. And in the far corner, the Kazans of the Ionian Sea. My father says Nikos and Chara are always the voice of reason. Good people."

The head of each Venerable Bloodline wore an amulet unique to their own house. Candlelight illuminated blood-red rubies, the prismatic shimmer of diamonds, dark green emeralds, oceanic sapphires, and other precious stones set in gold and silver, each piece exquisitely crafted.

"Who's that?" I whispered. "The old man in purple?"

"Vito Grimaldi," Adrien replied with a narrowed gaze. "And he looks like he just sat on a stinging nettle."

Grimaldi was staring across the room with a sour expression—directly at Richard, who had just walked in with "Mrs. Voss." A murmur went through the wizards as they turned to study him. Richard pretended not to notice. He was tall and dashing in black and silver. The moonstone amulet gleamed at his throat, and I saw him as the others must—the last heir of a powerful, controversial house, returned from twenty years of exile.

"Your young man cuts quite a figure," Jean-Marie remarked. "The very image of his father at that age. There was never a more loyal friend or a more formidable ally." He patted my hand. "Come, we must take our seats. Happily, tradition dictates that the Ravencrofts and Questels sit together."

We approached our table, where kobolds in grey

uniforms were pouring wine into crystal goblets. Richard caught my eye and gave a tight smile. Mrs. Voss cast her imperious, flinty gaze across the room and sailed toward us in her flowing caftan and turban. She'd traced her eyes in black kohl, making them appear even larger. At least she wasn't toting the cat carrier. I imagined Barbarossa's doleful howls drifting through the dining room and swallowed a laugh.

"Richard," Jean-Marie called, arms opening in welcome. "It has been far too long since you graced our table."

Richard's handshake turned into a warm embrace as Jean-Marie pulled him close. "Uncle Jean," he said, his voice carrying more emotion than I'd expected. "It's good to see you."

"Look at you," Jean-Marie held him at arm's length. "Your mother's son in every way. And who is this enchanting lady?"

Layla extended a gloved hand. "Mrs. Voss, spiritual advisor and Vedic astrologer," she announced, pitching her voice to be audible at the nearby tables—whose occupants were avidly listening. "My late husband was a cousin to the Fontaine-Schönborns of Vienna. Lord Ravencroft and I met at a rare book auction. We both bid on the 1654 edition of *Opus Astrologicum*. I saw immediately that he was destined for greatness."

"Fascinating," Jean-Marie replied, his blue eyes twinkling with amusement. "I must consult you later on the retrograde of Venus. It's been troublesome this season."

"Ghastly," Mrs. Voss agreed languidly. She produced a cigarette and fitted it into a long holder. Several Questels jostled to light it for her.

We took our seats, and I found myself sandwiched between Théo and an elderly aunt whose name I'd already forgotten. Richard sat across the table, with Layla on one side and Jean-Marie on the other. I wished we were closer, but it was amusing to watch Mrs. Voss hold court. She was legally blind without her glasses, but you'd never know it. I just hoped she didn't accidentally put someone's eye out with the cigarette holder she was waving about.

The Questels absorbed Richard into their circle as if he'd never been away, speaking rapid French that I couldn't follow. Richard responded in kind, his accent flawless (to my tin ear, at least).

"I had no idea he was fluent," I said to Théo.

"Tutors," Théo replied with a wink. "Plus Richard spent every summer with us until he was ten. Our mothers insisted we all be bilingual."

"He never mentioned it," I said, watching Richard laugh at something Jean-Marie had said, his usual reserve melting away in the warmth of family connection.

Kobolds appeared with the first course—flaky vol-au-vent pastries filled with mushrooms that released a heavenly aroma when broken open. Next came a hearty vegetable soup and braided loaves of sweet brown bread hot from the oven. They were flavored with rosemary and other herbs I was unfamiliar with. Briar would know, and I suddenly wished she were here. Her frank manner and brash American laugh would have been the perfect antidote to all these stuffy wizards.

"What about the Tempestarii?" I asked Théo. "Do they attend the opening ceremony?" I looked around eagerly, hoping for a glimpse of our mysterious fae hosts.

"You will not see them here," Théo replied. "They administer the Riddle, but remain behind the scenes."

I was about to ask more when a kobold whisked away my dirty bowl and replaced it with a leek and potato stew called *papet vaudois*, followed by fried cheese balls, a crispy potato hash called *rösti*, and various other creamy, heavy dishes that started to make my dress strain at the midsection. Especially after I shamelessly stuffed myself with cheese balls.

By the time dessert arrived—some sort of cherry brandy cake and a rich tart filled with caramelized walnuts and yes, more cream—I could only groan . . . and accept small pieces of both.

Between bites, I studied Vito Grimaldi, who continued to fire off venomous glances our way. He must have been eighty, but his back was straight as a wand and his black eyes glittered with malice.

"Regretfully, he is the host of the Riddle this year," Théo remarked. "It rotates among the houses."

"He looks as if he wants to throw Richard out into the snow," I muttered.

"Well, he cannot," Théo said firmly. "The rules are clear. Richard's parents have been banned, but he committed no crime and has every right to be here."

"What is Grimaldi's affinity?" I asked, thinking of the storm that pursued us. "I mean, his magical path."

"He is a stone wizard. "

"What does that mean exactly?"

Théo took a bite of cake, considering the question. "Stone wizards are builders. They create marvels of engineering with earth and rock. The bridge to the Chalet was made by a stone wizard. I do respect their abilities, but they tend to be unyielding and boastful—both qualities that Vito Grimaldi has in abundance," he added dryly.

"Hmmm." So the old man wasn't a storm summoner. "Are all the Grimaldis stone wizards?"

"No, they are a mix—like every house. Talents can skip generations, or appear out of nowhere."

I nursed a cup of strong coffee, which would probably

keep me up all night but prevented me from going face-first into the remains of the walnut tart.

"So one of them could be a storm summoner?" I asked.

"Oh yes," Théo agreed. "In fact, Dario Grimaldi—the grandson at the end of the table, with the big ears—he is a storm summoner, I think."

The boy looked hardly out of his teens, but I filed this away.

When the meal concluded, the kobolds passed around tiny glasses of clear liquid that smelled like it could strip the paint from a boat's hull in thirty seconds flat. I demurred, but the Questels tossed them back like water. Then Vito Grimaldi rose from his seat. A glass floated up beside him, and a spoon tapped it insistently until the hall fell silent.

"Friends, colleagues, esteemed representatives of the Venerable Bloodlines," he began, his Italian-accented voice carrying to every corner of the vast space. "It is my honor to welcome you to the five hundred and twenty-third Riddle."

He proceeded to drone on about tradition and the agenda for the coming days, but my attention soon wandered. Between the wine, the food, and the long journey, not even black coffee could fend off my postprandial fog. To stay awake, I studied the other tables, trying to memorise the distinctive colours and styles that marked each house.

The Ab Owains in their forest greens, with oak leaves embroidered on their cuffs. The Footes in russet and gold, their cloaks trimmed with intricate Celtic knotwork. The boisterous MacLeods in lavender and blue, the colours of heather and Scottish lochs. The Montabas in light blue, all smiling with perfect teeth. The Drexlers severe in navy, with the women wearing copper bracelets and torques around their necks.

The Kazans were the plainest, in soft shades of brown.

While the others pretended to listen while whispering behind their hands, only the Greeks seemed attentive to Vito Grimaldi's speech. When he finally wound down, there was rustling of silk and velvet. The formal dinner might be over, but the evening's social maneuvering was just beginning. Small groups formed and drifted among the tables.

I covered a yawn, wishing for my oldest, softest pair of tracksuit bottoms. In extra large.

"You look tired, cousin," Adrien said, appearing at my side. "Shall I escort you to your room?"

I glanced at Mrs. Voss, who gave me a tiny nod. She would keep an eye on Richard while we slipped away.

"Yes, please," I told Adrien, thinking of the promise I had made to Clove before we left the Vale. It was hard to imagine a more horrifically awkward conversation, but I'd given my word.

Ginger came bounding up with a joyful bark when we entered the Questel suite. No one else was there. The rest of them had stayed for the networking after-party.

"I see you're wearing the Questel amulet," I said, sinking into one of the couches and kicking my heels off. Ginger hopped up beside me, resting her chin on my knee, and I played with her velvety ears to hide my nervousness.

Adrien nodded. "It is the first time. Usually, my father wears it at the Riddle, but he is grooming me to take his place someday. He decided that the others will take me more seriously if I wear the amulet." Adrien smiled. "I am not certain his plan is working, but it's lucky I had it during the journey, eh?"

He couldn't have given me a better opening.

"So lucky," I agreed. "I was wondering if Grimaldi might be the storm summoner, but your brother said he was a stone wizard."

"That much is true. I will keep an eye out when I go back downstairs." He fiddled with the amulet, clearly eager to return but not wishing to seem rude.

I cleared my throat. "Speaking of amulets and the, ah, Vale of Cherry Blossoms . . . I . . . well . . ."

His gaze cooled. "Let me guess. You know all about the curse. Clove has begged you to convince me that I must never return."

I exhaled out a pent-up breath. "Thank you for sparing me. Yes, that sums it up."

He sighed. "She does that to everyone who comes. I have not visited in a long time, and I do not plan to in the foreseeable future. So you see, there is nothing to worry about. *Ça va?*"

All this was said briskly and without emotion, in a rehearsed sort of way.

"Are you just saying that so I'll drop the subject?" I asked.

"Is it your business either way?" he countered.

"No," I conceded. "And I know we've just met. But you are family to me now. And Richard cares for you, too, even if he'd never admit it."

Adrien's face softened. "You are family to me, too, Kitty. I don't mean to be rude. But this is not something I wish to speak of further."

Ginger rolled over and gave me a side-eye plea to rub her belly. I obliged. "Then we won't," I said. "I promised Clove I'd mention it, and now I have."

He snorted. "Never have I met a woman so bent on interfering in my affairs. She is like a meddling fishwife."

"It's only because she cares about you," I said.

"Yes, I know," he muttered. "Well, I must go do my duty. Do you need anything?"

I patted my belly. "I am content. Go have fun."

He rolled his eyes. "My father already has three or four future wives picked out for me. I fear I shall be passed around like a box of cigars."

"Oh, you poor thing," I commiserated. "All of them hideous and with an abundance of facial hair, I'm sure. However shall you manage?"

Adrien laughed and blew me a kiss. Then he checked himself in a mirror, fluffing his golden locks, and strode out the door. But beneath the banter, I knew that his heart was already spoken for—and could only imagine the fights he must have with his parents about it.

"Well, Ginger," I said. "It's you and me, lady."

She licked my hand. I felt a surge of gratitude for the non-human company. To clarify: I'm not a full-blown introvert. I enjoy chatting with clients on my walking tours, and with the guests at the inn. But I do better in small settings, with just a few people. More than that makes me tired.

My room had a canopied bed and a window seat overlooking the dark spine of the mountains. A fire crackled cheerfully in the grate, and a thoughtful kobold had even laid out my nightgown on the turned-down bed.

Which had a square of Swiss chocolate on the pillow.

I picked it up and started to unwrap the gold foil. Then I thought of Mr. Creosote in *The Meaning of Life* (if you don't know, look it up), and slipped it into the bedside drawer instead.

I changed into the nightdress, washed my face, and was brushing out my hair when I heard a soft knock. Not from the door, but from the wall nearest the window seat. I froze, hairbrush caught in a tangle.

"Hello?" I ventured, feeling thoroughly foolish addressing a stone wall.

A section of the wall slid open with a whisper of well-oiled hinges. Richard stepped through, still in his formal clothes. His expression wavered between happiness and exhaustion.

"Secret passages?" I laughed, setting down the brush. "Well, of course there are secret passages! It's a wizard castle."

"The Questels and Ravencrofts have always maintained private routes between their quarters," Richard said, crossing to take my hands in his. "Our families were thick as thieves long before my parents married."

"Another thing you never mentioned," I said, letting him pull me closer. "Along with your fluent French."

He looked abashed. "I suppose I've been secretive. I'm sorry, Kitty. I'm not trying to shut you out. It's just force of habit. But not all the memories are painful." His thumb traced circles on my palm, sending shivers up my arm. "Seeing my cousins tonight—being welcomed back as if I'd never left—it brought back the good parts I'd forgotten."

I leaned into him, breathing in the familiar scent of his skin beneath hints of woodsmoke and alpine air. "They adore you. Especially Jean-Marie."

"He was like a second father to me," Richard admitted. His hand slid to my waist. "What did you make of all that?"

"I think wizards are not as different from regular people as they would like us to believe," I said. "Did you try the cheese balls?"

Richard arched a brow. "I would have, except there were none left."

"How mysterious. I wonder how that happened? Maybe Mrs. Voss sent them to the astral plane."

"Mrs. Voss!" Richard barked a laugh. "Do you know how hard it was, sitting next to her, to keep a straight face?"

"She warned you. Layla really was the founding president

of the Little Groating Amateur Drama Club. You should have seen her in *Little Shop of Horrors.*"

Richard gave a last chuckle and pulled me closer. "And Adrien behaved himself? No flirtations or knee-grabbing?"

"Perfect gentleman," I assured him. "Well, that's one night down with no horrible mistakes. Only two more to go."

His gaze traveled over my face, lingering on my lips. "I've missed you."

"It's barely been a few hours," I teased, though in truth, I'd felt his absence like a physical ache.

"An eternity," he murmured.

He leaned in to kiss me, gentle at first, a question rather than a demand. I answered by winding my arms around his neck, drawing him closer until there was no space left between us. We moved to the bed without breaking apart, his hands warm through the thin silk of my nightgown, mine working at the buttons of his formal shirt.

"Stay," I whispered against his mouth.

"Until dawn," he promised, his voice rough with desire. "No one will miss me before breakfast."

The candle on the bedside table guttered and went out, leaving the golden glow of the firelight. Outside, the alpine night pressed against the windows, stars wheeling in their ancient patterns above the Chalet, where we found magic of an entirely different kind.

12

SKY AND STORM

I woke to pale light filtering through the tower's mullioned windows. Richard's arm lay heavy across my waist, his breath tickling my neck. For a moment, I let myself linger in the warm cocoon of our bodies.

But somewhere in this vast castle was the Tempestarii archivist who held the key to freeing Mr. Deen from his feline prison—and there were only two days left of the Riddle.

I snuggled against him and rubbed my cheek against his beard stubble until he opened his eyes.

"Morning, cariad." Richard gazed at me with a tenderness that made my heart contract.

"Weren't you supposed to leave by dawn?" I teased. "I believe you're already running late."

He glanced toward the window and sighed. "So I am. The first Riddle Session begins at nine, and I fear Vito Grimaldi will send out a search party if I fail to appear. Though I'd much rather spend the day with you."

He kissed me, then sat up and scrubbed a hand through

his dark hair. I reluctantly crawled out of bed and dug through my suitcase for something suitable to wear.

"So what sessions did you sign up for this morning?" I asked.

"Um, *Applied Theory of Hex Transference*. And *Working Safely with Borrowed Time as an Ingredient*."

I frowned. "Like the herb?"

"No, t-i-m-e."

"Ha! That sounds interesting." I dragged a brush through my snaggly hair. "Any more ideas on who might have sent that storm after us? I found out that one of the Grimaldis is a storm summoner. He looks very young, but Vito could have put him up to it."

Richard slowly shook his head. "I'm not sure how we could prove anything. Now that we're here, I do think it's safer. Too many witnesses to try again." I could see the worry in his eyes, and knew it wasn't for himself. "But be careful today. Stay close to Layla, and if anything feels wrong—"

"I'll find you," I promised. "All the wizards will be at the morning sessions, which means fewer prying eyes. But you be careful, too. Especially of the Grimaldis. I don't trust them."

Richard nodded and quickly dressed in his clothes from the night before. "I'll see you at dinner, if not before. I'll be thinking of you both. Let us hope there's good news for Mr. Deen." With a brush of his lips against mine, he strode to the hidden panel beside the fireplace, pressed something I couldn't see, and slipped through the opening. The wall slid closed behind him.

I dressed in one of Madame de Berry's outfits—a warm woolen dress in Questel blue with subtle green embroidery at the bodice collar. My feet still ached from last night's heels, but happily the dress was long enough that I could get away with black trainers. Downstairs, I found the dining hall empty save for a group of splotchy teenagers whispering together in the far corner.

Layla was the lone adult. A purple scarf covered her hair, and she wore a glittery satin pantsuit that looked like it had strolled out of 1978.

"On your way to a Bee Gees concert?" I asked, dropping into a seat opposite.

"Just Stayin' Alive," Layla replied.

I groaned and poured myself a cup of coffee. "How's Barbarossa?"

"Well, he hid under the bed all night, but he finally came out this morning when the kobolds brought stinky sardines. He was napping on the bed when I left him."

"I suppose that's good," I said. "How late did you stay up?"

"Not too. Richard and I left shortly after you did." She adjusted her glasses. "That dinner was lavish. Like a medieval banquet."

"I know. I'm definitely going light for breakfast—"

A kobold appeared at my elbow, setting down a plate heaped with cinnamon coffee cake, porridge drizzled with honey and blueberries, potato hash, and more of that fantastic braided bread with pots of butter and jam.

"But then again, I don't want to seem rude," I added, digging in with gusto. "And who knows when we'll eat again?"

Layla appeared to be surviving on black coffee. I made her eat half my hash and we formed our plan of attack.

"Gilcarren told me that the Tempestarii live in a palace adjacent to the Chalet," she said.

"Okay. How do we get there?"

"He promised to give me directions when we go pick up

Barbarossa." Her voice was a bit higher than usual, and she kept fiddling with the salt cellar.

"They're going to help us," I said firmly.

"But what if they demand a bargain?"

"Then we'll consider the terms carefully. Fae can be negotiated with. And you know all their tricks."

She exhaled. "You're right. We can do this."

"Have a coffee cake," I suggested. "The crumb is heavenly."

Layla made a sad face. "They just make me think of Briar."

"I miss her, too." I reached across the table and took Layla's hands. She'd borrowed a stack of Nan's silver bracelets and they tinkled as we gripped fingers. "She'll be so excited to meet your Dad, and vice versa. It's time to end this enchantment." I gazed into her eyes. "So enough Jive Talkin'."

Layla snorted. "I'd keep this going, but don't know any more Bee Gees songs."

"Yes, that about exhausts my knowledge too . . . wait—Night Fever!"

Layla glanced around at the empty dining hall. Then she stood and flung an arm into the air. *"Night feevah, night feevaaahhhh,"* she belted out.

"We know how to do it," I sang in a breathy falsetto.

"Night fevah, night fevevaaahhh." Her voice dropped to a throaty growl.

"We know how to show it!" I came around the table to bump her hip.

The bored teenagers snickered as we danced the hustle out of the dining hall and made our way, cackling, to the Ravencroft tower. Once we arrived, I decided that I didn't mind staying with the cheery hearth wizards, because the suite was austere bordering on dismal, with dark wood paneling and blackout drapes.

Plus it smelled faintly like cat pee.

Barbarossa sat on the bed. He allowed Layla to scratch behind his ears, though he refused to purr.

"I'm not sure you understand," she said awkwardly, "but there's a faerie here who knows every spell ever created. If anyone can break your enchantment, it's her. So that's where we're going this morning."

Barbarossa gave a trill that could be interpreted as agreement.

"Brilliant," she said with relief. Layla retrieved the carrier from a closet. At the sight of it, the cat froze. His ears flattened.

"Now, listen," she said reasonably, "we'll be walking through common areas and I can't have you scampering off again. Your little travel house is the safest way." She unzipped the door and chucked a tattered catnip mouse inside. "Look how cozy it is! And your favourite toy is waiting!"

She reached for him. Barbarossa backed away, tail lashing. Then he hissed and shot under the bed.

"Oh, for God's sake," Layla muttered, pushing her glasses up her nose.

"Don't worry," I said. "I'll get him."

I lay on my stomach and groped around under the bed, but he snuck past me and started running frantically about. It wasn't that large of a room, and you'd think two people in their twenties could catch one geriatric cat with ease. But I'd eaten too much cake, and Layla had the caffeine jitters. By the time we cornered him, Barbarossa was making awful, deep moans and I was bleeding in three places.

"Barbie," Layla scolded, seeming to forget in her frustration that it was her dad. "This is for your own good!"

"You call him Barbie, too?" I panted.

Layla nodded with a scowl. "Psychotic Breakdown Barbie, in this case."

The cat glared at us from the carrier, where we'd finally managed to stuff him. He started chewing at the mesh door and I felt a twinge of pity.

"I don't blame you," I told him. "But if this works, you'll never have to ride in a carrier again. How does that sound?"

Barbarossa ceased his gnawing to stare at me with contempt.

"Let me see," Layla said, examining my scratches. "We ought to put something on these first."

"Maybe there's a first aid kit in the bathroom?"

She rummaged through the cabinet and found a box with a red cross on its lid. I was hoping for plasters and antiseptic, but instead it had vials filled with liquids in various colours.

"Wizard medicine." Layla squinted, holding a vial of swampy-looking fluid up to the light.

I eyed it dubiously. "How do you know it won't turn my hair green?"

"Or make you grow a third boob," she murmured. "Richard would like that."

"Ha-ha."

Before I could stop her, Layla dabbed some on my arm. I'd always been her guinea pig.

"Ow!" I protested. "That stings."

"Sorry." She patted my hand. "That just means it's working, love."

"How do you know—" I broke off as the pain faded and a cool, tingling sensation crept across my skin. Before my eyes, the scratches healed, leaving faint pink lines.

"Richard should stock this at his surgery in the village," I said. "It's brilliant stuff!"

"I doubt the NHS would approve." Layla returned the box to its cabinet. "Now, shall we hunt down Gilcarren?"

The brownie was sitting on the floor of an enormous

walk-in closet in the master bedroom, polishing the silver buttons on Richard's evening coat. He wore Ravencroft livery, tufted ears protruding from his cockeyed top hat.

"How may I be of service?" he asked with a toothy grin.

"We're seeking the Tempestarii archivist," I explained. "The one who keeps records of spells."

Gilcarren's bushy eyebrows rose. "Deema, the Keeper of Histories." He set down his cloth. "As I told Miss Deen, she dwells in the Cloud Palace, accessible from the highest spire of the Chalet."

"Can you tell us how to get there?" Layla asked, adjusting her grip on the carrier, from which disgruntled meows emerged every few seconds.

He rattled off a long series of incomprehensible directions.

"—and then you must turn left at the statue of Hans Von Winteregg, but only if his staff points east. If it points west, you must continue straight until you reach the Chamber of Dawn, where you should speak the word 'ascension' three times," Gilcarren finished, briskly polishing the buttons again.

"Er, perhaps you could draw us a map?" I suggested.

The brownie shook his wizened head. "The paths to the Tempestarii change with the weather. A map would be obsolete by the time the ink dried."

"Very well," Layla said. "Thank you, Gilcarren."

"Godspeed!" he replied with another impish grin.

Armed with these baffling instructions, we set off into the labyrinth of the Chalet. Left at a four-way intersection where a suit of armor held a gold shield, then right at a stained-glass window depicting what appeared to be a wizard turning himself into a cloud.

"What comes next?" I asked Layla.

"Winteregg, I think," she said. "Or was it a sun and moon set into the floor tiles?"

"The second," I said confidently. "Winteregg comes after. And we are to take the fourth crossing after that."

"Lefthand," she said.

"Most certainly left," I agreed.

Soon we were lost, wandering through corridors that looped back on themselves or led to dead ends. Worse, Barbarossa's unrelenting howls were drawing attention. A trio of Drexlers in navy robes stopped conversing in rapid German to stare as we passed, their eyes lingering on the carrier.

"My familiar!" Layla called breezily over one shoulder. "I am afraid he ate some bad fish this morning." We rounded the corner and she turned to me. "We're going in circles," she muttered. "This is bad."

Barbarossa unleashed another plaintive cry, even louder than the last.

As if summoned by our desperation, a familiar figure appeared around the corner—Gilcarren. He feigned surprise, but his eyes glittered with amusement and I reminded myself that he had been a boggart not so long ago. Some of the mischief clearly remained.

"You are far from the route I gave you," he remarked.

"Lost, you mean?" Layla said flatly, setting the carrier down. "Yes, we are."

Gilcarren gazed up at the buttresses along the corridor's ceiling. They resembled the ribs of some fossilized leviathan. "The Chalet was built by a wizard, and a diabolically clever one at that. He is long gone, but some say his spirit lingers in these halls—and likes to play tricks."

"That's a shame," I said. "I'll have to tell Richard that we couldn't find it."

Gilcarren looked alarmed. "Of course, I will escort you myself," he said quickly, straightening his top hat. "It would not do for Lord Ravencroft to learn you were left to wander."

I glanced at Layla and hid a smirk. When Richard had first returned to Ravencroft Hall, Gilcarren held a grudge at the family's long absence and did all he could to drive him away. And when we went to see Lord and Lady Vael to beg their aid, Gilcarren made everything worse by telling them about Richard's ambivalence toward his magical heritage.

I didn't blame Gilcarren for the last part since he'd been forced to testify, but I knew he still felt bad about the whole thing and took pains to ensure Richard was never angry at him again.

"Thank you, Gilcarren," I said warmly. "You're a lifesaver."

The brownie's good side reasserted itself and he preened under the praise. "It's my pleasure, Miss Kitty. This way."

He led us through corridors and staircases I was certain we hadn't passed before, occasionally stopping to murmur under his breath. As we climbed into the highest reaches of the Chalet, the windows grew narrower and the stairs tighter. At last, we reached the very pinnacle of a tower—and what seemed to be another dead end.

"The Tempestarii realm begins here," Gilcarren said, halting before an arch of billowing fog. "I can go no further. Brownies are creatures of earth and hearth, not sky and storm."

Layla and I inched forward, through the fog, to a small hoarding. Beyond it, a slender bridge extended across empty air—about two hundred feet or so—to a palace suspended by chains of pure gold. It appeared to be hanging from the sky.

The bridge itself was made of mist. It looked barely substantial enough to support a beetle, let alone two women and a howling cat. I stared into the abyss on either side, immediately regretted it, and clutched Layla's arm. She was holding Barbarossa's carrier with white knuckles.

"Oh, hell no," she said.

My stomach lurched. "Gilcarren, is this another prank? Because it's not funny."

He eyed us seriously. "The bridge is safe if your intentions are pure," he assured me from the safety of the stone turret.

"Can you define *pure*?" I asked.

Another howl drifted from the carrier.

"You don't intend harm, do you?" Gilcarren said.

"No," I said.

"You will approach the Tempestarii with honor and respect?"

"Yes."

"Then I am almost certain you will be fine," he replied cheerfully.

I didn't care for that *almost*.

"There must be another way across," I pleaded.

"Not unless you have the ability to sprout wings," Gilcarren said.

Layla squared her shoulders. Sunlight glinted heroically off her tortoiseshell glasses. "We've come too far to turn back now, Kitty."

"Have we, though?" I asked, my throat dry.

She frowned.

"No, of course you're right," I muttered. "This is the test. Should have expected it really. Like the Castle of Corbenic in Arthurian mythology. Did you know that seventy-two knights died seeking the Holy Grail?" A manic laugh escaped me. "Put quite a dent in the Round Table."

"On three?" Layla suggested.

"Sure," I agreed. "Three. I mean, it's a quest, so there has to be last-minute trials. Separate the deserving from the sniveling cowards."

"One . . ." she counted.

"If you survive me, I want you to know that I love you, and that you can have my Pink Floyd CD collection . . ." Layla grabbed my hand with an ungainly lurch that made the soles of my feet tingle. "What happened to *two*?" I squawked.

She didn't reply, just dragged us both onto the bridge of mists.

13

DEEMA

My trainers sank a few gut-clenching inches into the mist before meeting resistance. Whatever was underfoot felt squishy. Like wading into Nelly's Pond, where you never knew what might be lurking beneath the surface.

"Don't look down," Layla advised, though of course I did —again.

Between gaps in the cloud bridge, I glimpsed mountain slopes, stands of dark pine, and valleys with silver threads of river. Sunlight glanced off the snowy peaks, throwing dazzling shards into my eyes. The wind did its best to sweep us both sideways, but we clung together and the bridge held, bowing beneath our steps.

Tendrils of mist swirled around my skirt, growing thicker until I could no longer see much of anything—only the endless bright arc of the sky above. We inched forward, step by step. Barbarossa had gone dead silent, apparently too petrified even to complain.

"My glasses are fogged," Layla replied, squinting. "What do you see, Kitty?"

"We're nearly across," I said. "Oh, it's beautiful!"

The Tempestarii headquarters coalesced like a mirage, suspended on chains of pure gold that vanished into the heavens at some inconceivably distant point. The whole palace was made of puffy white clouds, slowly billowing and reforming. Hundreds of storm petrels wheeled around it, diving in and out of the vapour.

A kobold waited at the end of the bridge. It looked like the ones from the Chalet except that its pointy hat was not red but grey. "Greetings, mortals," it said gruffly. "Speak your business."

Layla bowed, Barbarossa's carrier banging against her knee. Somehow, her sparkly disco pantsuit fit right in. "We seek an audience," she said, "with the keeper of the archive."

"Deema?" The kobold studied us, then gave a brief nod. "Follow me."

We trailed the faerie into the cloud castle. Petrels flew overhead, carrying tiny scrolls in their beaks. Occasionally, one would swoop down, deliver its message to a half-seen recipient, then glide away.

It was chilly and damp, and I was glad for my stout wool dress. There were galleries and staircases, all made of mist, that wound upward to dizzying heights. I couldn't see the ground due to the dense fog that rose to my knees. What if there was no ground at all? My heart began to race.

Don't think that. Have faith. It's perfectly solid . . .

"This is the archive," the kobold announced.

The chamber just ahead was large and circular, open to the sky. Spaced at regular intervals were huge blocks of glass-clear ice with artifacts frozen in their depths. The chill deepened and I rubbed my arms.

A figure waited, tall and brown-skinned with curly hair the blue-grey of thunderheads. She wore a tattered greatcoat that shimmered with dew and a floppy, broad-brimmed hat. At her feet crouched a small snow leopard.

Barbarossa caught its scent and growled deep in his throat. The snow leopard bared its fangs and replied in kind.

"All is well, Ghost," the archivist said, laying a hand on its head. "These visitors are expected." With a graceful motion of her hand, a nearby cloud formed itself into a plump sofa. "You will find it quite solid," Deema added, noting our hesitation.

Expected? I wondered how much else she knew. Could the Temtestarii be the ones who tried to stop us from reaching the Riddle? But Deema did not look hostile, just mildly curious.

Layla and I perched on the edge of the cloud-sofa. Damp immediately soaked through my bottom. Barbarossa's carrier sat between us, the cat inside issuing periodic growls.

Something drew my gaze to a block of ice at Deema'a left. Suspended within was a length of dark red fabric. Like a fly caught in amber, it had been frozen upright and rippling like a bloodstained curtain. Tiny forks of lightning flickered along its edges. Beside it, in the same block of ice, hung a necklace with a huge ruby.

I immediately got bad vibes from both items.

Deema noticed. "Our most infamous treasures," she said. "They are guarded night and day."

"What are they?" I asked.

"The storm cloak and amulet of Hans Von Winteregg," she replied. "He was the wizard who built the Chalet centuries ago. It was his stronghold." Deema moved to the ice, her snow leopard padding silently at her heels. "Winteregg made a bargain with the Tempestarii. He was the most powerful storm summoner of his age. Perhaps of any age.

But power breeds ambition, and ambition unchecked leads to evil."

Layla leaned forward. "I've read the name, but his crimes were never specified. What did he do?"

"Winteregg tried to bind multiple fae courts to his will, secretly pitting them against each other to sow chaos." Deema's hand hovered near the ice, not quite touching it. "When we discovered his betrayal, we stripped him of his amulet and cloak—the sources of his greatest power."

"What happened to him?" I wondered.

"He fled into the deeper realms of Faerie before we could seize him," she said. "Winteregg never showed his face again, and many believe him dead. But rumors surface time and again." She turned back to us. "I keep these items as a reminder of our duty to protect both the mortal and fae realms against threats—and to remember that sometimes it is those closest to us who are the most dangerous."

The words chilled me, though Layla, naturally, seemed fascinated. "He could be still alive?" she asked.

"Anything is possible," Deema agreed. "Though many centuries have passed since he vanished. Even the greatest mortal wizards do not live so long." She let her hand fall and stepped away from the cloak and amulet. "But you did not brave the path to our realm for a history lesson. I sensed your approach, but I still do not know your purpose."

Layla drew a breath and whisked the covering from the carrier. Yellow eyes gleamed in the dim interior. "My father has been under an enchantment for twenty-three years," she said. "I hoped you would have the knowledge to break it so he can return to his family."

Deema crouched down to peer inside. "This is sophisticated magic," she said, "bound with safeguards. Whoever cast it was a master."

Layla's face went taut. "Can you untangle it?"

Deema looked regretful. "The Tempestarii don't intervene in affairs between mortals and fae unless we have a compelling reason. It is not my place to undo a spell that another fae has wrought when I do not know the circumstances that led to it. Can you tell me who cast this enchantment?"

My heart sank.

"No," Layla said quietly, "I haven't a clue. But I can assure you that my father was blameless. He was a kind and caring man who always respected the fae. Whoever did it was wicked!"

"I truly am sorry," Deema said. "If you could discover who cast this enchantment, I might reconsider."

"But he cannot speak," I protested. "And there were no witnesses! What you're asking is impossible."

"You could ask a Faun-tongue wizard to aid you," Deema suggested.

"But we don't know any," Layla said. "As you must be aware, I'm here with Richard Ravencroft."

Deema's lips quirked. "Pretending to be . . . ah, what is the name? Mrs. Voss?"

"Yes," Layla admitted, her light brown skin flushing slightly. "The point is that the other wizards are all hostile to us. And even if one did help, my dad might not remember anything."

Deema tipped her floppy hat back and scratched her blue hair. "Still, I cannot—"

She broke off at the appearance of a kobold, bending down to listen as it whispered urgently in her ear. Deema's face darkened. "When was the last contact?"

The kobold murmured something, too low for me to catch.

"I see," Deema said, her voice tight. "Send word to our other agents. We must know what happened." She turned to us. "I'm afraid I must cut this short. One of my mortal couriers has vanished."

Layla cleared her glasses on a sleeve—the lenses kept steaming up—and peered at Deema. "Did you say courier?"

Deema nodded distractedly "The Tempestarii employ a small corps of mortals to carry messages to places we cannot go ourselves. Some are warded against fae, and in others, our presence would draw unwanted attention. Couriers travel the hidden roads between realms, bearing sensitive information that cannot be trusted to other means of communication."

"Sounds like dangerous work," I said.

"It can be," Deema agreed. "The faerie roads have many perils, and the information our couriers carry often has significant value to various interested parties." She heaved a gusty sigh. "We've lost three in the past year, an unprecedented number."

Layla bit her lip. "What qualities do you look for in couriers?"

Deema studied her. "Intelligence. Courage and resourcefulness. Fluency in a number of languages. A firm understanding of etiquette, both mortal and fae."

I knew what Layla was about to do before she opened her mouth. It was obvious from the determined glint in her eye. And Deema's list was basically her exact résumé.

"I'll deliver your message," Layla said. "If you agree to aid me."

Ghost wandered over and rubbed against her pantsuit. She smiled and patted the snow leopard's muscular flank. Deema adjusted her hat again, thoughtfully tugging the lobe of one pointy ear. She didn't look surprised at Layla's offer, and I wondered if we'd just walked into a trap.

"You would risk the faerie roads for a chance to free your father?" she asked. "With no guarantee of success?"

Layla unzipped the carrier and stuck a hand inside. Loud purring drifted out. "For him, I would risk anything."

14

A DOOR TO ELSEWHERE

"Where would I need to go?" Layla asked Deema. "To retrieve this message?"

"A contact within the Holy See has information I need," the Tempestarii replied. "*Why* is not your concern."

"The Vatican?" she blurted. "You have spies in the *Vatican?*"

Deema frowned. "Not spies—allies. The pope quietly maintains relations with the Tempestarii. He is aware of our mission to monitor fae meddling in the mortal world and approves of it. However, fae are not permitted within the walls of Vatican City. Thus I require a courier for the job."

"Is that a yes?" Layla asked.

Deema smiled. "Not quite. Tell me your qualifications first."

Layla answered in rapid Italian. She was that kid who got perfect grades and used their birthday money to hire tutors in niche subjects like Renaissance demonology. I didn't understand a word, but Deema looked grudgingly impressed. "So you're fluent in five mortal tongues. What else?"

"I've studied the habits and customs of the Fair Folk my entire life," Layla said. "Both courtly and trooping fae, as well as solitary fae. I have written six books on the subject and am well-regarded by my peers. I am also discreet and trustworthy."

Deema studied her for a long moment. Then she reached into her greatcoat and withdrew a book. It was bound in red cloth with gold lettering.

"This is the *Atlas of the Otherworld and its Various Byways,*" Deema said. "It lists every faerie door in the mortal realm and its corresponding door in the lands of the Folk. The way from one place to another is often shorter—or longer—using the doors. The Atlas does not include ephemeral passages that come and go, but it is otherwise complete."

Layla blinked several times. She eyed the book like it was the Holy Grail—and I thought of all those valiant but dim-witted knights who had perished in pursuit of the holy relic.

"If I bring back your message," Layla said, "do you vow to help my father?"

Deema's expression grew solemn. "I vow to try my best," she clarified. "I cannot promise success. And even the attempt carries risk." Her gaze drifted to the carrier. "At least you and he are together after a fashion. But if you lose your way, you might wander forever and never see him again."

Layla knew how real this possibility was. So did I. The chamber fell quiet. I watched Ghost, the Tempestarii's snow leopard, pace restlessly among the blocks of ice that guarded the archive's secrets.

"I understand," Layla said at last. "But I must try. If there's a chance to have him back, no matter how small . . ."

Deema nodded approval. "Your courage does you credit." She gazed through the drifting clouds, where a shaft of afternoon sunlight slanted into the archive. "You have until midnight to retrieve the message and return it to me. Go to the Porta Sant'Anna. The Gate of St. Ann. My contact there will recognise the Atlas."

Deema tucked the book into a waterproof satchel and passed it over. Layla slung the bundle over one shoulder.

"I'll do my best to return by midnight," she said, "but time passes differently in the Otherworld, as of course you know."

"Do you carry a timepiece?" Deema asked.

Layla nodded.

"As long as you have the Atlas in your possession, time will behave itself," Deema said with a twitch of her wide mouth. "You may judge the hour by your watch."

"Excellent." Layla stood, gripping the cat carrier like it was an attaché case and she'd just concluded a business meeting. "I'll be in touch," she said briskly.

"I wish you safe passage," Deema added, "but choose your route wisely. As I said, three couriers have failed to return in the last year. I fear something might be hunting them."

With those foreboding words, our audience came to an end. I clambered to my feet, damp and stiff and glad to be freed from the clutches of the soggy cloud-couch. The same kobold escorted us to the bridge of mist. It was no less terrifying the second time around, though now I kept my gaze firmly fixed on the Chalet ahead. Halfway across, Barbarossa decided to rouse from his stupor and start yowling again.

"Maybe we can just rent a car," I suggested once we were back inside the solid walls of the Chalet. "Drive like maniacs to Italy and back."

"We?" Layla shot me a sidelong look as we hurried to the Ravencroft tower.

"I'm coming with you. Obviously."

"Kitty, no," she began, but I cut her off.

"It's not up for debate," I said. "You need me."

Layla might be brilliant, but she was an armchair scholar. The only faerie she knew well was Quince, the inn's brownie. He could be prickly, but his worst revenge was to hide all your socks. Compared to wild fae, who might make live toads fall out of your mouth every time you speak.

I swallowed hard. Suddenly, the scariest of Nan's stories seemed all too real. There were creatures in the deep regions of the Otherworld that could drive you to madness with a single glimpse.

"Are you all right?" Layla squinted.

I cleared my throat, which had gone bone dry. "Just swallowed a cat hair. Listen, I'm not letting you travel the faerie roads alone. Briar would murder me with that egg-beater she's always brandishing if I went home without you."

Layla looked about to argue, but then her expression softened. "Thank you. To be honest, I'm slightly terrified."

"We should tell Richard and Adrien," I said as we panted our way up another staircase. "They'll worry if we miss dinner."

Layla shook her head. "If we tell them, they'll insist on accompanying us. And if Richard misses the evening ceremonies, the other wizards will think he's plotting against them." She shifted the heavy carrier to her other hand. "We'll make up some excuse later. But you know I'm right."

I gave a reluctant nod. Richard's protective streak had only grown stronger of late, and he wouldn't let me walk into danger without him—whatever the cost.

Once in Layla's room, we freed Barbarossa from the carrier. He shot straight under the bed with a puffed tail that conveyed his opinion of our recent adventures. Coaxing him out took another ten minutes and several sardines, but eventually he settled on a cushion near the fire.

"He'll be fine," Layla said, arranging the remaining

sardines on a plate that she set on the floor. "We'll be back in a few hours."

Maybe, I thought, but I didn't say it.

She sat down and took the Atlas from the satchel. The moment Layla opened the cover, I felt the air stir. It smelled of dusty roads and wild roses and . . . cardamom? I peered over her shoulder. The front page had an ornate border of flowers and strange beasts, coloured in vibrant amber and scarlet, lapis blue and fern green.

THE ATLAS OF THE OTHERWORLD AND ITS VARIOUS BYWAYS
A TRAVELER'S GUIDE TO THE KNOWN DOORS OF FAERIE
BY MAGISTER MARIA BECHER
VIENNA, 1542

"I've heard that name," I said. "I'm pretty sure she was an Italian alchemist. That's what they called wizards back then."

The first map showed Abyssinia, now Ethiopia. It was old and drawn by a fine—and magical—hand. Sunlight glistened on flowing rivers and the spines of mountain ranges rose up from the page. We shared a look of wonder.

"She must have enchanted the paper," Layla said. "Quite a trick. Let's see the rest."

She flipped through the maps. In Germania, I could hear wind whispering through the firs of the Black Forest. In the lands of the Norsemen, the sea heaved with currents and tiny longboats. All the maps were wildly outdated, with nations and borders that no longer existed, so it took some digging to find the land of the *Schwitz*. After consulting the index, Layla followed a set of coordinates to a miniature castle in the canton of Bern, about forty miles north of the Eiger. Tiny cursive script identified it as *The Chalet of Hans Von Winteregg.*

Layla tapped the castle and the view zoomed in on several faerie doors marked by squares. Each had a number and a cryptic notation that led back to the index—which held thousands of entries.

"Ha!" Layla said triumphantly. "Now we just have to find the fastest route from here to the Vatican."

"Can you figure this out?" I asked. It reminded me of those horrid maths questions about trains moving at different speeds towards the same station, except worse, because in this problem, the trains would be going down faerie rabbit holes.

"Piece of cake," Layla muttered, hunching over the Atlas like a troll under a bridge.

I changed out of my dress into leggings, a jumper, and the good waterproof shoes I wore on my walking tours, then packed a rucksack with some nut bars, water, and a few other necessities.

"I've found a route that should get us to Rome and back before midnight," Layla said. "It leads through three faerie realms."

"Which ones?"

"Sylvonia, Hanter Noz, and the Cinnamon Sea."

I leaned over her shoulder. The Atlas lay open to a double-page spread depicting a few realms of Otherworld. A compass offered four nonsensical points: East of the Sun, West of the Moon, North of Nowhere, South of Summer. Borders were entirely absent. Notations littered the maps in Maria Becher's cramped handwriting.

They sing here at nightfall.
Here are horned children.
Here do the Sidhe make the water of life.
The Fortunate Isles lye beyond Night's Labyrinth.
Here do they kennel nightmares.
Here Cadmus soweth dragon's teeth.

"Can we avoid the place where they kennel nightmares?" I said. "Also, the horned children. I could skip that."

"Mindmeld," Layla said. "Let's bypass Hanter Noz. That's where the children live. Ditto for Castle Warlock, whatever that is." She checked her watch. It was the same one she'd worn since we were ten, with a picture of Snoopy as the Red Baron in goggles and a jaunty red scarf. "It's already one-thirty. We'd best be off." She returned the Atlas to its satchel and patted Barbarossa's bony rear end. "Be good, love. I'll be home soon."

He looked at her with watery eyes, sneezed, and went back to sleep.

"The first door is at the base of the Questel tower," Layla said as we hurried down the stairs and into the main part of the Chalet. The wizards seemed to be at lunch and the corridors were mostly empty.

"Are you sure? I never noticed anything."

"That's the point," Layla replied. "Faerie doors are not meant for mortal eyes. Not unless you know exactly what to look for. Now hurry, we don't want to run into Adrien."

Once we reached the foot of the Questel tower, she consulted the Atlas again, then approached a blank wall. "There!" Layla whispered with a note of triumph.

"There what? I don't see anything."

"Unfocus your eyes," she said. "It's like an optical illusion."

"Oh, I hate those things," I muttered. "I can never see what everyone else does."

I squinted and unfocused and focused again and was about to give up when it suddenly leapt out at me. Hairline cracks that suggested a doorway. About waist-high.

"How do we open it?" I crouched down, feeling like Alice after she drank the wrong bottle.

"I think we just crawl through." Layla turned to me, her dark eyes serious. "Last chance to back out. It's okay. I won't hold it against you."

I slipped my clammy hand into hers. "Where you go, I go."

She gave a taut nod. Together, we crawled through the brick wall, the faerie door sealing itself silently behind us.

15

THE HOUSE OF ECHO

Layla and I crawled through dusty darkness. Presently, the stone of the Questel tower softened to moss under my palms. I blinked in a sudden spill of sunlight. We were on a faerie road sunk deep between its banks like a dry riverbed. Garlic mustard grew in white profusion on either side. The air tasted clean and sweet, like icy water from a spring.

I rose to my feet and looked back. The door was gone.

Layla already had the Atlas open, and started walking and reading at the same time. That was one of her superpowers. I'd seen her countless times on the High Street with her face buried in a book as she strode between the Dancing Toadstool and Sugar & Sprites, unerringly avoiding every obstacle without once looking up.

It drove her mother crazy. Mrs. Deen said she'd get hit by a car, or trip and break her neck. Layla claimed her peripheral vision was uncommonly acute. Since she was half-blind, we took this with a grain of salt—but she did seem to possess some sort of bat sonar that guided her around obstacles.

"Where are we?" I asked.

"Silvern," she said, eyes scanning the text. "Forested realm, generally benevolent, known for falling stars and white deer."

"That sounds nice."

"Ha." She pointed. "There's one now."

"How did you even see that?" I asked.

At the edge of a meadow to our left, camouflaged amid the flowers, stood a pretty white doe. She regarded us for a long, considering moment, then flicked her tail and bounded away.

"Well, we're in the right place," Layla said.

We walked on, the road meandering through gently rolling woods. Layla paused to tap a page and the map enlarged. "There should be another door about a mile ahead."

"Look up Little Groating," I suggested. "Just for fun."

She flipped to the index and ran a finger down the pages. "Not there. I don't even see England."

I thought for a moment. "The Atlas uses the old names for places. Try Anglia. Or Britannica."

A minute passed. "You're a genius. Found it! Now let me zoom in . . . Oh, Little Groating has loads of doors."

"I'm not surprised," I said, moving closer to look down at the Atlas.

"There are six in the village alone . . . One in the inn—that must be Quince's pantry. But oh, there's another in the old abbey. Didn't know about that one."

The page was beautifully illustrated. Green grass for the Long Meadow and a tiny, detailed drawing of the old monastery. Not far off, I saw the faerie door in the hillside of Arthur's Barrow—

Something caught my shoe and I nearly went sprawling.

"Careful, Kitty," Layla murmured, her eyes glued to the page.

"Three deer," I reported, pointing to a small herd just visible through the trees.

"Yes, they infest the place," Layla replied absently. "Silvern used to be the hunting preserve of a fae king named Geldric of the Bloody Fist, but the stories say he came across an orphaned fawn one day and decided to raise it as a pet. He loved it so, he became much nicer and gave up hunting altogether."

"Good," I said. "Oh, there's two more." These deer were not fleeing. They stared at us boldly, for deer. "How far did you say the door was?" I asked, staring into their dark, unblinking eyes.

"Not far." She closed the Atlas and returned it to the satchel, which she slung over her shoulder. "I wonder what this message is from the Vatican?"

"No idea. But the fact that Deema has a contact within the Holy See at all is remarkable. The Church's position on magic has shifted so many times over the centuries, it's hard to keep track." We rounded a bend and the white deer vanished from sight. I felt oddly relieved. "Rome used to persecute wizards relentlessly—though the wizards dished it right back. In 1163, they cursed Pope Gregory to squeak like a mouse every time he saw a piece of cheese. It was the shortest reign of a pope ever. Nine days."

"The Gorgonzola Wars?" Layla said.

I nodded. "Five centuries of mutual hostility followed. They finally reached a truce in 1687, which has held more or less since—though there was some unpleasantness in the 1870s over a bishop changeling in Perugia." I skirted an enormous root snaking across the road. "These days, as long as magic isn't being used for harm, it's quietly tolerated."

"Hmm," Layla said. "Though that plot against the queen was a black mark against England's wizards . . . More deer. How many are we up to now?"

"I've lost count," I said, eying the largest herd yet in a meadow ahead. At least a dozen. "Are you sure they're not carnivorous?"

She squinted. "Aren't they eating clover?"

"So it seems," I muttered.

"Well, I just hope Richard proves his parents' innocence someday," Layla said.

I thought of his face when Adrien said the evidence against them was fabricated. That hunger for it to be true, carefully controlled. He had tried so hard to bury the past, but its weight would never leave him until he reconciled with them.

"I think he will," I said. "Eventually."

The path curved just then, revealing a tree wider than a house, its roots snaking out in all directions. Circles of mushrooms nestled around the base.

"There," Layla said. "That's our next door."

It was built into the trunk and actually *looked* like a door, about three feet high with fresh green paint. A little plaque said *Private: Keep Out,* but Layla ignored this and turned the brass knob. It opened easily. We barged inside.

"Bloody hell," she muttered, fending off a gang of chittering hazel faeries. They waved yellow catkins about, swatting at us as we blundered through their abode to another door at the back. The catkins were soft and did little harm, but they tickled, and I was glad when we popped out of Silvern and onto a bluff.

It rose above a jewel-bright sea. The day was hot, but the trees growing near the door were conveniently shaped like umbrellas and we moved into the shade. Flying fish played in the waves below, their scales throwing off shards of red and gold as they launched themselves skyward.

"The Seaglass Isles," Layla said with satisfaction. "They share the same ocean as the Vale of Cherry Blossoms. I'm two for two, Kitty!"

"Well done," I said, taking out our water bottles. "Here."

We refreshed ourselves and she checked the Atlas. "The next door is at the high tide line. We need to find a way down to the beach."

"There!" I pointed to a narrow track that wound through the scrub.

The bluff gave way to grassy dunes and then to sugary sand. I found the flying fish mesmerizing to watch. They frolicked in groups, breaching and diving like dolphins. I stopped to watch one explode from the water and hang glittering for an endless moment, then plunge back down into the frothing waves.

"Do you hear that?" Layla asked, her brows knitting together.

It might have been the fish, or it might have come from something else further down the beach.

Singing.

Wordless and bewitching, like a half-remembered lullaby.

The song made my limbs heavy, yet I felt a deep contentment, like the moment just before you tip over the edge of sleep, when the world loses its urgency and staying awake feels absurd. I became dimly aware that we'd veered off the track and were walking into the ocean.

If I hadn't spent so much time rambling through the Wild Wood, I fear we would both have drowned. But I'd developed a sixth sense about faerie magic, and that awareness slapped me like a gout of icy water.

I grabbed Layla's arm. Waves lapped at our shoes. Her

brown eyes were soft and unfocused. "Cover your ears," I said, my voice harsh. "Sing something—anything!"

She blinked slowly.

"Ears," I shouted. "Like this!"

I jammed my fingers into my own ears and launched into the first song that came to mind, which was one of Nan's bawdy sea shanties about a merchant of Cadiz and his three comely daughters.

Layla revived enough to imitate me and belt out something—I couldn't make out what over my own raucous singing—but we were moving again, which was the important thing.

We ran and ran, until we rounded a cove and encountered a pile of driftwood. It must have taken centuries to accumulate—bleached branches and planks worn smooth by the sea, all tossed into a pell-mell mound that stretched down the beach for thirty yards. A gap yawned, barely wide enough to crawl through.

I jerked my chin toward it and stopped singing long enough to mouth, *Door?* Layla nodded vigorously. We dropped onto our hands and knees.

Of course, crawling meant we had to remove our fingers from our ears.

The singing was fainter but not gone. Layla only made it about ten feet inside the mound before she stopped moving. Her shoulders had that same heavy quality, her chin dropping.

I reached out and pinched her on the back of her upper arm. Hard.

"*Ow!*" She twisted around to glare at me, then seemed to realise. "Oh . . ."

"Keep going," I urged, blowing hair from my face.

We wriggled and squeezed our way through the tangle of

flotsam. Besides wood, it had buoys and barnacle-encrusted bits of rope and even a rusty teakettle. There seemed to be no particular route, so we took any gaps we could fit through. At least the sand was dry—and that terrible undertow of melody gradually faded to silence.

"What sort of realm is this leading to?" I asked, squinting in the stripes of sunshine that penetrated the mound.

Layla glanced back over her shoulder. "The Land of the Savage Bees," she replied.

"That doesn't sound very benevolent," I said.

"The bees don't suffer thieves," she replied. "But if you don't bother them, they don't bother you. They just named it that so people would leave their hives alone. You know how much fae love honeycombs."

"The *bees* named it," I said.

"Naturally. They're smart bees."

We muddled along for a while, and I thought about clever bees and wondered what sort of behavior they would interpret as "bothering." Then the light changed, growing murkier, and Layla made a sound of triumph.

"Door," she whispered. "Don't worry, we won't be amongst the savage bees for long. The next one leads back to our world. Straight to Rome! I am *so* getting a gelato."

She fast-crawled to a dark hole, and I followed her. A discomfiting sensation, like baby spiders walking on my arms, made me tense as I crossed the threshold, but it came and went quickly.

I straightened up on the other side. We were in a lane between tall hedges that had curved thorns as thick as my thumb. There was nary a flower or hive in sight.

"Is this where the bees live?" I asked.

Layla tilted her head back, looking beyond our thorny prison. Mountains loomed in the distance. Dark, sinister ones, hemming us in on three sides. She cleared her throat. "We may have taken a wrong turn."

"How wrong?" I said with what I felt was admirable restraint.

"I hate to say it, but this looks like Hanter Noz."

"Oh no." A cold feeling settled in my chest. "Not the horned children. I specifically said I didn't want to go there."

"You did say that."

"I thought I was very clear on that point."

"You were, Kitty, and I apologize. We'll just go back to the Seaglass Isles and start again." Layla gazed about expectantly. The door was gone. Or hiding itself exceedingly well. "Damn," she said.

We stood in silence for a moment.

"Right," I said. "Fine. Look for another door."

"Good idea." She consulted the Atlas. "Ah. Yes, indeed. Now I know *exactly* where we are," Layla said with forced cheer. "Night's Labyrinth!"

"Is that in Hanter Noz?"

She nodded.

"Wonderful." I rubbed my arms and looked around.

"Well, it could be worse. There is another faerie door, and it's dead in the middle." She slammed the Atlas shut. "So we just have to find the centre."

"Easy," I said sarcastically. "It's not like a *maze* or something designed to keep us lost."

She adjusted her glasses. "Before you get snippy, mazes and labyrinths are different. A maze has many solutions, a labyrinth only one path to the centre."

"Sorry," I muttered. "Let's just start looking. Before . . . " I lowered my voice further. "*They* show up."

We started walking. The Atlas was no use. It had a miniature drawing of the labyrinth, but we didn't know exactly where we were. The path kept dead-ending at walls of thorns.

"We must be getting closer," Layla said confidently after a while. "Time for a snack break. Might I have one of those nut bars, love—"

She cut off at a high-pitched giggle. It came from behind the hedge.

"Damnit," I hissed. "They'll make us play with them forever!"

Layla grimaced. "Yes. It's why no one comes to Hanter Noz."

"Except for us," I snapped. "Because we're idiots."

They scampered towards us, about a dozen or so, looking just as I'd imagined. The horned children were white-skinned, with pointed ears and sly eyes. Black branches grew from their heads.

"Oh god," I said.

The children surrounded us, spouting nonsense rhymes and entreating us to play with them. They had dainty little hooves for feet, I noticed. The leader grasped Layla's hands. His yellow hair was a wild nest of twigs and berries, his mouth sullen as he examined her sparkly disco pantsuit.

"Are you a princess?" he demanded.

She raised her chin. "Yes, I am Princess . . . Fiona. And this is my faithful servant . . . Donkey."

I gave a small wave. It was the only movement I could manage.

"We seek the door at the centre of Night's Labyrinth. If you do not lead us there," Layla said, "I will be *very* cross."

They didn't seem impressed by this threat. "You will come to Mother Mora," the leader said, his wide mouth grinning in a way I didn't much care for. "She will show you the door."

"Yeah," I muttered to Layla. "The door to her oven."

We shared a worried look, but the children pressed in from all sides, lowering their heads to prod us along with their branching horns. They herded us through turn after turn. I kept close to Layla and watched for any chance to escape.

"Have you heard of this Mother Mora?" I whispered.

Layla shook her head, also whispering. "She isn't mentioned in any folklore I know of. But keep an eye out. If we find the door at the centre of the labyrinth, we can make a run for the savage bees."

"The savage bees sound *so* good right now," I whispered back.

Of course, this supposed door might prove to be another "wrong turn." I contemplated taking door after door, getting ever more hopelessly lost, while the midnight deadline to deliver Deema's message ticked down. Then Layla gripped my arm.

I looked up from my reverie and saw a tilting, cockeyed structure ahead. A thatched cottage, all overgrown with thorny vines. Smoke drifted from the crooked chimney. A weathered board hanging above the door named it *The House of Echo*. Definitely the dwelling of an evil witch.

"Mother Mora, Mother Mora!" the horned children cried, running toward the cottage.

Their hoofs clattered against a flagstone path leading through a front garden—lavender and thyme, bee balm and thick clumps of bright yellow coreopsis. Moths fluttered among the flowers. It was quite pretty, and the lavender smelled divine. Suddenly, the ramshackle cottage seemed quaint, the chimney smoke welcoming instead of ominous. I imagined an apple-cheeked woman in a kerchief and apron opening the door to greet us. She would give us cups of hot tea and order her unruly brood to escort us to the next faerie door, posthaste.

Then something drew my gaze to the casement on the upper story. A black-veiled figure stood there, watching through the window. She was tall and thin and faceless, yet I felt the weight of her regard.

A thrill of dread rippled through me.

Layla and I exchanged a look and wordlessly turned to flee back into the hedge maze. Or labyrinth. Whatever.

An angry screeching went up among the horned children. We dashed down long, gloomy tunnels at random, taking any turn that seemed like it wouldn't lead back to Mother Mora. Dead end. Back. Left. Dead end. My sleeve caught a thorn. It raked my arm but I barely felt the sting. Wee hooves pattered nearby, keeping pace on the other side of the hedge. The moment we reached a gap . . .

Layla dragged me to a stop. Her glasses were askew. Wisps of sweaty hair had escaped her braid, but her eyes were steely. "I've got an idea," she said, very quietly.

"Yeah?" I breathed, glancing left and right.

"Hanter Noz is a place of make-believe. Magic here responds to any form you choose, as long as you're playing a game."

"Okay?"

"Let's pretend we're giants," she said. "But you have to really *believe* it."

I made a panicked small animal noise. *Urrrhm*?

"You can do this!" Layla whispered urgently. "Remember when we were kids?"

We had no tellies in Little Groating and very little supervision. So after school, Layla and I would pack a basket of her mum's crispy coconut cookies and go to the Long Meadow by the orchard. We'd amuse ourselves by recreating our favourite fairytales—and sometimes rewriting them entirely. I knew we were meant to be best friends because we'd argue over who got to be the hungry witch, or the cruel stepmother, or the scheming wolf. We both knew the villains were the juicy roles.

"Like *Jack and the Beanstalk*," she said.

"You were always the giant."

Layla took my hands. "I know, Kitty, and it was selfish of me to hog that part. Now you can be the giant, too."

The pitter-patter of little hooves grew closer. I closed my eyes and tried to remember. At first my heart was beating too fast, but then I caught the edge of something. A golden summer afternoon in the meadow. How the high grass tickled my bare legs, and the buzzing song of the katydids. Layla stomping around and bellowing *fee-fi-fo-fum* while I ran away, screaming with laughter.

She did hog the role. Layla had always been smaller than the other kids, and she *loved* being the giant so much I usually let her. But I'd played it a few times, and I remembered how enormous the world felt when you were being enormous in it.

Fee-fi-fo-fum . . .

A rush of wind hit my face. I opened my eyes.

The hedges had shrunk rather dramatically.

Or . . . they weren't small. I was big. Thirty feet tall. The terrible thorns barely reached my great knobby knees. Layla stood beside me, colossal, her face full of wonder and something fierce. The horned children craned their necks to gaze up at us. They looked about the size of kittens.

"Run along or I shall grind your bones for my bread!" I snarled, my voice booming against the mountain peaks, and they shrieked in delight, scattering through the tiny passages of the labyrinth.

I could see the middle of it clearly from this new vantage, and covered the distance in six earth-shaking strides. Once there, I crouched down, poking around with a huge finger.

There was nothing but an old well. Slimy leaves drifted on the surface.

"Stop," a cold voice commanded.

It came from a dark gap in the hedge, and it dropped me back to my own size like a pin in a balloon. My knees buckled and I fell, landing hard in the brown grass. Layla thumped down next to me in an ungainly heap. She banged her head on the stone coping of the well, and her eyes turned glassy.

Mother Mora. I still could not make out the witch's face behind her black veil, but her gown was woven from intricate knotwork. It reminded me of something, some distant warning, but fear dried my mouth and the thought slipped away.

I looked frantically around for the faerie door. It had to be here. It had to!

The witch walked forward with a deliberate, unhurried step.

"You will not leave Night's Labyrinth," she said. "Not now, nor ever."

I dragged my gaze away from her black veil and the silhouette of a face behind it.

Leave . . . That was the key word. So there *was* a door!

Oh. The well?

Gah.

Maybe the Atlas was wrong and there was no door at all. Maybe it was just an old well, in which case we'd drown. Mother Mora didn't seem like the type to dive in and heroically save us.

No, she seemed like the type to bake us into pies. Or one extra-large pie that all the children could share.

I grabbed Layla with my right hand and the satchel holding the Atlas with my left. She peered up at me. "Jack? Is that you?"

"Yes," I said, "hold your breath," and threw us both into the well.

16

CHARLIE

In the interest of keeping things moving along, I'll give you the short version of our visit to the Land of the Savage Bees.

After we fell out of the faerie well and shook the slimy leaves from our hair, I made Layla sit down and drink some water from my canteen. Then we both ate nut bars. She had a bump on her head, but it wasn't bleeding.

The bees turned out to be surprisingly polite, and we found the next faerie door after half an hour of wandering about a pretty goldenrod meadow.

That door—round and reeking of cheap wine—took us into a dim tunnel of rough-cut stone blocks. Roars echoed from somewhere up ahead. They were deep and powerful and made the little mammal at the centre of my brain curl into a tight ball.

"Lions?" I whispered, wiping sweat from my forehead. It was hot as blazes. "Layla, dammit, are those lions?"

She consulted the Atlas and scrunched her nose. "You

know, they might be . . . I think some of these doors lead into temporal loops."

"Deema did *not* mention that." I paused. "What does it mean?"

"It means that we're in the right place but the wrong millennium."

Another roar sounded, followed by thunderous cheers. The tunnel curved and filled with daylight. The tumult ahead grew louder. It sounded like a football match, except with lions running about, and also a few screams that I felt sure didn't come from the onlookers.

I stopped walking, mutinous. "Layla, I am *not* going out there."

"Of course we're not, darling," she said, squeezing my arm. "There's another door . . . that one!"

She dragged me away from the main tunnel and through a narrow crevice into fading sunlight. A big man wearing leather armor and a helmet with a scarlet crest loomed before us. Italian, judging by the olive skin and dark eyes. My stomach clenched until I saw he was posing for photos with a group of frat boys in baggy shorts and backward baseball caps.

"Fifty euros," the centurion said, "or I stab you with my sword."

The Americans laughed nervously and pulled out their wallets.

"Christ Jesus, we made it," Layla exclaimed, staring up at the crumbling arches of the Colosseum. "We're in Rome!"

It was about an hour's walk to Vatican City so we stopped for gelato on the way. I picked chocolate hazelnut and Layla, the daring one, ordered ricotta and fig. The rush hour crowds and cold, sweet ice cream banished the last lingering shadows from our misadventure in Hanter Noz. Something about the witch, Mother Mora, still nagged at me, but I resolved to worry about it later, after we'd collected the message for Deema.

Once at the Tiber, we crossed the Ponte Vittorio Emanuele II, a stone footbridge with the circular hulk of the Castel Sant'Angelo on the far bank. I had never been to Rome. It was amazing, and I wished we could stay and see everything. I was so busy looking around that I was nearly run over by a sexy girl on a moped. Layla yanked me out of the way.

"Watch out," she scolded. "They drive on the other side here." Her gaze followed the miniskirted rider down the street. "I know Italians are hot, love, but they're not worth dying for. Now help me find St. Anne's Gate . . ."

We passed a bookstore and a travel agent promising luxury holidays, then paused at a cobbled street with a fountain. Layla consulted the Atlas. "We're *so* close," she said. "It's just up there."

"Are there actually time-travel rabbit holes?" I asked. "That's rather odd, don't you think?"

"You heard the lions," she said, slamming the book shut.

"Yessss, but I mean . . . was that really the ancient Colosseum? Like, the fight-to-the-death arena?"

My memories of the day were starting to blur together like a fever dream.

"We could pop in on the way back," Layla suggested. "Satisfy your curiosity."

"No, that's all right," I said quickly. "Short on time, aren't we?"

She checked her Snoopy watch. "It is getting late. Come on."

Two short blocks later we arrived at the outer wall of Vatican City. St. Anne's Gate was just past a McDonald's. It was made of ornately wrought iron with double pillars on either side. A lone Swiss Guard stood at the entrance. He wore a black beret, a doublet with puffy sleeves, and flowing pantaloons with bright blue, red, and yellow stripes.

"Well, my contact's hard to miss," Layla said.

"Be careful," I told her. "And hurry back."

She approached the guard with a confident stride. They spoke briefly and she opened the satchel. His stony expression didn't alter—I imagine the Swiss Guard have to look as lethal as possible given their medieval fair costume—but he waved her through.

I wandered over to the vast expanse of St. Peter's Square and sat by the Egyptian obelisk in the middle. Dusk was falling. I watched in silent awe as a flock of starlings whirled above the basilica's dome in a perfectly choreographed tornado-like murmuration.

Murmuration was a fantastic word. I also liked orangery, squall, vainglorious, and aghast.

I sat there thinking about starlings and words. After a while, I began to feel quite strange. Like I'd lost time—a big chunk of it. I knew *why* I was in Rome (fetch something for Deema), but I couldn't remember how I'd gotten there. Or why I was alone with no money and nut bar wrappers in my pocket.

After a minute of two of quiet panicking, the phrase *Saint Anne's Gate* popped into my head. It seemed important to go there. I asked directions from another guard and then hung about on the corner, pretending to look in the window of the nearby McDonald's, whilst ignoring the voice in my head ordering me to find the nearest hospital since I'd obviously sustained a concussion.

When I turned and saw Layla, overpowering relief made me run up to her like a lost child.

"Got it," she whispered, linking her arm through mine. "A cardinal was waiting in a private study. He gave me a scroll sealed in wax with his ring. Of course I haven't a clue what it says." She grinned. "But we're halfway there!"

I was about to ask how we planned to get back to the Chalet when Layla pulled out a large red book—*the Atlas,* I recalled—and memories started slotting themselves into the appropriate cubbyholes of my brain.

Creepy white deer . . . kids with antlers . . . not-so-savage bees . . .

"Good news," she said. "We don't need to trek all the way back to the Colosseum. There's a faerie door just over there."

She jerked her chin at the dark alley behind the McDonald's. I trailed her to a big dumpster that smelled of ancient grease.

"Layla," I said, "when you were in the Vatican, did you forget what happened today? All the places we went?"

She looked puzzled. "No. It was clear as a bell."

"I think it's because you had the Atlas," I said. "Because I nearly forgot *everything* while I was waiting for you. Thank God I remembered Saint Anne's Gate."

Layla nodded slowly. "That makes sense. We know it has magical properties—it makes time run the same no matter where you are. So it must also help mortals keep our wits."

"Deema might have warned us," I muttered, a bit shaken at how close I'd come to being stranded in Rome.

"True, but she didn't know you planned to come along, or

that we'd get separated." Layla took my hand and gave it a squeeze. "So let's make sure we don't again."

"Also, I don't want to go to Hanter Noz again," I said, "so please tell me there's a detour."

"Yes, I could skip a reunion with Mother Mora," Layla said. "According to the Atlas, we have a number of possibilities. I'll sort it once we're through the first door."

The mention of Mother Mora sent my brainwaves humming. After what just happened, I knew I needed to remember it *now*. If I didn't, I might lose it forever—whatever *it* was. I closed my eyes, trying to pinpoint the thing that kept nagging at me. I visualized her black veil, and the gown with its intricate knotwork . . .

"Kitty, the smell in this alley is giving me flashbacks to my worst uni hangovers," Layla said. "Can we just—"

The knotwork. *That was it.* And if I was right . . .

"Listen," I said in a low voice. "I think I know who she really is! When we were in the Vale of Cherry Blossoms, Clove told me about a curse on her sister. It's why Elowyn and Adrien can't be together, even though Adrien clearly loves her—"

"What?! You've been holding out on me."

"I know, I'm sorry, but I'm telling you now. The aunt who cursed Elowyn in her cradle was named Morana. She disappeared and no one knows where she went. But Mother Mora's dress was woven with intricate knotwork just like they make at the Vale. It can't be a coincidence!"

Layla's brows rose further. "What's the curse?"

"That anyone who loves Elowyn will die within a year."

She winced. "Oh, that's a nasty one. Poor thing."

"Clove said that only the person who laid the curse can take it back. Which I'm sure is Mother Mora. We have to tell Adrien she's at the House of Echo!"

Layla nodded. "The instant we return." She glanced at the dark mouth of the alley. "So let's go."

The door behind the McDonald's dumpster was another of those barely perceptible connect-the-cracks situations, but I was getting better at noticing them. We passed through and I immediately smelled the sea. We were partway up a flight of stone stairs. A single torch burned in a bracket, its flame bending in a draft.

"Hmmm," I said. "Up or down?"

"Up first," said Layla.

We climbed.

The stairs wound tight and steep, the brick walls pressing close as the tower tapered. After a dozen turns, I heard a sharp crack of thunder. We emerged into the lantern room of a lighthouse. Sheets of rain lashed the windows and, far below, surf pounded the rocky islet that the lighthouse stood upon. I saw no land in any direction.

"Ah!" Layla said sagely. "The Amberjack Ocean."

I stared at the heaving seas. "Is it where we meant to go?"

"Of course it is, darling. And this lighthouse is a sort of roundabout for a bunch of different roads. I suppose the doors are at the bottom."

We trudged back down the winding stairs, all the way to the base of the lighthouse. The doors were there—seven, set at intervals like numbers on a clock face. One was covered in scales, another had green light leaking from its keyhole, and the next smelled of sulphur. The rest looked relatively normal, but that meant nothing.

Layla sat on the bottom step and propped the Atlas across her knees, angling it toward the torchlight. She began to mutter under her breath, tracing paths with a fingertip, then squinting at the index and starting again. She looked tired—I was dead on my feet—but she was the sort who would quietly keel over before admitting it.

I sat on the step just above her, unwrapped the last nut bar, and broke it in half. She ate without looking up.

"Some of these are *not* viable," she said, chewing. "That one—" she jerked her chin at the scaly door, "—leads to a court where they worship enormous snakes. And I'm fairly sure the one reeking of sulphur goes to—"

The door flew open.

We both shrieked. Layla shoved the Atlas into her satchel as a young man burst through the portal. He wore jeans and a black hoodie and carried a crossbow at his hip. He turned to us, breathing hard.

"Could you do me a massive favour," he said in a thick Scottish accent, "and put your backs against this door for a wee moment?"

Something crashed into it from the other side, hard enough to rattle the hinges.

Layla and I shared a look. We put our backs against the door and braced our feet. There was a brutal scraping sound, like claws being dragged down the wood.

The newcomer rummaged through his satchel—identical to Layla's, I noticed—and pulled out a thick rubber wedge, which he jammed into the crack at the bottom. Whatever was on the other side went quiet.

"That oughta hold," he said cheerfully, studying us with shrewd hazel eyes. "Let me guess, youse came through the door behind the Maccy D's? Someone ought to do something about it. Tourists are always blundering through and getting lost."

Layla bristled. "We are *not* lost," she said indignantly.

"Aye, right." He sounded amused.

I could imagine what we looked like—Layla in her dirty

Liberace jumpsuit, me with my torn leggings and wild hair, picking nut bar out of my teeth.

He dragged a hand through his shoulder-length dredlocks. Then he noticed her satchel and gave a start. "Ah! Sorry—youse must be new couriers. I'm Charlie Maikori."

He held out his hand. I'm an expert at guessing people's ages by their hands. Charlie's placed him in his mid- to late twenties. He had an open, amiable face and I liked him immediately. We all shook and made introductions.

"So where youse off to, then?" Charlie asked, one eye on the rubber wedge holding whatever lurked beyond the door at bay.

"The Tempestarii cloud palace," Layla said. "We were just . . . taking a quick rest."

I gave her a look. We needed help, and I wasn't too proud to admit it. "Maybe you could point us back to the Chalet," I said. "And er, what was chasing you?"

"Ah that, yes. 'Twas a Foireaux Cat," Charlie said.

Layla covered her mouth. "Dear God," she said faintly.

"What's a Foireaux Cat?" I asked, glancing between them. I knew most of the fae species in Britain, but there were hundreds around the world. Thousands, probably.

"Well," Layla said, "they slip in through cat flaps and pretend to be the usual cat who lives in your house. Then, when your guard is lowered, they spit in your soup and poison you. Once they've dragged your soul to hell, they relax by the flames, toasting their fur."

"Surely not," I said, trying to gauge if she was having me on.

"It's a fact," Charlie said. "If you mix a dram of their blood with wine, it cures pneumonia."

"And if you swap eyeballs with a Foireaux Cat," Layla said, "you can see through walls and find buried treasure."

"They grow tall as a man on the Sabbath," Charlie said. "Sometimes they wear armor stolen from their mortal enemies, the Matagot Cats. You can find them—"

"In the Ardennes," Layla interrupted. "Bigorre. And the American state of Maine."

The two of them locked eyes. Then Charlie gave a delighted laugh. "You're a faerie scholar! They're rare these days."

She preened and waved a hand. "It's just a hobby, love. Though I might have written a book or two on the subject."

"She's famous in folklore circles," I said. "Look her up."

"Pish," Layla said, though her eyes sparkled and she'd clearly found a second wind.

"I absolutely will," Charlie said. "There's always something new to learn." He gave us a wry grin. "Like the fact that Foireaux Cats sometimes hang about crossroads like this one."

Layla chewed her lip. "You know, I did read that somewhere, but I didn't think of it until just now. Deema wasn't joking when she said the faerie ways are dangerous."

Charlie nodded. "You can't really avoid the crossroads, but you have to watch your back. They attract all sorts of things. Anyway, I'm going back to the cloud palace myself. Just picked up some books for Deema at the Bodleian Library in Oxford." He patted his satchel and winked. "I know a shortcut, we'll be there in a trice."

I was relieved to follow a seasoned courier the rest of the way home. He chose one of the nondescript doors, and we crossed through to a faerie road that looked wonderfully ordinary—a sunken track of packed earth through a forest of silver birches.

Layla fell into step beside Charlie and peppered him with questions about how he became a courier. It turned out that his mother was from Glasgow, his father from Lagos. They were both economics professors at the University of Edinburgh and tried to be supportive, though they seemed a bit baffled by the direction their son's career had taken.

"I found my first faerie door in the toilet of a pub in Strathbungo," Charlie said as we walked. "Just stumbled through it by accident." He tucked his hands into his jeans pockets. "I'd been wandering about for a while when I heard someone calling for help. There was a woman on the bank of a mire. She'd broken her ankle. A thing stood over her. Old man, white beard to his knees, dressed in rags."

"A Tiddy Mun!" Layla exclaimed. "What did you do?"

"Well, I could see right away it wasn't human and that it meant her harm. A bow and quiver had been thrown up on the bank. I picked it up, nocked an arrow, and shot the Tiddy Mun through the left eye."

"Bloody hell," Layla said, looking impressed. "Had you shot a bow before?"

Charlie shook his head. "I was terrified, but I s'pose I have a talent for it. I found out later that my mum's second cousin in Nigeria had been a fae courier when she was young. So apparently it runs in the family. Anyway, I carried the injured courier back to Deema. After she hired me full-time, I eventually switched to this for protection." He patted the small crossbow at his hip. "Lighter and easier to carry."

"How long have you done it now?" I asked.

"Four years." He smiled. "Never the same day twice."

Presently, the birch forest turned to pine and spruce, and I recognised the grey walls of the Chalet's lower outworks peeking through the trees ahead. Charlie led us into a door at the bottom that opened directly to the turret with the cloud bridge (don't ask how, it makes me dizzy just thinking about it).

We shook hands again, and he promised to look up Layla's books. "I'm off to the eighteenth level," he said, flashing a grin. "Got another job that can't wait. Cheers, see ya later!"

Before I could thank him, he was jogging across the bridge, crossbow bouncing against his hip as he vanished into the swirling mist.

"I like Charlie a lot," I said.

"So do I." Layla sounded wistful. "He's got a fantastic job, the lucky sod." She turned to me with the glassy eyes of someone running on adrenaline fumes. "We did it, darling."

I squeezed her hand. "And I finally got to play the giant."

She laughed and blew out a breath. "Right. Let's go tell Deema we have her message."

17

BAD DOG

The archive was as I remembered it, a jumble of ice blocks with mysterious, shadowy relics frozen in their depths. Deema stood in her floppy hat and greatcoat flipping through a stack of books on a pedestal—perhaps the ones from the Bodleian library that Charlie had dropped off before dashing away on his next assignment. The little snow leopard Ghost crouched at her feet.

"I am glad you returned safely," she said with a smile.

Layla stepped forward and handed Deema the scroll. The Tempestarii briefly examined the cardinal's wax seal, then nodded. "You made excellent time. I didn't expect you back so soon."

It felt to me like we'd been gone for days, but when Layla had checked the time on her Snoopy watch before crossing the bridge, it was barely suppertime.

"I managed all right with the Atlas," Layla admitted, "but Charlie Maikori helped us. I suppose you know that already."

Deema didn't reply, but her storm-coloured eyes drifted to me. I wondered if she would refuse to honor the bargain since Layla brought me without permission. That was my fault, and I was ready to fall on my sword but Deema simply nodded.

"You have fulfilled your part. Now I will honor mine. Bring your father here and we shall see what can be done."

Layla's shoulders sagged. "Thank you."

"Don't thank me yet," Deema cautioned. "He is not restored to himself."

And might never be, I added silently—then berated myself for being a cynic. But it did worry me. After all Layla had gone through, to fail now would be unspeakably cruel.

We turned away and Deema cleared her throat. "The Atlas, please," she said firmly.

Layla blinked. "Right, sorry, of course." She turned over the satchel with a rueful smile. "Long trip, you know."

Nice try, I mouthed when Deema wasn't looking. Layla shrugged.

We knew the way back to the bridge by now, and Deema did not bother summoning a kobold servant to escort us. Once we'd left the archive, Layla voiced my own fear.

"What if it doesn't work?" she said quietly. "What if the enchantment is too powerful?"

"Then we try something else."

She shook her head, grim. "This is the end of the road. We both know it."

"Then don't give up hope," I said. "Not until we *know.*"

We walked the rest of the way to the Ravencroft tower in silence, our buoyant mood deflated. Kobolds had been in to stir the coals and Layla's room was toasty. Barbarossa dozed in his basket by the fire, nose tucked under one paw. I thought of the Foireaux Cats dragging people down to hell and suppressed a shiver.

"Okay," Layla whispered, "I'll pet him and keep him calm while you get the carrier ready."

Her voice was barely audible, but Barbarossa's eyes opened at the word "carrier." He hopped down with a soft thump. I watched the tip of his tail vanish under the bed.

"Dammit," Layla said. "We need a code word."

"Maybe if we explain that it's for his own good—" I cut off at a knock on the door.

"Who is it?" Layla called, frowning.

"Thank all the gods, we've been searching everywhere!" The door burst open and Adrien strode inside. "There you are!" He shot us an accusing look. "Richard is worried sick."

I felt a pang of guilt, but before we could formulate our denials, the Questels' hound pushed past him, tail wagging furiously.

"Ginger, no!" Adrien lunged for her collar, but it was too late.

The dog, exercising a profound lack of judgment, bounded over and stuck her nose under the edge of the quilt. Claws lashed out. Ginger gave an injured yelp and swiftly backpedaled, giving Barbarossa the opening he needed. Like a bony streak of midnight, he shot from under the bed, between Adrien's legs, and out the door.

Layla cursed and dashed after him, briefly tangling with Adrien in the doorway. After a scuffle, he managed to snag Ginger's collar before she joined the chase. "A thousand pardons! I didn't realise the cat . . . Ginger would never harm him, I swear—"

"Not your fault," I assured him. "But we need to find him, fast. The Tempestarii agreed to break the enchantment, and she's waiting for us."

There was something else I meant to tell him . . . something important . . . but I couldn't think of it. I shook my head, frustrated.

"But this is wonderful news!" Adrien said, holding tight to a lunging Ginger. "Ah, you are a bad dog!" he scolded. "I am taking you home at once."

Her ears drooped at the words "bad dog" and I gave her a quick rub so she wouldn't take it personally.

"Go," I said. "Catch up with us later."

Adrien clipped Ginger's lead on and tugged her away. I was partway down the tower's spiral staircase when I ran into Richard coming up.

"Kitty!" His dark hair was rumpled and I knew he'd been dragging his hands through it. The moonstone amulet at his throat pulsed with an agitated light.

I hugged his stiff body, and got a lukewarm pat on the back in return. "I'm sorry, I didn't mean to worry you. I'll tell you everything later, but Barbarossa escaped and we need to find him—"

"Where the *hell* have you been?" The relief in his voice gave way to something sharper. "You disappeared without a word, all day, no one knew where you'd gone—" He broke off, studying my face. "What's happened?"

Even on my best days, I don't take kindly to being chided, and this was not my best day. I was so tired, I could hardly think straight.

"We went to . . . " I rubbed my head. Where on earth had we gone again? There were starlings . . . "Rome! That's it." A few salient details came rushing back. I recited them before they, too, vanished. "Deema of the Tempestarii needed a message picked up from the Vatican. In exchange, she agreed to try breaking the enchantment on Mr. Deen. So we had to. There was no time to tell you first."

"How," Richard asked, "did you get there?"

I lifted my chin. "Faerie roads."

The colour drained from his face. "You ventured into the Otherworld alone?"

"With Layla," I corrected. "And everything went . . . just fine." *Did it, though? I really couldn't recall, dammit.* "I'm standing here right now, aren't I?" I said before he demanded details.

Richard's hot gaze traveled from my filthy shoes to the rat's nest of my hair. "The *Otherworld*," he repeated, his voice dangerously soft. "Without telling me. Without telling anyone."

"Deema knew where we went." I was losing patience. "And we didn't have time. If we'd told you—"

"I would have tried to stop you," he finished. "Can you blame me? People disappear there. Forever!"

"I know that," I snapped, stung by his tone. "But I'm not a child who needs your permission to take risks."

"This isn't about permission," he retorted. "It's about not letting the people who love you think you're dead in a ditch somewhere!"

The hurt beneath his anger penetrated my defensive shell. I took a deep breath and forced myself to see the situation from his perspective. We'd vanished without explanation on the same day he was facing the most difficult challenge of his life at the Riddle.

"You're right," I said. "And I *am* sorry. At the very least, I should have left you a note."

His face softened. "I don't mean to be controlling, Kitty. I know how much it means to you to see this enchantment broken. And I know you can handle yourself with fae." A muscle ticked in his jaw. "But I don't trust these wizards. I was terrified they'd done something to you."

I took his hands. "Forgive me. But right now, we need to find Barbarossa."

Richard bent his head and kissed me, then pressed his forehead to mine. "We haven't had a row in a while," he said softly. "I'll have to make it up to you later." A little tingle of anticipation went through me. "Now which way did the cat go?"

"I'm not sure. He bolted too fast. But I think Layla went that way," I pointed down. "Maybe we should check the upper floors?"

Richard nodded, and we started to climb. I glanced at him sideways. "How was *your* day?"

He sighed. "It's been lovely to see the Questels, and Adrien's done his best to shield me, but the rest . . . Well, the Ravencroft name doesn't inspire much goodwill. The Drexlers refused to sit at the same table when we took a coffee break. And the Montabas all pretended not to hear when I spoke directly to them."

"That's awful," I said, outraged on his behalf. "You were ten years old when your parents were exiled! How could they hold you responsible?"

"Wizard politics has a long memory," he said with a grimace. "And family is everything. The sins of the parents and all that." We paused at a landing, checking behind a tapestry for any sign of Barbarossa. "I managed to keep my temper until lunch, when Vito Grimaldi suggested that perhaps the Ravencrofts should be stricken from the registry of Venerable Bloodlines altogether."

"He didn't!"

"He did." Richard's expression darkened. "In front of everyone. I may have suggested, equally publicly, that for a family so obsessed with pure bloodlines, the Grimaldis had produced a remarkable number of squibs and failures in recent generations."

I grinned. "Good for you. I'm sure he took it well."

Richard snorted. "I thought he'd have a stroke. But I did make one ally—Thaddeus Foote. His parents were part of the same conspiracy as mine. He's been getting the cold shoulder treatment too."

I vaguely remembered Adrien pointing out a man in his thirties with sandy hair and a gentle, crooked smile at the opening dinner. "What's he like?"

"Seems a nice enough bloke. He was raised by his aunt and uncle in Donegal after his parents disappeared." Richard's voice lowered. "They fled the country before they could be arrested. He doesn't even know if they're alive."

My heart twisted. "Poor man."

Richard was silent for a moment. "Anyway, at least Thaddeus found his wizard path," he added, trying to sound cheerful. "He has a gift for speaking with animals—Fauntongue, they call it—

A familiar moaning echoed down the staircase.

"Speaking of which," I said, cocking my head.

"That was definitely Barbarossa," Richard agreed.

18

A MERRY CHASE

The throaty yowl came from somewhere in the upper reaches of the Chalet. Richard and I exchanged a look and hurried to the next floor, which was all meeting rooms. Placards announced the evening Riddle Sessions in flowing purple script:

Substitutions in Spell Components: When You Don't Have Moonwort (Again)

Fae Court Calendars and Seasonal Spell Timing: Spring Forward!

The Foote-MacLeod Symposium on Problematic Ancestral Bargains: Contracts You Didn't Sign and Still Owe

That last one made me want to stop and take notes, but we had more pressing concerns. Richard checked his watch. "It's nearly eight. The evening sessions will be breaking for dinner soon, and then we'll have hundreds of wizards milling about."

"Poor Barbarossa," I said. "He'll be terrified. We need to find him fast. He can't have gone *too* far—"

A faint moan led us down the corridor to *Advanced*

Elemental Transubstantiation: Theory and Emerging Practice. The door stood ajar, and drifting through the gap came the authoritative drone of someone who had spent decades perfecting the art of sounding important.

Before I could squeeze inside, a black shadow came streaking out and fled around the corner. We hurried in pursuit, checking behind a suit of armour, a likely-looking sofa, and a heavy velvet curtain that turned out to conceal nothing but an affronted kobold who was dusting the windowsills.

I muttered apologies and we jogged around the next bend —where the corridor met a dead end.

"He must have gone into another meeting room," Richard said with a wince, surveying the line of open doorways we'd just passed.

"Then we have to check them all." I stepped aside to avoid being jostled by a group of young Ab Owains, their emerald robes swishing as they filed into *Shadow Ethics: A Modern Wizard's Guide to Not Accidentally Conjuring Abominations.*

We followed them to the room and peered inside. The latecomers had joined two dozen wizards seated in a semi-circle, their attention fixed on a woman drawing pictures of monsters on a chalkboard. Several heads turned toward us in irritation. There was no sign of Barbarossa.

"Sorry," I said brightly. "Wrong room."

We worked our way methodically along the corridor. One of us would wander in by mistake while the other loitered, craning for a view under chairs and tables. I became expert at pretending to have dropped something—patting my pockets with an expression of mild concern before crouching down for a quick look at floor level, then straightening with a sheepish smile and backing out.

The third time I performed this manoeuvre, in the

doorway of *Cauldron Bottom Thickness: The Overlooked Crisis in Potion-Making,* a very old wizard with a beard so long it looked like a companion animal turned from the front of the room and stared at me with eyes like two grey stones. His lips began to move and I beat a hasty retreat.

"I never realised magic could be so boring," I whispered as we passed a door marked *Standardized Spell Nomenclature Committee: Year 347 of Deliberations.*

"You've no idea," Richard whispered back. "I fell asleep this morning in *Maintaining Neutrality in Multi-Court Research Environments.* When I woke up, I was the only one still there. Stop laughing, Kitty, it was embarrassing."

I bit my lip. "Sorry. I just hope you didn't snore."

"I never *snore,*" he protested.

"Layla's worse, so don't feel bad," I said. "Oooh, try that one."

He shot me a dark look and walked into a session called *The Art of Culinary Transfiguration.* Unfortunately, the instructor—a Montaba with a formidable bosom and curling black hair—took umbrage at his tardiness and Richard found himself "volunteered" to demonstrate the proper technique for turning treacle into Tabasco sauce. I crawled around the back of the room, peering between legs, as he fumbled through the demonstration.

Richard finally managed to extract himself and we met up in the hallway. "Well, now I know seven ways *not* to transfigure treacle," he said. "Ugh, I'm all sticky."

I leaned in and sniffed. "Mmmmm. You do smell a bit off. Sweet and spicy—just how I like my men."

He snorted and ducked into a lavatory to wash his hands. Then we pressed on, the search becoming more urgent as time slipped away. Five minutes before the sessions were due to end, I glimpsed a black tail furtively vanish into *Contempo-*

rary Management of Ancient Curses: Breaking Bonds Without Breaking the Law.

Ah, the irony.

I grabbed Richard's arm. "There!"

We peered through the door into a crowded auditorium where at least a hundred wizards were listening to a lecturer drone on about the ethical implications of curse modification. On the fourth tier, hiding under the chair of a plump woman with red hair—an Ab Owain, judging by the oak leaves embroidered on her robes—was Barbarossa. He met my eye, gave a guilty blink, and looked away.

"We can't let him bolt again," I whispered.

Richard assessed the room with a strategist's eye. "I'll create a distraction. You grab him when everyone's attention is on me."

Before I could ask what sort of distraction he had in mind, Richard straightened his tie, adjusted his black and silver cloak, and strode into the room as though he'd been invited to give a guest lecture. All eyes turned to him.

I slipped inside and made my way up the sloping ramp, thankful that the plush carpet muffled my approach.

"Pardon, but I have a question!" Richard announced loudly.

The lecturer, a short, wiry man in light blue robes—a Kazan?—scowled. "There will be a Q&A session afterwards, Lord Ravencroft—"

Before he could finish, Richard launched into a spectacular coughing fit. "A thousand pardons," he choked out, pounding his chest. "Must be the—" another wracking cough "—alpine air."

I studied my quarry. He had chosen his hiding spot with uncanny shrewdness. The next seat over was occupied by Vito Grimaldi, Richard's nemesis. The wizard sat straight-backed as ever, an old lion with a flowing white mane who might be past his prime but was still dangerous. He watched Richard gasping for air with a narrow, speculative gaze.

"Perhaps some water, Lord Ravencroft?" the lecturer ventured, sounding concerned.

"Yes, water would be—" Richard erupted into more wracking coughs, keeping everyone's attention on the centre of the auditorium.

I lunged for Barbarossa. He tried to slink under the hem of Vito Grimaldi's purple robe, but this time I was too quick. My fingers closed around his bony haunches. I tried to pull him backwards and he hooked into the carpet, clinging on for dear life. I was forced to reach around and detach his claws, one by one, all the while expecting Vito Grimaldi to look down and demand to know what on earth I was doing.

Barbarossa emitted an outraged growl that thankfully coincided with another of Richard's coughing fits. He saw me out of the corner of his eye and gave a brief nod as I sidled down the ramp, Barbarossa writhing like a basket of eels in my arms.

"Well, go on, Ravencroft," Grimaldi declared, his voice dripping with derision. "Now that you've caused a scene, what exactly is your question?"

The room fell silent. Everyone stared at Richard. He cleared his throat.

"Thank you, Vito," Richard said, his voice stronger. "I'm curious about the intersection of binding curses and time-dilation effects in pre-Renaissance spellcraft. When Arch-mage Dobrovnik claimed that temporal anchoring was essential to maintaining cross-generational hexes . . ."

I didn't hear the rest of Richard's impromptu question because I was slipping out the door. Halfway down the corridor, I glanced back to see Richard walking briskly to catch up. As soon as we turned the corner, we both dissolved into hysterics.

"Griamldi's face," Richard gasped, leaning against the wall. "He had no idea you were practically *underneath* his robe . . ."

"Your coughing!" I countered, struggling to hold the moaning cat. "I thought you were about to hack up a lung!"

Richard wiped his eyes. "That was more fun than I've had since we arrived."

"How did you know what to ask?" I said. "It was brilliant."

He shrugged. "I just made it up on the spot."

We fell over laughing again.

Barbarossa had lapsed into sullen silence, but now he launched an explosive escape attempt. I managed to keep hold of him with Richard's help—just barely. "We'd better get this troublemaker back to Layla," I said. "Also, I need more of that healing potion."

"Give him to me," Richard offered.

Barbarossa screamed like a lynx, a bone-chilling cry that literally sounds like a person being murdered.

"Bloody hell," Richard said, "perhaps not."

We half-ran to the Ravencroft tower. By the time we reached Layla's room, where she was pacing with Adrien, I had a fresh collection of scratches.

"You found him!" Layla cried, rushing forward.

"Quick, the carrier," Richard urged.

At the hated word, Barbarossa seemed to sprout an extra set of legs, all of them flailing. Adrien held the carrier open while Richard and I performed a complicated transfer that miraculously resulted in Barbarossa ending up inside. The mesh door zipped just as bells throughout the Chalet began to chime, announcing the end of the day's sessions.

Layla knelt beside the carrier, her expression soft. "It's nearly over," she said. "We're taking you to Deema."

The only answer was a long, mournful cry.

The archive looked different at night. Moonlight silvered the ice holding Hans Winteregg's cloak and amulet, and I could make out a scattering of bright stars through holes in the shifting clouds.

Adrien and Richard came with us. I drew strength from their presence, and I think Layla did, too. Both of them had played a role in discovering Barbarossa's true nature. They ought to be here for the end.

Deema waited alone in her storm-grey greatcoat. The silence amplified the swift beating of my heart as Layla set Barbarossa's carrier down. Her fingers shook slightly as she unzipped the door.

"Watch out," I cautioned. "He's been temperamental—"

Barbarossa lashed out, his claws catching her finger. A bead of blood welled up, and Layla jerked her hand back with a hurt expression.

"Allow me," Deema said firmly. She gestured and tendrils of cloud seized the hissing cat, lifting him into the air. "Be still," she commanded. "Your time of hiding is over."

Barbarossa made a plaintive sound and allowed Deema to run her dark hands through his fur. "The enchantment runs deep," she said. "It is rooted in his very being. There will be pain in the breaking, but it can be done. His physical form can be returned to what it was. Whether he will be *wholly* a man in both mind and spirit, I cannot say."

I moved to Layla and put an arm around her waist. It all

seemed to be happening so fast, and I was terrified at the outcome. But only Layla could stop Deema now, and I knew she wouldn't.

The Tempestarii's hands moved in intricate patterns, leaving faint trails of lightning in their wake. Barbarossa gave a last anguished howl. The clouds around him billowed, darkened, concealing him entirely. Then Deema pursed her lips and blew like a child scattering dandelion fluff, and the mist dissipated.

My breath caught. A naked man with light brown skin crouched on the floor, blinking.

"Dad?" Layla's voice broke on the word.

I quickly looked away.

"Allow me to help you, sir." It was Adrien's voice, solemn and kind. There was a rustle of cloth. He had been thoughtful enough to bring an extra shirt and pair of trousers. Layla's hand gripped mine so tightly it hurt.

"You may turn around," Adrien said, after a minute that felt like an eternity.

We turned to find Arush Deen leaning on Richard's arm. The clothes hung loosely on his thin frame. Grey threaded his hair and his face was lined, but he looked much as I remembered from the old photographs at the inn.

Except for one thing—his eyes were the same golden-yellow as the cat's.

He stared at Layla, wonder and confusion on his face. "My dear girl . . . but you're all grown up." His voice had the same Sri Lankan-British lilt as Layla's mum. "Of course you are. I knew that. I *do* remember, but it's all so strange . . ." He reached out a hand, then let it fall. "Layla. My Layla."

With a sob, she flung herself into his arms. He staggered but held her tight. I found tears pricking my own eyes. He *knew* her, and that's all that mattered for now.

After a long moment, Mr. Deen gently disengaged himself and looked around with bewilderment. "Where are we?"

"The palace of the Tempestarii fae," Layla said, wiping her eyes. "This is Deema, the archivist. She broke the enchantment."

Deema smiled at him. "You have courage and fortitude. Not all would have survived with their mind intact."

"Thank you," Mr. Deen said. "I remember . . . being *him*. Being me, but also . . . *not* me." He frowned, rubbing his temples. "Birds and mice I recall very clearly." A small smile crossed his face. "And that blasted parrot."

"What do you remember of mortals?" Deema asked.

"Well," he replied slowly, "I understood some words, but they seemed unimportant. Like background noise. I knew my family, but it was as if . . . as if I was watching them from behind thick glass."

"Do you remember who cursed you?" Deema asked.

I tensed. So did Layla. I wanted to know, yet somehow I feared the answer.

Mr. Deen's expression darkened. "That part is clearer." He took a deep breath, steadying himself. "I was gathering mushrooms in the Wild Wood. Milkcaps and Fool's Funnel. Then I heard voices. Something about the hushed tones made me wary. I crept closer to see who it was.

"Six figures stood in a clearing. They wore cloaks with the hoods raised and I couldn't make out their faces. But I caught enough to know they were speaking about the queen. About stealing her away and placing a faerie changeling on the throne."

Richard turned white as curdled milk. I shook my head slightly in denial. It couldn't be. Oh God, no.

"I realised then that I was in grave danger," Mr. Deen

continued. "I tried to sneak away, but a twig cracked beneath my foot." He shuddered. "The next thing I remember is running through the undergrowth on four legs with the cloaked figures chasing me. But I was cunning and sly, and managed to lose them in the Wild Wood."

There was an awful silence. Then Richard spoke, his voice hollow. "My parents," he said. "I fear . . ." He couldn't finish the sentence.

Mr. Deen studied him with dawning recognition. "You're the Ravencroft boy! I saw your mother down in the village occasionally. How is she . . . ?" He trailed off at the pain on Richard's face. Of course, Mr. Deen had disappeared before they were arrested and knew nothing about it—though he had unwittingly overheard them plotting.

Or he'd heard *someone* plotting, I reminded myself. Right at the edge of the Ravencroft estate.

"What happened after you got away?" I asked quickly.

He squinted at me. "Kitty Boot?"

I swallowed hard and nodded.

"Kitty . . . I'm sorry I scratched you."

"Oh that, it's nothing. You were upset. The carrier . . ."

He winced, a brief spasm. "As for your question, I lived wild for a time. Catching frogs and voles. But then winter came. It was a cold, hungry life."

"Oh, Dad," Layla said, wiping her eyes again.

He smiled. "But eventually, some instinct drew me back to the village. To the inn."

"I believe that instinct saved you in more ways than one," Deema said. "Being among those you had loved as a man helped preserve the human part of you."

"I remember the day Barbarossa—you—showed up," Layla said. "You were soaking wet from the rain, meowing at the back door. Mom thought you might belong to someone in the village, but when no one claimed you . . ." Her voice broke. "We kept you."

"I was so happy to be home," Mr. Deen admitted. "Being near you all . . . it sparked memories of being a man, though they felt distant, like they had happened to someone else."

"Quince knew," Layla said.

Mr. Deen nodded. "He recognised me right away, but I . . . I was ashamed. And I didn't want to upset you more." His expression grew wistful. "I was very glad to have a warm place to sleep. Of course, I couldn't help but sneak out. But I came back the next morning. And the next."

Layla was weeping again, silent tears tracking down her cheeks. "Don't, dearest. I was where I needed to be," Mr. Deen said. "With my family."

They embraced. Richard stepped a dozen paces away, his face a mask of controlled anguish. I followed

"We don't know for certain it was your parents," I said softly. "And even if it was . . . Well, all that matters is that we have Mr. Deen back. Look how happy they are."

Richard gave a curt nod, but I could see this new evidence of his parents' guilt—and their callous treatment of an innocent man—had torn open the old wounds.

Adrien joined us. "We'll get to the bottom of this," he vowed. "I'm sure—"

"No," Richard interrupted sharply. "We won't speak of them again. Never, do you hear me? It's over! They're dead to me."

Adrien and I exchanged a look. He looked unhappy, but he knew better than to argue with Richard when he was in a mood like this.

"Of course, cousin," Adrien murmured. "I don't blame you at all."

I covered a huge—and inappropriate—yawn. It was all

catching up to me and I was literally swaying on my feet. Layla too, judging by the happy exhaustion on her face. We thanked Deema again and made our way back across the cloud bridge. There was an extra room in the Ravencroft quarters for Mr. Deen.

"Stay with me," I told Richard as we'd bid the others goodnight. "I'll probably pass out on you, but I'd still like the company."

His face softened. "So would I," he said.

19

FEENACHT

I woke to the chill light of dawn filtering through the window. Richard slept beside me, one arm draped across my waist. The events of the previous night hardly felt real. Layla was reunited with her father, our mission accomplished against all odds.

The Riddle was almost over. One more day and we could go home, back to the gentle rhythms of village life where the biggest excitement was quiz night at the Dancing Toadstool.

So why did I feel unsettled, like the moment before thunder rolls across a summer sky?

I'd always had an instinct for magical mischief. Leading walking tours in the most faerie-infested part of England gave one a sixth sense about these things. But perhaps this time it was simply nerves.

Richard stirred beside me. His hair was tousled, his jaw bristly. I especially loved him in the early mornings when he was most relaxed. Now his face softened into a smile that made my heart skip.

"Good morning," he murmured.

I nestled closer. "Sleep well?"

"Better than I expected after hearing Arush Deen's tale last night." A shadow crossed Richard's face, but he shook it off. "Never mind, I refuse to dwell on that."

"We still don't know it was your parents who—"

"It doesn't matter. Truly." He gave me a dazzling smile and stretched, the sheet sliding down to reveal the lean plane of his chest. "I'm just glad the Riddle is almost over. I miss Little Groating and the Hall."

I grinned. "Well, my nefarious plan to win you over has come to its full fruition. If the old Richard could hear you now, he'd be appalled."

He pulled me close. "Then who needs him?"

I laughed. "I love you both. But yes, I was just thinking the same thing. I enjoyed the adventure, but I'm glad it's over. You've done brilliantly, you know. Despite Vito Grimaldi's worst attempts."

Richard's smile faded. "Do you still think he was behind the attack on the faerie road?"

"I don't know. But whoever it was hasn't tipped their hand with another attempt. Maybe they've given up. They tried to intimidate you and it didn't work."

Even as I spoke the words, my foreboding returned. A voice whispered that it wasn't over—not just yet. I didn't say this aloud. And I doubt it would have changed anything if I had.

Richard caught my hand and brought it to his lips. "Well, it was all worth it to bring Layla's father home as himself."

I thought of Mrs. Deen and how she'd never remarried despite being courted by various hopeful suitors over the more than two decades of her husband's absence. She'd never worn black or called herself a widow. Never took off her wedding ring or packed the old photos up in boxes.

Arush was her one great love, and even if he never returned, she would rather live out her days with his memory than make a new life with someone else.

"If I lost you for twenty-three years and then got you back again," I said to Richard, "I can't imagine what that would feel like."

"You'll never lose me," Richard said firmly. "In fact, I look forward to parading you about on my arm tonight."

I frowned. "What's tonight?"

"Feenacht," Richard said. "Remember? The wizard equivalent of All Soul's Night when the boundary between realms grows thin. It's the traditional closing fete of the Riddle. There will be a formal ball, followed by the Night Market."

I sat up. "A formal ball? Tonight?" Panic fluttered in my chest as I mentally inventoried my wardrobe. There were the two dresses I'd worn to dinner, but nothing suitable for a ball.

Richard's lips quirked into a mischievous smile. "I might have informed Madame de Berry before we left," he said, looking far too pleased with himself. "Gilcarren will bring the gown by later. Apparently, it's stunning."

I arched a brow. "Dr. Ravencroft, you are entirely too smug."

"Entirely," he agreed, sliding his hand behind my neck and pulling me down for a kiss that deepened, sending pleasant shivers down my spine.

When we broke apart, both breathing a little faster, he looked regretful as he glanced toward the window where sunlight now streamed in earnest. "I ought to go. The final sessions start in an hour, and I'm signed up for something called Low-Impact Spellcraft for Shared Spaces. It sounded . . . relaxing."

I watched him dress, transforming from the warm, sleep-rumpled man who had shared my bed into Lord Ravencroft, wizard and heir to an ancient magical lineage. The moonstone amulet gleamed at his throat as he adjusted the chain. "I'll see you tonight," he promised, pausing at the door. "Save me a dance?"

"Every dance," I replied, feeling a flutter of anticipation.

After he left, I lay in bed for a while, doing nothing. Tomorrow we would leave for home, Layla and her father reunited. A happy ending worthy of Nan's fairytales.

I SPENT THE DAY LOUNGING ABOUT THE QUESTEL SUITE. I figured I'd earned it after our trip to Rome, although I could scarcely remember a bit of it now. When I asked Adrien why I could still remember the details of our journey to the Chalet—the magical storm, the Vale of Cherry Blossoms, Clove and Elowyn—he said that a spell had been woven into the coach to ward off the temporal anomalies that affected mortals in Faerie.

He'd told his father he had a headache to get out of the last Riddle Sessions. We curled up with Ginger and played cards for hours—not Barbu, which was far too complicated, but Go Fish and Gin Rummy. Every so often I found myself studying Adrien's face with the strong feeling that there was something I'd meant to tell him. But each time the thought drifted away like smoke.

In the late afternoon, I slipped away to check on Layla and her father. I found them in her suite, Mr. Deen dozing in an armchair while Layla read a book.

"I don't want to disturb you—" I began.

"No, no," she said softly. "Come in."

We went to the adjacent sitting room. "So how's it been going?" I asked.

"Fine, I guess. He sleeps a lot. Not much difference from before, really."

"He must be exhausted," I said. "Not just the physical part but from a mental standpoint. Everything looks different. And all that lost time . . ."

Layla nodded. "Sometimes he seems like himself, sharing stories about mum and the inn. Other times he just sits there staring at nothing." She leaned forward and lowered her voice to a whisper. "After breakfast, he licked his hand and started to wash before catching himself."

I wasn't sure what to say, so I fell back on an empty cliche. "Er, old habits are hard to break, I suppose."

"Do you think he'll get better, Kitty?" she asked.

There was such hope in her eyes. "I'm certain he will," I said. "Just give him time."

"We're not coming to the ball tonight," she said after a moment. "Dad needs rest, and I want to stay with him. The crowds will be too much. Besides, I'm not in the mood to play Mrs. Voss."

"Do whatever you please," I told her firmly. "And tomorrow we go home and see your mum. She'll be over the moon."

"Yeah," Layla said, smiling. "She will."

"What about your brothers?"

Layla had older twin brothers who were thirty-two and shared a flat in London. Their names were Darwin and Mendel. When they were born, Mr. Deen had high hopes that his sons would become famous biologists, but it wasn't in the cards. Darwin managed a trendy boutique hotel in Notting Hill and Mendel was an underwear model. Layla joked that they might technically be straight, but they were *far* gayer than she was.

"I didn't tell them a thing," she said, gnawing on a thumbnail. "Didn't want to get their hopes up, you know? But I'll ring as soon as we're back with the good news."

"It'll be a bang-up Christmas this year," I said with a grin. "We'll throw a big bash at the Hall. Sugar & Sprites can cater."

"And miss all the fun?" Layla laughed. "We'll see." She sobered and suddenly pulled me in for a hug, her voice thick. "Thanks, Kitty. You're the best."

We embraced for a long moment. Layla had the softest hair, and it always smelled good even when it was dirty. I finally untangled myself and sat back. "Does that mean I get to ride Rainbow Dash at the Pride Parade?"

JUST BEFORE SUNSET, GILCARREN ARRIVED AT MY DOOR bearing a garment bag and a shoebox. "From Madame de Berry, with her compliments," he said.

I unzipped the bag. The dress was shimmery black silk, its bodice sewn with tiny silver beads that caught the light like stars against an inky night sky. The shoes matched perfectly—silver slippers with delicate beadwork. And inside one of the slippers, Richard had tucked a stunning bracelet of freshwater pearls, three strands that felt heavy and smooth in my hand.

"Lord Ravencroft wanted you in his own colours tonight," Gilcarren said, baring his sharp teeth in a smile.

I felt a flutter of anticipation as I thanked him. Then I went off to bathe and get ready for the evening's festivities.

The Chalet's ballroom had been transformed into a frozen forest with trees and flowers, foxes and stags and hares, all carved from blocks of ice. I knew the Tempestarii had crafted them for they were too exquisitely lifelike to come from mortal hands.

The silk gown left my arms bare, but I felt warm thanks to glowing white orbs that drifted through the room, radiating heat.

"My cousins made those," Adrien whispered. "Trust me, it is no easy task to keep the temperature pleasant while not melting the decor."

"Well, then," I replied, "I hope Richard is a hearth wizard, too. We could use those globes. Ravencroft Hall gets quite draughty in January."

Adrien sniffed. "The whole country gets draughty—and stays that way. If you ever wed, it must be at the Villa du Soleil. We shall have the ceremony on the beach!"

I made a noncommittal noise. Not about marrying Richard, but I knew he'd want to do it at his ancestral seat—despite his complicated feelings for the Hall.

As always, the Questels entered en masse, their blue and green finery bright as peacocks against the icy decor. A classical orchestra played on a raised platform, something by Strauss, I think.

I spotted Richard standing alone across the room. The moonstone amulet nestled in the hollow of his throat, and his hair was winsomely rumpled. He looked every inch the dark wizard, powerful and assured.

I wasn't the only one who noticed. Several women in the colours of Drexler and MacLeod studied him with undisguised interest, and a handsome man in Grimaldi purple flashed him a flirty smile, apparently unmoved by the ancient feud between their families.

There was a buzz of excitement in the air I hadn't felt before. Young people laughing too loud, touching hands and arms, their elders standing on the sidelines in watchful groups. As we crossed the floor, I understood the true purpose of Feenacht. The sons and daughters of the Venerable Bloodlines were here to make matches and forge alliances that would shape wizard politics for generations.

"May I borrow your companion for one dance before you steal her away forever?" Adrien asked when we reached Richard.

His gaze lingered on me. "It's up to Kitty. She doesn't need my permission."

I knew he was trying to make up for our row, and I loved him even more, if that was possible.

"Of course I don't," I said evenly, "but I do think it's fair that I tell you in advance that I intend to dance with Adrien. So you know where I've gone."

Adrien glanced between us. "Do you two need a lawyer to draw up a contract? Or may we simply dance?"

I gave him a playful push and dragged him out to the dance floor. Of course, Adrien was a wonderful partner. My feet barely touched the ground as he guided us gracefully through the turns, the music swelling. He also unleashed his razor wit to great effect, sharing the gossip he'd picked up about the other dancers. By the time we returned to Richard's side, I was breathless with laughter.

"I shall retire to the punchbowl," Adrien announced. "Ah look, there's Anna Montaba. I fear she plans to knock me on the head with her cane and drag me to her room." He shrugged. "Once I am deflowered, I shall be entirely in her power."

"Somehow, I think that ship already sailed," Richard said dryly. He turned to me and bowed from the waist. "Miss Boot, may I have this dance?"

He held out a hand. I took it. Another waltz began and Richard drew me close, one hand resting lightly at my waist. He guided me across the floor, his steps sure and confident. Unlike Adrien's playful style, Richard danced with intensity, his dark eyes never leaving mine.

"You took my breath away when I first saw you tonight," he said as we spun beneath a shower of enchanted snowflakes.

I felt my cheeks heat. "Only because of Madame de Berry's magic."

"No," he whispered in my ear. "The dress is pretty, but the woman wearing it is ravishing."

We danced until my head spun. When the waltz ended, we found a kobold carrying a tray of crystal flutes filled with blue liquid. I was parched and dying for a drink.

"You try," the kobold urged, grey eyes sparkling beneath its pointed red hat. "A special distillation of juniper berries and frost lilies that bloom only on Feenacht."

I had a cautious sip. "Blimey," I choked out. "That packs a punch."

Richard took a glug and coughed, eyes watering. "It tastes like a glacier soaked in alcohol."

My grin felt lopsided. "Exactly!"

"Shall we visit the Night Market?" he asked.

I nodded eagerly, and we left the ballroom through a wide archway that led to a vast open courtyard under a canopy of stars. The Night Market spread before us, a magical bazaar with a hundred stalls selling everything from crystals to cauldrons. A frozen rink occupied the centre, with skaters gliding in pairs and trailing streams of white light behind their blades.

We browsed for a while, pausing to try out enchanted quills that automatically translated text into different languages. There were apothecaries stocked with rare spell ingredients in tins and jars. There were antiquarian booksellers and pale, wizened men peddling secret formulae to turn lead into gold.

We were examining a display of coloured candles when excited murmurs rippled through the crowd. People were pointing, their faces alight with anticipation.

"What's happening?" I asked.

"Frost imps," Richard said. "I heard they put on a show for Feenacht every year."

A moment later, they appeared—leering, leather-skinned creatures riding small sleighs across the night sky. They swooped above the market, pelting each other with snowballs that burst into glittering crystals on impact.

The crowd shouted and clapped as the display grew more elaborate. The imps conjured roaring snow dragons and prancing unicorns and tentacled krakens. A few of the families had brought young children, who cheered with delight as the imps performed daring aerial acrobatics, racing the sleighs around an invisible track high above our heads.

Then one of them hurled a snowball down at the rink. When it struck, jagged shards of ice exploded outward, sending the skaters scrambling for safety.

"What the devil," Richard muttered.

Another volley rained down, aimed at the market. People screamed and scattered beneath the onslaught. The chandler's stall collapsed, impaled by a spike of ice as thick as a tree branch, its owner barely escaping in time. The frost imps bared their silver teeth. With chittering screeches, they hurled hailstones down on the milling crowd.

I grabbed Richard's arm. "We need to get back inside!"

But the archway was blocked by panicking wizards. All around us, the Night Market dissolved into chaos as the frost imps descended, leathery wings beating the air as they swooped toward their prey.

20

A REEK OF DARK MAGIC

I chanced to look up and saw two imps diving toward us. They gnashed their silver teeth and hurled little lightning bolts that crackled and boomed.

"Over there!" Richard cried.

We ran to a mostly intact stall and crawled under the table. Across the courtyard, a flash of blue caught my eye. Adrien stood with raised hands, his golden hair tossed about by the wind. Flames leapt toward a cluster of marauding imps. The creatures scattered, but a moment later the flames guttered and they came surging back.

My heart sank as I saw it was the same everywhere. Wizards were trying to repel the imps, but their spells fizzled like damp matches. I recalled what Adrien had said about the Riddle being held on neutral ground. Wizards were strongest on their own estates. The farther they traveled from their ancestral land, the weaker their power became.

And the imps clearly knew it.

A thin scream cut the air. It was a child, cowering inside a giant cauldron that had tipped to one side. Two imps circled above her, preparing to land.

"Wait here!" Richard said. He darted across the open ground and scooped her into his arms. The moonstone at his throat flared with blinding light, and the imps screamed and flew off. A moment later, the girl's parents—Kazans, I thought, in light blue robes— rushed forward and carried her away. Richard doubled back, throwing himself down next to me as a squadron of at least twenty imps passed overhead.

"How could this happen?" I whispered. "Doesn't the Chalet have defenses?"

"I've no idea," Richard said. "But it can't be random. I wonder what they're after—"

There was a hard thump above our heads as an imp landed on the table. Clawed feet scraped against wood, knocking satchels of dried herbs to the ground. We pressed together so tight I could feel Richard's heart thrumming against mine. The creature sniffed the air. Then it took flight, perhaps distracted by easier prey.

"We'd better get inside," Richard whispered. "If we stay here, they'll find us."

I chewed my lip. "It's a long way to the door."

"Then we'll head for the stall over there." He pointed. "See?"

It was about halfway across the courtyard. I drew a deep breath. "Yes."

"We'll take cover and then try for the next one." His fingers interlaced with mine. "Now!"

We ran past one of the pale alchemists trying desperately to gather his potions and stuff them in a sack. The frost imps circled overhead, screeching maliciously. I looked for Adrien, but he had disappeared. At least the scrum to get through the archway into the Chalet had mostly calmed down. I flung myself through the torn flaps of the stall, landing on hands and knees as Richard tumbled in behind me.

We crawled beneath another table as a barrage of hailstones struck. Rare books tumbled from their shelves, pages fluttering like wounded birds. Richard pulled me against him as ice fragments pounded the floor.

"I'm sorry," he whispered.

I twisted to look at him. "For what?"

"For being bloody useless. If I'm a storm summoner like my parents, I might be able to stop these creatures. But I haven't a bloody clue if that's my path. Or if it is, how to tap the power."

"This isn't your fault! Don't be a ninny." I peered into the darkness. "The Tempestarii will deal with them. We just need to stay hidden."

I could smell that reek of dark magic in the air, like burning electrical wires. Ghostly fingers of hoarfrost crept across the ground. A vicious cold gripped me. Something was happening—

The imp landed before us with a flap of its leathery wings. Eyes like colourless chips of ice fixed on Richard. A shriveled hand reached for his throat, fingers closing around the moonstone amulet. With a hard jerk, it snapped the chain.

Richard lunged, but the imp danced away on nimble feet, clutching its prize. The amulet gleamed in its little monkey hands, catching the dim light. The imp made a wheezing sound that might have been laughter and turned to flee.

Without thinking, I pulled off one of my slippers and used it to swat one of the heat globes that was drifting past. I aimed for the imp's face, remembering how they had scattered from Adrien's flames.

The effect was immediate. The imp shrieked in fury, its skin blistering where the heat globe touched it. It scrambled backward to escape the burning orb.

"Richard, the amulet!" I cried.

He made a frantic dive for it, fingers grazing the chain. For a heartbeat, I thought he might reclaim it—but the creature was too quick. It shot upward, the moonstone still clutched in its claws. Richard was on his feet in an instant, bursting through the ragged stall entrance in pursuit.

"Wait!" I cried.

By the time I caught up, he was standing in the centre of the market, his face white with fury, and the sky was full of fleeing imps, like a flock of misshapen birds. The Night Market lay in ruins. Dazed wizards were emerging from their hiding places. Several figures lay still, encased in ice. I recognised Vito Grimaldi, his purple robes frozen into stiff folds like fondant. *A wizard ice cream cake,* I thought, followed by, *I'm a very bad person. Let's blame that blue alcohol.*

Richard sank to his knees. He cracked the thin layer of ice and pressed his fingers to the man's throat, searching for a pulse. "Alive, thank God," he said.

Adrien came running up, his face ashen. "My father was attacked," he said, pausing to gulp air. "Frozen . . ."

Richard stood and gripped his shoulders. "You're a hearth wizard. Your magic might be weak but it's not gone. Focus whatever warmth you can summon and get them inside. But do it gradually. Too fast, and the shock could kill them."

Adrien gave a shaky nod and hurried to tend to Jean-Marie, while Richard knelt beside Vito Grimaldi. "Anyone with medical training or healing skills, please come over here. The rest of you, go find blankets, cloaks, anything warm. We need to move them to the great hearth in the dining hall."

The shock that had paralyzed the crowd broke. Wizards rushed to help, lifting the frozen forms—there were eight—and using the stall coverings as makeshift litters. Richard directed the triage with calm authority, moving between victims and checking vital signs.

I helped a young Drexler carry thick woolen blankets from inside the Chalet. As I passed them to waiting hands, I caught sight of Richard conferring with one of the MacLeods. His face was calm, but I knew him well enough to see the anger simmering beneath. His amulet was gone, and with it the key to the Court of Silver Shadows.

And not just his. From what I could tell, all nine amulets of the Venerable Bloodlines appeared to have been taken in the attack.

Inside the dining hall, kobolds were building up the fire. The frozen wizards were wrapped in blankets and laid out near the flames. Some were already reviving. There were a few minor injuries, but no one had died.

I helped where I could, fetching hot drinks, laying heated stones wrapped in cloth near the victims' feet. It was Vito Grimaldi who woke up first. He tried to sit but was restrained by his wife, who murmured words in Italian.

But Grimaldi wasn't looking at her. His gaze fixed on Richard, who was examining Merwyn Ab Owain. A vein pulsed in the old man's forehead. "You," he spat, his voice hoarse but carrying enough venom to draw every eye. "You did this!"

Richard straightened and eyed him wearily. "I have no idea what you're talking about, Grimaldi. I'm trying to help—"

Grimaldi struggled to a sitting position despite his wife's gentle protests. "How fortunate! The Ravencroft heir survives unscathed while the rest of us are attacked." He looked around the room, which had gone dead silent. "His treasonous parents were storm summoners—a rare talent. Those were creatures of ice and wind who robbed us! Do not insult our intelligence by claiming it's a coincidence."

A murmur ran through the gathered wizards. I stepped forward before it got out of hand. "Don't be ridiculous," I snapped. "Richard lost his amulet too. An imp stole it right in front of me!"

"Perhaps," Grimaldi retorted. "But if he controlled them, wouldn't he do so to maintain the illusion of innocence?"

Instead of pointing out how ridiculous the charge was, Richard kept an icy silence. How familiar I was with that side of him! Adrien let loose a torrent of French that I didn't understand but definitely had curses in it. An argument erupted among the families both for and against Richard's guilt, with Thaddeus Foote taking Richard's side.

At last, a rolling boom of thunder silenced the room.

Deema strode in, her storm-grey greatcoat billowing in a gust of rain. Ghost prowled at her side, teeth bared in a silent warning. "Enough of your bickering," she snapped. "The imps are gone and will not return this night. The Cloud Palace was also attacked. Hans Von Winteregg's cloak and amulet have been stolen."

Grimaldi seemed struck dumb by this news. I shared a worried look with Richard.

"Impossible," someone called. "Winteregg has been dead for centuries. How could he—"

"I do not know," Deema cut in. "But either he has returned, or someone has taken up his mantle. Those imps did not carry out this assault on their own. No, they were ordered to do it, and we shall discover who and why." She moved to the centre of the room, her gaze pausing on

Richard before sweeping past. "The Riddle is over. You will return to your estates at first light."

"But our amulets—"

"We can't leave without—"

"Who will recover—"

Deema raised her hand. "You are welcome to hunt the frost imps, but they move constantly, like the storms they ride."

A few wizards muttered, but none dared to contradict her.

"The Tempestarii shall convene our own council to determine what must be done," Deema said. "But I expect the Chalet to be empty by noon." Ghost gave a low growl. The pair of them turned and left, the silence filling with anxious whispers.

Richard looked grim. I knew he didn't give a fig about Grimaldi's wild claims, but without his amulet, he had no way to reach the Court of Silver Shadows. No way to renew the bargain that had bound his family for generations.

And no way to keep the promise for which I was the forfeit.

21

BITTER FAREWELL

When I went to Layla's room, which was on the far side of the Chalet and faced a peaceful view of the mountains, I found her still in her pyjamas. Mr. Deen sat by the window, amber eyes fixed on a cute little alpine bird with reddish wings and a long beak. His fingers twitched against the chair's armrest, but he didn't look over or acknowledge my presence in any way.

"He's been like that all morning," Layla whispered. "I offered him yoghurt and muesli, but he just made this . . . humming noise and went back to watching birds." She eyed me up and down. "You look terrible, Kitty. What happened last night? I saw lights in the sky, but I assumed it was part of the Feenacht celebrations."

I sank into a chair and related all that happened. The frost imps diving from the sky, the attack on the wizard elders, and worst of all, the theft of the amulets.

Layla blanched. "The key to the Court of Silver Shadows is gone?"

I nodded wearily.

"But that means—"

"Richard can't fulfill his promise to dance with Maeryn Vael at the Frost Moon," I finished.

"Oh no! Oh shit!"

"Yes. And there's more. Deema said the frost imps also stole two items from the Cloud Palace—Hans Von Winteregg's cloak and amulet."

"The rogue wizard?" She frowned. "The one from hundreds of years ago?"

"Deema believes he's either returned or someone is trying to make us think he did. Either way, it's connected to the attack." I rubbed my eyes. "The Riddle is over. Everyone's been ordered to get out by noon."

Layla cracked her knuckles. "Okay, don't worry, love, we can solve this. I need access to my laptop. All my notes." She was already kicking into overdrive. "There's bound to be other ways to reach the Vaels' court."

"The Frost Moon is two weeks away," I reminded her.

Layla fell silent, her brow furrowed. After a moment, she stood. "Let's ask Deema first. If anyone knows another way to reach the Court of Silver Shadows, it would be her."

Hope flickered. "Do you think she'd help us again?"

"We won't know unless we try." Layla glanced at her father, who hadn't moved from his vigil. "Dad will be fine."

Mr. Deen hummed low in his throat as the bird hopped closer to the glass.

"If he still had a tail, it would be twitching," Layla muttered. "But you know what? I'm grateful he's here. Even if he's . . . a bit off."

"He'll get back to normal," I said. "It would be peculiar if he didn't have a few . . ."

"Quirks?" she finished wryly.

"Little Groating has more than its share of eccentrics. He'll fit right in."

Layla barked a laugh and threw Mrs. Voss's kaftan over her pyjamas. "Come on. If they're kicking us out, we'd better hurry."

THE MORNING SUN PAINTED THE CLOUD BRIDGE IN BRILLIANT white and gold, a sight I would have appreciated under different circumstances. Now, with my future dangling by a frayed thread, the splendour felt like cruel mockery.

Inside, the palace hummed with activity. Storm petrels darted overhead, clutching small scrolls and messages in their beaks. Tempestarii moved with purpose between the towering ice blocks, their expressions grave. In the centre of it all stood Deema, her broad-brimmed hat tipped back on her head as she issued terse orders.

She looked up at our approach. "I didn't expect to see you again. Is it your father? It takes time for the enchantment to fully wear off—"

"It's not that," Layla said.

Deema waited, looking impatient. She clearly had bigger fish to fry than helping mortals.

"The frost imps stole Lord Ravencroft's moonstone amulet," I said. "It held the key to the Court of Silver Shadows."

"Along with the amulets of eight other Venerable Bloodlines," Deema said dryly. "I am well aware."

"Without it, he can't fulfill his bargain to the Vaels," I said. "And well, if he forfeits, I'll be bound to Lady Seraphine's service forever."

Deema's expression softened. "I am sorry, but there is nothing I can do."

"Surely you know another way to reach the Court of Silver Shadows?" Layla pressed. "A back door?"

"It is the most closely guarded of the fae realms. The barrow is the only access granted to mortals, and that is limited to those who have the key."

"But there must be something—" I began.

"As you well know, I am bound by ancient pacts of neutrality," Deema interrupted, an edge to her voice. "The Tempestarii do not interfere in the bargains between mortals and fae courts. We observe, we record, we maintain balance —but we do not intervene."

"What about the Atlas?" Layla asked. "If you loaned me one, I'm sure I could find another way. No one needs to know."

Deema's brow furrowed. "The Atlases of the Otherworld are not trinkets to be handed out at whim. In the wrong hands, they could be used to cause great mischief. They are entrusted only to our couriers."

"Then let me become an official courier! I've proven I can navigate the faerie roads."

Deema studied her with luminous eyes. "It is true that you possess courage, intelligence, resourcefulness—all qualities we value."

"So it's a deal? You don't have to pay me—"

"But I cannot take you into my service knowing your true motive," Deema said. "You do not wish to serve out of dedication to the balance between realms. You wish to use the Atlas to find a door for Lord Ravencroft."

"What does it matter?" Layla argued. "I would deliver your messages faithfully. And if, in my free time, I happened to search for another entrance to the Court of Silver Shadows—"

"It matters greatly." Deema frowned. "Couriers must be neutral, as the Tempestarii are neutral." She shook her head. "The answer is no."

Layla opened her mouth to argue further, but Deema cut her off. "We are hunting the thief. If I find them, I will likely recover all the stolen amulets, including Lord Ravencroft's. That is the best hope I can offer you."

"And if you don't find them in time?" I asked.

"Then the bargain will unfold as it must."

Before either of us could respond, Charlie Maikori burst into the archive, crossbow dangling from one hip and a bulging backpack slung over his shoulder. A trio of storm petrels fluttered around his head.

"Deema!" he called, slowing as he spotted us. "Word from the Court of Gilded Dusk—they've rejected the summons to council. Calling it 'a wizard affair.'"

He flashed us a distracted smile as he hurried past, following Deema to a large table covered with scraps of parchment. They bent their heads together, Charlie nodding as she relayed new messages.

"Let's go," Layla said angrily. "There's nothing more we can do here."

I swallowed my disappointment as we made our way back to the bridge. Layla, never one to give up easily, had a determined gleam in her eye. "Don't worry, we'll find a solution. Lady Vael is *not* stealing you away."

We stepped into the swirling mists. I tried to mirror her confidence but found only dread. Somewhere, frost imps carried Richard's amulet to a wizard who should have been dead centuries ago.

Hans Von Winteregg.

What kind of dodgy name was that anyway?

THE WALLS OF MY ROOM IN THE QUESTEL TOWER CLOSED IN AS I stuffed my belongings into suitcases. All was not lost, I reminded myself. If Deema found the thief before the Frost Moon, I'd be fine. Even if she didn't, we still had two weeks to find another way into the Court of Silver Shadows.

But there would be no mercy from the Vaels. That I knew for certain.

A knock interrupted my spiraling thoughts. I opened the door to find Adrien's brother, Théo. His flaxen curls wanted brushing and his blue coat was buttoned askew, but his smile was warm.

"May I come in?" he asked, hesitating at the threshold.

I forced a smile. "Of course."

He entered, Ginger trotting at his heels. The dog came to my side and rubbed against my leg, as if sensing my distress.

"I wanted to check on you," Théo said, leaning against the bedpost. "After everything that happened last night . . . well, we're all a bit shaken, but I imagine you and Richard have more cause for worry."

Everyone knew that all nine amulets had been stolen, but only a handful understood what it meant for us. I knew Théo meant well, but I didn't want to talk about it.

"We'll manage," I said, stroking Ginger's ears.

"The whole family wants you to know that we stand with Richard. This accusation from Grimaldi is absurd. We all saw him saving lives last night, organizing the rescue effort. It's unbelievable! The man should be grateful."

"Yes, well, it was just the excuse he needed," I said bitterly. "But I appreciate your kind words."

"Father is speaking with the other families now," Théo said. "The last thing we need is to turn on each other when some hidden enemy is trying to weaken us." He sighed. "Though I admit, we do have our own problems."

"Your amulet opens the way to the Vale of Cherry Blossoms."

"*Oui*. It's been in our family for many generations."

I closed the trunk. "What will you do?"

"Return to Sainte Marguerite and await word from the Tempestarii. What choice do we have?"

A kobold appeared in the doorway. "Master Questel asks if you are ready for your trunks to be taken down."

"Yes, thank you," I replied.

"I'll help with the rest," Théo offered, picking up my smaller bag.

We followed the kobold down the winding staircase. More hurried past, carrying luggage and packages. The Chalet hummed with a hasty collective departure—doors slamming, voices shouting, the occasional muffled argument as tempers snapped.

In the entrance hall, we found Adrien directing several kobolds who were loading a massive trunk onto a trolley. He looked pale and drawn.

"Don't worry, Kitty, this thief will be found and punished." Adrien lowered his voice, stepping closer. "Richard is in the courtyard with Gilcarren. Fair warning—the mood out there is tense. Grimaldi has been shouting accusations all morning—ever since the old crow could start squawking again."

My stomach tightened. Adrien patted my arm. "Don't

worry. The Questels stand with the Ravencrofts. Always have and always will."

Jean-Marie approached in a robe of deep blue and forest green. He planted a quick kiss on each cheek. "I am so sorry the Riddle ended this way, Kitty. Please know you are welcome in our home any time."

"*Merci*," I replied, touched by the gesture. "You've all been incredibly kind."

He glanced at Adrien. "We believe in Richard's integrity, regardless of what others may say."

Outside, the courtyard had transformed into a staging area for departure. Wizard coaches jammed the courtyard, loaded with trunks and cases. The MacLeods' was pulled by six enormous corvids with blue-black feathers. The Ab Owains had a team of green wyverns snorting puffs of smoke, while the Drexlers had mechanical horses fashioned from brass and copper.

I spotted Richard, Layla, and Mr. Deen standing beside our dream team of Pip, Twilight Sparkle, Rainbow Dash, and Applejack. I made my way over to them. Richard turned as I approached, his face lighting with relief.

"I was beginning to wonder if you fell down another faerie hole," he said dryly.

"Just saying goodbye to your cousins," I replied. "How are you holding up?"

His gave me a grim approximation of a smile. "I think we'd better go before they break out the torches and pitchforks."

He glanced across the courtyard where Grimaldi stood surrounded by his extended family, all in purple. Even from a distance, the old man's violent gesticulations and stormy expression said it all.

"Ignore him," Layla advised. "Everyone's on edge."

Mr. Deen's yellow eyes slitted. "Fear makes people irrational," he said quietly. "Lord Ravencroft is right. We should slip away while we can."

Kobolds appeared with the last trunks, loading them onto the back of our coach. "All is ready, my lord," Gilcarren called from the driver's bench.

I heaved a sigh of relief and was about to climb into the coach when Grimaldi's voice cut across the courtyard like a whip-crack. "Ravencroft!" He strode toward us, his face white with fury. Several offspring trailed in his wake.

Richard drew himself up. At over six feet, he towered above Grimaldi. "If you've come to wish us a safe journey—"

"Don't play coy with me," Grimaldi spat, stopping a few paces away. "Every Riddle for four centuries has concluded without incident. Then *you* attend and it's a disaster! Every one of us was attacked except for you, boy. How do you explain that?"

I stepped closer to Richard. The rest of the Venerable Bloodlines paused to watch.

"I *was* attacked," Richard said in exasperation. "But Miss Book had the presence of mind to drive the imp off with one of the heat globes."

"It still took Lord Ravencroft's amulet," I added. "He's in the same boat you are. And he helped to save your life!"

Grimaldi sniffed. "A convenient tale." His cold grey eyes studied Richard. "Your parents were traitors. It seems the apple hasn't fallen far from the tree."

Richard stiffened. Even Vito's sons looked embarrassed. I think that if the stone wizard had been a few decades younger, Richard would have punched him in the nose.

Before it came to blows, Adrien stepped forward. "That's quite enough, Grimaldi," he said sharply. "We've all been robbed. It does not give you license to hurl baseless accusations."

Vito's eyes narrowed. "The Questels have always been too quick to defend the Ravencrofts. Blood loyalty blinds you to their true nature."

The confrontation was drawing a larger audience now. The Footes had paused their departure, watching with wary expressions. The MacLeods whispered among themselves, the corvids shifting restlessly in their harnesses.

"You have no evidence," Richard said. "Only suspicion fueled by ancient grudges."

"Evidence?" Grimaldi's laugh was harsh. "Your entire bloodline is tainted! Storm summoners with a history of treachery. Those imps were under the control of someone with an affinity for weather magic."

"Then perhaps we should look to your own bloodline," Richard countered. "Or the McLeods and Owains. They too have weather affinities."

This suggestion did not go over well. Merwyn Ab Owain, who had been about to enter his coach, turned back with a scowl. "Careful, Ravencroft. You'd better watch your tongue!"

The situation was spiraling out of control. Grimaldi's accusation was a spark tossed on the tinder of fear and suspicion. I was about to suggest we make a run for it when a deep, calm voice cut through the muttering.

"Lord Ravencroft makes a valid point." The crowd parted to reveal a tall man with dark olive skin and piercing green eyes, wearing a brown cloak. Beside him was a striking woman with long dark hair.

"Who is that?" I whispered to Adrien, who stood beside me. "They look familiar."

"Nikos Kazan and his wife Chara," Adrien murmured.

"Tree wizards from Greece. Chara is actually Grimaldi's niece by marriage."

Nikos Kazan carried a stout walking stick which tapped the stones as he approached. "There is no evidence implicating Lord Ravencroft." His voice was a deep rumble that carried without being raised. "Only fear and old grudges."

Grimaldi flushed. "His amulet could have been stolen as part of the deception! To make him appear a victim rather than a conspirator."

"That would be an elaborate ruse indeed," Nikos observed. "But a simpler explanation is all nine amulets were taken because all nine were the target."

Grimaldi opened his mouth to argue, but Chara Kazan stepped forward. "Uncle," she said, "we are all shaken. But accusing one of our own without proof will not recover what was lost. It only weakens us further, which I suspect was the true purpose of the attack."

A murmur of agreement rippled through the crowd. Some of the younger Grimaldis nodded, seeing the wisdom in her words.

"We should be uniting against our common enemy," Chara said, her gaze sweeping across the gathered wizards. "Not fracturing along fault lines of suspicion and resentment."

Vito Grimaldi stared at Richard for a long moment, his expression still hard. "This isn't over, Ravencroft," he said. "But for now . . ." He glanced at his niece, then turned away with a dismissive gesture. "We all have more pressing concerns."

The tension in the courtyard ebbed as Grimaldi strode to his own coach, his family closing ranks around him. Conversations resumed, the sounds of departure once again filling the air.

"Thank you," Richard said quietly to Nikos and Chara.

Nikos inclined his head. "Hasty accusations benefit none of us in these uncertain times."

"I wish you a safe journey," Chara added, her gaze troubled. "May you find what was taken from you."

"May we all," Richard replied.

They moved away, returning to their own modest coach drawn by four piebald mares that stood calmly amid the chaos. "We should go," Richard said, "before someone else decides to waylay us."

Layla and her father were already waiting inside the coach. Gilcarren perched on the driver's bench with the reins in his hands. Richard and I settled on the plush velvet seat. As the door closed, I caught a last glimpse of the Questels. Adrien raised his hand in farewell as the coach lurched forward. Through the window, I watched the Chalet recede, its turrets wreathed by fog.

"What now?" Layla wondered.

Richard's hand found mine, our fingers interlacing. "We go home and find another way."

I tried hard to believe it. But as the Chalet disappeared from view, I couldn't shake the conviction that we were leaving behind our best chance of solving the mystery of the stolen amulets—and with it, my only hope to escape Lady Seraphine's claim.

22

REUNIONS

Gilcarren took us along secret ways that shortened the journey by two full days. None of us talked much. Richard was preoccupied with the theft of his amulet, and I think Mr. Deen was getting nervous at the prospect of returning to the inn where he had lived so long as a cat, for his fingers kept twitching. As for myself, I was happy for Layla and her father and didn't want my own circumstances to dampen their reunion.

I must have dozed off, for next thing I knew we were rolling down a familiar lane bordered by blackberries. The spire of Little Groating's church was visible in the distance, and my throat tightened at the sight of home.

Moments later, the Dancing Toadstool appeared around the bend. Smoke curled from the chimney, and the windows glowed with light. As our coach neared, the front door flew open. Mrs. Deen stood there, one hand pressed to her mouth. She must have been watching for our arrival—Gilcarren had sent a message ahead with a half-goblin cousin named Hairy Meg.

The coach drew to a stop before the inn, but Mr. Deen sat frozen. Layla squeezed his hand. "It's okay, Dad," she said softly.

"Arush?" Mrs. Deen called, a tremor in her voice.

Richard opened the door and jumped out. At another firm nudge from Layla, Mr. Deen followed. He crossed the yard and stood uncertainly before his wife. For a long moment, they just stared at each other. She took in the grey threading his dark hair, the strange cast to his eyes.

"Sanaja . . ." he ventured.

She flew into his arms with a wordless cry, clutching his shoulders to assure herself he was real. He held her just as tightly, burying his face in her hair.

"I thought you were gone forever," Mrs. Deen sobbed. "All these years—"

"I was here," he replied, his voice rough with emotion. "Right here beside you, my dear."

The sound of footsteps made us all turn. Briar came running down the High Street in her flour-dusted apron. "It's true?" she panted. "Your father—?"

"Is back," Layla said with a grin.

Mr. Deen smiled at her. "Thank you for all the scraps of fish you slipped me when Sanaja wasn't looking. I could not ask for a better daughter-in-law."

Briar blushed to the roots of her red hair.

"Let's all go inside," Mrs. Deen suggested, clinging to her husband's arm as if afraid he might vanish again.

"I should get back to the Hall," Richard said. "There's research to be done."

"I'll come up later tonight," I promised. "After I've seen Nan."

He bid goodbye to the Deens and climbed into the coach.

Gilcarren clucked his tongue, and they set off for Ravencroft Hall.

Inside the Dancing Toadstool, Mrs. Deen was in the midst of cooking a welcome-home dinner of her husband's favourite Sri Lankan dishes. After he gave Nan a long hug, the whole family retreated to the kitchen to chop and peel and stir—and get to know one another again.

"Well, you did it!" Nan exclaimed. She was puffing on a briar pipe in her usual chair by the fire. Her smile faltered. I could never hide anything from her. "What's happened?"

I sank into the chair and told her everything—the frost imps, the stolen amulets, my impending servitude to Lady Seraphine.

"Well," she said gravely when I had finished, "that's a pickle, no mistake. But we're not beaten yet, my girl."

"Deema said the barrow entrance is the only one granted to mortals."

"Hmmm. She could be right. But the Tempestarii are Folk of the sky and air. They've got as much connection to the earth as a butterfly has to a badger's den. I doubt they know every single thing there is to know in this world."

Despite everything, I felt a small flutter of hope.

"I think Richard Ravencroft is a stubborn man who won't lose you without a fight," Nan continued. "Besides which, you're a Boot, and we're too pigheaded to quit." She squeezed my hand, her grip strong for a woman of ninety-two. "There's always another door, Kitty. You just have to know where to look."

Nan had lived through two world wars, the loss of her first husband, and countless encounters with the fae. If she believed we could find another way, perhaps it was true.

THE NEXT WEEK PASSED IN A BLUR OF DEAD ENDS. RICHARD pored over ancient texts for any mention of back doors to the Court of Silver Shadows. He tried a dozen different finding spells to locate the amulet, but they showed us nothing but impenetrable fog. I sought out my dryad friend, Nyx, to ask her advice, but she wasn't home (or refused to show herself). So I worked my shifts at the inn and passed my spare time with Layla, chasing down every bit of lore or half-remembered tale that promised a useful lead.

At night, I dreamed of silver doors that vanished when I reached for them and of Lady Seraphine's chilly smile.

"I am *such* a knob," Layla announced on a rainy afternoon six days before the Frost Moon.

We were gathered in the back room of Sugar & Sprites, surrounded by stacks of books, most borrowed from the library at Ravencroft Hall.

Richard looked up. "What?"

"The Atlas," she moaned. "I had it in my hands. I sort of recall looking up Little Groating. Right, Kitty?"

"Er, right. I half remember doing that too."

"But I forgot where all the doors were!" She chewed the tip of her braid, an anxious habit I hadn't seen since we were teenagers.

"Well, we know of two," I said. "The barrow entrance at Arthur's tomb. That one needs a key. Then there's Quince's house in the pantry of the inn. And . . . " A hazy thought began to form. Instead of trying to grab it, I let my gaze go soft and stared straight ahead the way you do when you're trying to see a faint star from the corner of your eye.

"Are you having a stroke, darling?" Layla asked. "Or maybe you've been smoking hash? If so, don't be stingy."

"Shush . . . Just wait . . . the cellar of the ruined abbey!" I shouted, triumphant. "That's the third one."

Layla's eyes lit up. "Yes! Now I do remember that!"

Richard was already on his feet, shrugging into his coat. "It's worth a try. But we might as well start with Quince."

The kitchen at the Dancing Toadstool was fragrant with the scent of baking bread. Mrs. Deen stood at the large wooden table, kneading dough. She looked up with a radiant smile. Mr. Deen sat nearby on a stool, sorting through a bowl of rice.

"Quince was just in here," Mrs. Deen said after we explained our errand. "He's been in a tizzy since Arush returned—reorganizing everything, muttering about 'proper household hierarchy.'" She winked. "But I think he's relieved not to be carrying the secret anymore."

"Will he mind if we bother him?" I asked, knowing how fussy the brownie could be.

"You? Never." Mrs. Deen gestured toward the large pantry built under the stairs. "Just be sure to compliment the décor. He's very proud of his button collection."

The space was cool and dim, lined with jars of preserves, sacks of rice and flour, and baskets of garlic and onions. At the very back was a small door no higher than my knee. It had a tiny brass knocker. I rapped on the door. "It's Kitty. May I have a word?"

Silence followed, then a shuffling. The door swung open to reveal Quince in all his finery—a potholder waistcoat and tiny breeches with silver buckles at the knee. His hazelnut-brown face creased into a smile. Then his gaze flicked to Richard.

"Well, well, Lord Ravencroft! What an honor!" Quince

chuckled nervously. "Do come in—though I'm afraid I haven't entertained mortals in some time. It's rather . . . You'll have to . . ."

He waved his hands and the doorway expanded, or perhaps we shrank—I wasn't sure which. The sensation felt familiar somehow, and I didn't resist. We all squeezed into Quince's home, a single room that contained everything a comfortable dwelling needed, all in perfect miniature.

The floor was covered with a patchwork of sewing scraps, and shelves displayed Quince's treasures—buttons of every description, silver thimbles, tiny glass bottles that caught the light from a lamp made from a hollowed-out acorn cap filled with glowing embers. A bed stood in one corner, crafted from a velvet jewelry box with cotton batting for a mattress. In another, a small hearth held a cheerful fire, with a tiny copper kettle bubbling away above it.

"What a lovely home," I said sincerely, and Quince preened.

"One does one's best," he replied. "Now, what can I do for you?"

Richard cleared his throat. "We're seeking a back door into the Court of Silver Shadows. The way through the Barrows is impassible with a key, but perhaps there's another path? A secret one known only to the Folk?"

Quince stroked his chin thoughtfully. "I'm afraid I know of no alternate passage. That court is most particular. Most particular, indeed. They don't like trespassers."

Disappointment soured my stomach. Quince gave me a sympathetic look. "I'm sorry, Miss Kitty. If there is another way in, it's well hidden."

We thanked him and took our leave, the door shrinking behind us as we emerged into the pantry. Our next destination was the abbey, a place I often took groups to visit but avoided close to dark, when lights floated among the broken stones.

The sun was just setting when we arrived, casting long shadows across the ivy-strangled walls. The roof had fallen in long ago, but the ruins were still majestic.

"Did you know that Brackwell Abbey was founded in 1131 by Cistercian monks?" I said. "At first, it was a simple stone church and cloisters, but the monks found a rich patron and by 1269, they started building the masterpiece of British Gothic architecture you see before you. Note the great west-facing front with its seven-lancet window and the soaring arches of the nave."

I paused for breath. "Sadly for the monks, the Reformation would sweep through England not long after the abbey was completed. Brackwell surrendered in the first round of Henry's dissolution of the monasteries—"

"You've gone into tour guide mode, darling," Layla said, flicking on an electric torch.

"Oh! So I have. Nervous habit."

"I think it's fascinating," Richard said loyally.

"Don't encourage her," Layla said with a wink for me. "She'll tell you the history of every single stone in this chilly heap."

"Not every single one," I protested. "But I will say that the abbey is built of Old Red Sandstone, a type of sedimentary rock that dates back to the Devonian age—"

I trailed off as Layla shone her torch down a crumbling staircase. I'd never gone into the cellar. Far too dark and terrifying.

"Must we?" I asked.

"Yes," she said firmly. "I'll go first."

The cellar was largely intact, protected from the elements by the main structure of the abbey above. Stone arches supported a low ceiling, and wooden barrels lined the walls, their staves dark with age. In the centre stood a massive wine press, its wooden screw green with moss. A sweet, fermented odor permeated the air.

"Where's the door?" Richard asked, as Layla swept the torch beam across drifts of dead leaves. "And what's that smell?"

She turned in a slow circle. "Who knows? I suppose it could be up in the church, but—"

There was a high-pitched, malevolent laugh.

"Oh no," I whispered. "Pixies."

More laughter came, decidedly drunken.

"Bloody hell, I think they're plastered," Layla said, wrinkling her nose.

One zipped past my ear, leaving a trail of sparkling dust. Another seized Richard's hair, yanking it violently before zooming away with a loud hiccup. The pixies were about six inches tall with wings and really nasty little faces.

"Bugger off," Richard snarled, flicking one away as it started peeing on his shoulder.

"These barrels must still have something in them," Layla said, squinting. "Hang on, I think I see the door."

It was behind the wine press. A small one, hanging on crooked hinges. It looked similar to Quince's door except not as nice. I crawled over and stuck my head through.

"Dammit," I called back. "It leads into the apple orchard."

Layla sneezed just then—she had a mild allergy to pixie dust—so hard that she stumbled into one of the barrels and knocked it over. The rotten wood gave way with a crack, and a gush of sour wine flooded the cellar. The pixies immediately flung themselves into the puddle, romping around and guzzling with abandon.

"Ugh," Richard said. "One of them just . . . Layla—"

She was backing up and swatting at the air. "Yes, run away!"

We fled, pursued by the drunken swarm. By the time we emerged into the twilight, we were splattered in a vile substance I feared was pixie sick.

Layla shook a fist at the stairs. "Now we know why no one uses that door," she said.

23

A HOLE TO PERDITION

The path into the Wild Wood was drenched in afternoon sunlight, the leaves still green even though it was mid-November and the air had a frisky nip to it. My time in the mortal world was almost over, and I wanted to visit the oldest tree in the forest one last time.

I also secretly hoped that Nyx would be waiting. That she would save me where others had failed.

The great oak towered over its clearing like a benevolent giant. My heart lifted when the dryad stepped from behind the trunk—or perhaps from inside it. She was dark and willowy. Hair like seed fluff peeked out from the cap of an acorn that she'd fashioned into a hat. She wore a shirt of moss and had long, knobby toes.

"Hello, Nyx," I said.

"Hello, Kitty Boot."

"I've been looking for you." I tried not to sound accusing or pathetic. "You weren't home."

"I was visiting my oak's daughter."

"Ah. It's growing strong and true."

She smiled. "Yes."

"I came to ask you something."

Her smile faded. "The Court of Silver Shadows."

"So you know."

Nyx nodded.

A sharp pain lanced through my heart. "Do you even care?" I demanded, hating the plaintive edge to my voice.

She seemed puzzled by the question. "For you? Yes, I care. But I cannot stop the bargain."

"Things are desperate," I admitted. "There's been no word from Deema of the Tempestarii. We've searched every book, tried all the doors in Little Groating. Is there another way? Some forgotten path known to the dryads?"

Nyx was quiet for a moment. "The Lord of Ravencroft should visit the sapling you planted together when your love was new. The daughter of my oak."

I frowned. "But the dryad there has never shown itself. Not once in a year. We've tried speaking to it, leaving gifts. It's too shy—or too young."

"Perhaps she is waiting for the right moment."

"Can you tell me the dryad's name? Maybe if Richard called to her . . ."

Nyx looked offended. "If she trusts him, she will tell him herself."

My patience, already thin after a fortnight of searching, now dangled by a hair. "Speak plainly for once. Does the sapling have a door to the Court of Silver Shadows?"

She shook her head. "No such door exists."

I wanted to kick something. "Then what's the use? Tonight is the Frost Moon. In a few hours, Lady Seraphine will claim me unless I find another way to her realm."

Nyx regarded me, unmoving. I began to doubt she would

reply when at last she spoke. "There is old magic in this land," she said. "Magic that runs deeper than amulets or doors. Magic that waits to be found, if your lord has the patience to find it."

Before I could ask what she meant, Nyx stepped backward, her slender form blurring against the bark. In the space between one heartbeat and the next, she was gone.

I muttered an oath and turned back toward the path with heavy steps. The sun was sinking, giving way to the cool blue of evening. I headed toward Ravencroft Hall, trying to make sense of Nyx's advice.

Old magic waiting to be found.

The irony wasn't lost on me. Patience was not Richard's strong suit. In fact, I'd put it near the bottom of the list of his virtues.

He was smart and brave and kind and knew how to think on his feet. But sitting quietly and waiting for subtle magic to reveal itself?

Ha.

We had run out of time for patience anyway.

When I reached Ravencroft Hall, a coach sat outside, emblazoned with the Grimaldi family crest of an eagle clutching a serpent. Next to it was another—this one forest green and bearing the MacLeod family's stag. A pair of enormous corvids stood in the traces, watching me with intelligent golden eyes.

I had the mad hope that the thief had been caught. Perhaps Grimaldi, in a sudden fit of magnanimity, decided to return Richard's moonstone himself and apologize for his baseless accusations.

Then I heard shouting inside, loud enough to carry through the heavy oak doors. I hurried up the steps, my fatigue forgotten.

"—for the last time, I don't have your damned amulets!" Richard stood in the centre of the foyer, rigid with anger.

Vito jabbed a finger at him. "Save your denials. I just want it back—no questions asked. This is your last chance to make things right. No one needs to be the wiser."

Beside Grimaldi stood a burly man with a shock of red hair. Angus MacLeod, head of the Scottish wizards. His massive arms were folded across his chest.

"What if the lad speaks truth, Vito?" MacLeod rumbled. "If he had our amulets, wouldn't he have tried to use the power by now?"

Grimaldi's scowl deepened. "His parents were masters of misdirection."

"For God's sake," Richard exploded, "I don't have them! Now get out of my house before I throw you out!"

I came to his side. "I suggest you listen to him, gentlemen."

MacLeod nodded gruffly. Grimaldi's scowl deepened. "This isn't over, Ravencroft. The other families will hear of your arrogance."

"Tell them whatever you like," Richard replied, his voice weary now.

MacLeod hesitated, looking between Richard and Grimaldi with a conflicted expression. He sighed. "Come, Vito. We're wasting time."

With a final glare, Grimaldi swept from the hall, MacLeod following behind. The front door slammed behind them.

So Deema had not found the thief. She had not recovered the amulets in the nick of time.

A strange calm settled over me. The one that comes when you've fought as hard as you can and must accept the inevitable. Despite our best efforts, we wouldn't find another door to the Court of Silver Shadows.

It simply did not exist.

Deep down, I had known this moment would come. Known it the instant Richard struck his unfortunate bargain with the Vaels.

That is how these stories always end.

"Did Nyx have any ideas?" he asked, desperate hope flaring in his eyes.

I told him what the dryad said about the young oak we had planted, about old magic waiting to be found if he had patience to seek it out. Richard looked frustrated.

"That's it? Visit a sapling and wait? Tonight is the Frost Moon! We don't have time for riddles."

"I know," I said. "But it's all I've got."

He drew a breath. "Then we'll try. Right now." He reached for his coat and I felt a surge of love for this man who refused to give up.

Richard drove us back to the village as the first stars appeared. We parked on the High Street and went to the sapling oak, which stood in a meadow. It looked so young compared to Nyx's ancient sentinel, which had been alive when William the Conqueror crossed the English Channel.

Richard knelt on the cold ground. "You should . . ." He cleared his throat. "You should say your goodbyes, Kitty. Just in case."

I smiled. "It's all right, really. I'm all right."

He nodded, unable to look at me.

I managed to sneak up the back stairs to my garret room and take a last look around. The creaky bed covered with one of Nan's handmade quilts, where I'd passed many contented hours reading and listening to rain dripping on the eaves. My film posters and piles of English guidebooks.

The Wellies I had bought with money Richard paid me last year, now nicely broken in with dried mud.

"Goodbye," I whispered, as I grabbed a couple of last things and went downstairs. They were all waiting in the common room. Briar and Layla, her parents, Nan and Dr. Singer, Charlotte de Berry in her silk shawl.

"There she is," Nan said, rising stiffly from her chair. "Our girl."

"Richard's trying one last thing," I said, "but I don't think it'll work."

"Nonsense," Nan said, pulling me into a fierce hug. "You'll be back before we know it."

"Like a holiday," Dr. Singer added with forced cheer. "A rather unusual one, to be sure, but nothing a Boot can't handle."

One by one, they embraced me—Mrs. Deen with motherly warmth, Mr. Deen with the awkwardness of a man still relearning human affection, Layla and Briar together in a crushing group hug.

"We'll find the stolen amulets," Briar promised. "However long it takes. That Winteregg prick is going down!"

"I know," I said. "But listen, just in case, here's my Pink Floyd CD collection." I pressed the stack into Layla's hands.

She flipped through them and gasped. "Even the bootleg Fantasio Club Amsterdam live show?"

"Yes," I said. "It's yours now."

Her eyes brimmed. "Your most precious possession."

From his perch by the window, Sir Francis Drake flapped his wings. "Not all treasure is silver and gold, mate!" he screamed.

I stared at Nan. "That's a quote from Captain Jack Sparrow. I was just looking at the poster for *Pirates of the Caribbean* on my wall."

"You still have that?" Layla asked.

"Been meaning to bin it, but yes." I rounded on Nan. "*Aha!* I *knew* you were teaching Sir Francis things!"

She feigned puzzlement. "I don't know what you're talking about, dear."

"Maybe Sir Francis's pirate owners *also* watched a lot of movies," Briar said with a knowing wink.

"I suppose it's possible," I allowed.

Nan sniffed. "Even that ridiculous bird will miss you," she said, her voice catching on the words.

Madame de Berry limped over with her cane and gave me a small bundle wrapped in midnight-blue silk. "A gift," she said. "For when you need it most." I started to open it, but she placed her hand over mine. "Later, before you sleep tonight." She whispered in my ear, then pulled me to her bosom in a cloud of Chanel No. 5.

"Thank you," I said, clinging to the shreds of my calm. "I love you all. And I . . . I will try my best not to forget you."

I kissed Nan once more and left before I started to ugly cry. The meadow behind the inn was empty. Richard didn't even have the patience to wait for me to come back out.

I gave a rather hollow laugh and looked up at the dark sky. The edge of the full moon peeked above the barrows. It was no great mystery where he had gone.

The night air slipped its fingers into the collar of my cardigan as I made my way along the path, hugging my silk-wrapped bundle. Mist rose from the ground, curling around my ankles like curious cats, then dissolving. After a few minutes, the rolling mounds of the Barrows appeared, their smooth contours outlined by the strengthening moonlight.

I'd walked this path hundreds of times during my guided tours, telling tales of ancient kings to wide-eyed tourists. But tonight the familiar landscape felt alien, as though the approaching Frost Moon was erasing the border between worlds.

I heard a few normal nocturnal sounds—the call of a barn owl, the rustle of small rodents bedding down in their dens before said owl caught and ate them. Yet as I crested the final hill, another sound reached me. A rhythmic scraping.

Richard stood in a shallow pit at the base of King Arthur's barrow, digging into the hillside with obsessive focus. His coat lay discarded on the ground. Dig, lift, throw, repeat.

"Richard," I called.

He glanced up but didn't stop digging. The look in his eyes chilled me. "I won't let them have you, Kitty." His voice was hard and flat, the words punctuated by another thrust of the shovel. "There has to be another way through. A forgotten passage. Some door that doesn't require the key."

The dirt beside him was mounded waist-high. He'd been at it for quite a while.

"Richard, stop," I said. "Please."

He paused, shovel suspended midair, his chest rising and falling. For a moment, I thought he might ignore me and continue his tunneling. Then he drove the shovel into the dirt with enough force to make it stand upright on its own.

"Did the dryad appear?" I asked, though the answer was obvious.

"No," he replied. "I tried to wait, to be patient. It wouldn't come. So I offered it bargains." A bitter laugh. "Even worse ones than the last. Firstborn children, all that. Finally, I threatened it, though I know how foolish that was."

I extended my hand, and after a moment's hesitation, he took it, climbing out of the shallow pit to stand beside me.

"Stop blaming yourself," I told him, brushing a smudge of dirt from his cheek. "You've done everything."

"Not enough," he said, his voice breaking.

I laid my hand against his cheek, forcing him to look at me. "Listen to me, Richard Ravencroft. Deema will find Winteregg. She'll recover the amulets. This won't be forever."

"You don't know that," he whispered, but he leaned into my touch.

"I do," I insisted with more confidence than I felt. "The Tempestarii are the most powerful neutral faction in Faerie. If anyone can track down Winteregg, it's them."

"And what if they never find him? If I never see you again except at the mercy of Lady Seraphine's whims?"

I swallowed the ache in my throat. "Then we'll have tonight. And the memory of it."

He pulled me against his chest, holding me with fierce protectiveness. I listened to the steady beat of his heart.

"You're the bravest woman I know," he murmured.

I pulled back to look up at him. "There's no point in digging a hole to nowhere. Come back to the Hall."

Richard cast one last frustrated glance at the barrow, then retrieved his coat from where he'd thrown it. We walked in silence, following a moonlit path that wound through silvered fields. Presently, the imposing silhouette of the manor appeared, its turrets and chimneys cutting sharp lines against the starry sky.

I tried not to think about Lady Seraphine's mirror-bright eyes. Instead, I focused on Richard's warm hand in mine, the way our shoulders brushed as we walked, the shared cadence of our footsteps. If these were my last hours in the mortal world, I wanted to fill them with something worth remembering.

Richard seemed to have similar thoughts. As we crossed the threshold into Ravencroft Hall, he turned to face me in the grand entrance with its marble floors and ancestral portraits glaring down from the walls.

"Kitty," he began, then stopped. Instead, he cupped my face in his hands, his thumbs tracing my cheekbones. Then he kissed me with an almost savage desperation. When we broke apart, we were both breathing hard. Richard's gaze darkened. Without a word, he swept me into his arms and carried me up the grand staircase to the master bedroom.

We lay down, silently clutching each other. "Whatever happens," he said, "whatever comes after—remember that I love you. With everything I am, with every part of me."

My eyes stung, but I would not let this be a time for sorrow.

"And I love you, stubborn man," I said, curving my hand along the strong line of his jaw. "No matter what realm I'm in, that won't change."

His mouth found mine again. Beyond the window, the Frost Moon rose higher in the night sky. And for a few hours, I found a happiness that Lady Seraphine's claim could not touch.

24

THE ICE ROAD

I sat up in the darkness, covered in icy sweat. I'd been running barefoot through a forest, dead leaves rustling beneath my bare feet. Lady Vael's amused voice echoed from everywhere and nowhere. *Come to me, child. A bargain is a bargain.*

Richard lay beside me, his breathing deep and even. But we were not alone.

The hair on my arms rose as I saw a hunched figure by the window. I didn't need to see his face to know who—what—he was. Halfglint, chamberlain to Lord and Lady Vael.

"The Frost Moon has set," he said roughly. "The bargain is forfeit."

Richard lay as pale and still as a marble statue. Fear gripped me. I touched his lips and felt a faint gust of warm breath.

"He lives," Halfglint said. "But he will not wake until morning."

I said nothing. What was there to say? This moment had been inevitable since Richard lost his moonstone amulet.

Perhaps since the first time I'd disobeyed my parents and ventured into the Wild Wood.

"You must come willingly," Halfglint said, stepping away from the window. "That too is part of the bargain."

He drew closer. What a peculiar creature he was. Half his hair frost-white, the other midnight black. One eye silver, the other onyx. Face narrow and cunning. Most Folk were beautiful, but Halfglint was grotesque.

"If I refuse?" I asked.

"The Wild Wood will fade and your village will die with it."

I looked at Richard one last time. His dark hair lay tousled across the pillow, his features smooth in slumber. I tried to memorise his face, terrified I would forget him.

"I will honor the bargain," I said, my voice breathy and dry.

Halfglint nodded as if he had expected this answer.

I reached for the dressing gown Madame Berry had sewn for me. The hem was embroidered with red thread soaked in an elixir of rowan and rosemary, a ward against fae enchantment.

"You may bring no possessions save the clothes on your back," Halfglint added sternly.

I wondered if he sensed the ward. Well, there was no point in arguing with a faerie, and certainly not one as unpleasant as Halfglint.

The floorboards were icy beneath my bare feet as I padded to the door, following him into the hallway. We moved down the stairs, silent as ghosts. I saw no sign of Gilcarren or Nettle or any of the house brownies. They rightfully feared him.

Then Halfglint opened the front door, and we stepped into the night. The Frost Moon must have just set, for its glow lingered above the trees. I shivered in the chill air, wrapping my arms around myself. Halfglint produced a cloak.

"Lady Vael does not wish you to suffer," he said stiffly, draping the soft fabric around my shoulders. The cloak was warm, as though it had been hanging before a fire. I murmured thanks and drew it tighter around me.

Halfglint inclined his head, then gestured toward the drive. Where the gravel path should have been, a road of ice now stretched away from the house, gleaming silver in the moonlight. It wound toward the edge of the Wild Wood, curving out of sight among the ancient trees.

Beside the steps waited a black sledge, its runners gleaming. Harnessed to it stood a pair of huge white stoats with red eyes. They grew excited when they saw their master, claws gouging the ice. Halfglint held out a gloved hand to help me into the sledge. I pretended not to see and climbed inside.

I was relieved when Halfglint took his place at the front. At least I would not have him staring at me for the journey. He lifted the silver reins. The stoats leapt in long bounds down the road, the sledge's runners hissing against the ice as we gathered speed.

We entered the Wild Wood, which was very dark except for the occasional will o' the wisp. I found a pile of blankets and heaped them all on top of me to fend off the bitter cold. The stoats drew us through the night. At some point, we crossed the boundary into Faerie, though I couldn't have said precisely when. But when dawn came, the air grew sharper, each breath painful in my lungs. Only the violet cloak kept me from freezing, its magic warmth a barrier between my mortal flesh and the killing cold of the faerie winter.

We topped a rise, and I caught my first glimpse of the

Vaels' castle, perched upon a hilltop. Dizziness washed over me—a sensation of standing at the edge of an abyss.

The sledge carried us down the slope and across a plain of snow, then up the winding path to the castle gates. Sentries I couldn't quite bring into focus stood on either side. They seemed made of shadow and starlight, with weapons that gleamed like the edge between dream and wakefulness.

We passed through the gates and Halfglint turned to me. His expression held an odd mixture of pity and satisfaction.

"Welcome to your new home, Katherine," he said, as the castle doors swung open to receive us.

I EXPECTED TO BE BROUGHT TO LADY VAEL AND PARADED before the court, but Halfglint led me deeper into the castle, past a great steaming kitchen and into tighter, meaner corridors that I took to be the servants' quarters.

"Lady Vael wishes you to settle in," Halfglint said. "Joan will attend to your needs."

We rounded a corner and stopped before a woman waiting in the corridor. She was young and apple-cheeked, with brown hair tied up in braids. Her mouth was arranged in a smile, but her eyes were empty, like a hollowed-out jack o'lantern.

"Joan," Halfglint said, "This is Katherine. Lady Seraphine's new handmaiden."

"And what a comely wench she is!" Joan exclaimed. She curtsied, the movement precise as a wind-up doll. "I shall take her under my wing at once."

Halfglint strode off without another word. I regarded my new supervisor warily.

"Come along," Joan said. "You're quite the lucky duckling. Lady Vael has given you a very fine chamber. She must think highly of you."

I allowed Joan to guide me down the corridor, trying not to flinch at her touch. There was no wood or anything that felt warm in this place. The keep was polished stone, and all the doors were silver or bronze. I wondered where the other servants were, for I saw no one about.

"Here we are!" Joan said, opening a silver door. The room was tiny, hardly big enough for the single bed and table. Upon which sat a slice of cake, golden and perfect, and a goblet filled with dark wine.

My stomach revolted just looking at it. Food and drink from Faerie bound one fully to this realm and hastened the forgetting of mortal life.

"You must be thirsty after your journey," Joan said. "Lady Vael commanded you to refresh yourself." She held out the goblet. "Drink, child."

"I—I'd like to change first," I said, pretending to admire the black dress that waited on the bed. Beside it sat a pair of velvet slippers and a silver net for my hair.

Joan's bright smile did not waver. "Lady Vael wishes you to refresh yourself after the long journey," she said again.

We stared at each other. "Of course," I said, accepting the goblet. "Her ladyship is very kind." I raised it to my lips. Then I looked past Joan's shoulder out the tiny window. "Oh goodness, what is *that*?"

Joan turned to follow my horrified gaze, and I seized my chance. My friends had not let me enter Faerie unprotected. I'd been forced to leave the dressing gown behind, but Madame de Berry had also sewn me a nightgown with concealed darts in the bodice that held small packets of table salt—the bane of faerie magic. I quickly extracted a pinch and dropped it in the wine. The dark liquid hissed, a wisp of vapor rising before dissipating.

"What did you see, girl?" Joan gave me a hard look.

"A frightful winged thing!" I exclaimed. "Didn't you see it too?"

She stared at me. "No. Perhaps it is just nerves. Now *drink*."

Under her watchful gaze, I raised the goblet to my lips. The wine was unlike anything I'd ever tasted. I thought of wild berries and quinces and heartache and moss. It warmed me going down, but beneath was a peculiar numbness that would have spread like poison without the salt's protection. The sensation faded quickly, leaving only a hint of fog.

I took another small sip, then lowered the goblet and gave Joan a vacant smile. "Delicious," I said. "Thank you."

She watched me closely, her head tilted like a bird studying a new species of insect. After a moment, she gave a satisfied nod. "Very good, dearie. Now don your kirtle and I'll return anon."

Once Joan had left, I sank down on the bed. My hands shook, but my head was clear. I had enough salt for several weeks if I used it sparingly. After that . . . well, I wouldn't think about it now.

I stripped off the cloak but kept my nightgown on, pulling the kirtle over it instead of changing. It was a small rebellion, but it felt important to wear something made by hands that cared for me. A soft knock came just as I finished arranging the silver net to hold my hair. I opened the door to find Halfglint waiting.

"Lady Vael desires your presence at once," he said.

I donned a vapid smile and stepped into the corridor, following him toward whatever revelry awaited.

25

MASQUES

Halfglint led me through a labyrinth of stone corridors, all polished to such a high gleam that I kept my face blank and stupid, but I cannot say if he even noticed. He probably thought we all looked like that anyway.

"You will serve Lady Vael," he said. "Speak only when spoken to and remember your place."

I nodded meekly.

Halfglint paused at a door carved with vines and crescent moons. They looked heavy, yet he pushed them wide with a flick of his wrist. I steeled myself for a great hall filled with the glittering Folk of the Vaels' court, but beyond lay a dark and twisted forest. Torches burned in a glade, their red light flickering on tables that groaned with food and drink. The revelers all wore masques, some of delicate lace, others sporting beaks and the muzzles of beasts.

I gave Halfglint a vacant smile. He gestured toward the far side of the clearing. "This way." We moved through the crowd, the courtiers parting before the chamberlain. None spared me a second glance—I was beneath their notice.

My new masters lounged upon thrones made from entwined branches of ivory wood. Lady Seraphine's white hair was so long it pooled around her feet, her gown shimmering between jet and silver. Beside her, Lord Thalen wore a cloak of eagle feathers and a gold and ivory horn around his neck. Neither were masqued, and they made a striking couple, he with golden-brown skin and his wife pale as milk. They were observing the festivities with a distracted air.

I sank into a deep curtsey, my heart drumming.

"Your Majesties," Halfglint said with a bow. "Allow me to present Lady Vael's new handmaiden."

I expected a bit of gloating. She had won, after all. But when I dared to glance up, she just nodded absently as if I had attended her every night for years. "Rise," she ordered.

There was no triumph in her voice. No pleasure at having acquired me. I was merely another transaction.

Halfglint gestured for me to sit on the cushion at her feet, then cast a pointed glance at her goblet. I was to keep it filled. Well, that was simple enough. And it allowed me to eavesdrop on their conversation.

As I settled onto the cushion, I noticed Princess Maeryn standing nearby, her hair floating about her shoulders like cobwebs. She wore a dress of layered silks and a harlequin masque with tiny silver bells that tinkled when she moved.

"That mortal woman is a poor substitute for Lord Ravencroft," she said unhappily.

Lady Vael sighed. "It's a shame that he failed to appear, but the terms of the bargain are clear. She is the forfeit."

"But I wanted to dance with him!"

"Peace, daughter," Lord Vael interjected. "We have more pressing matters to discuss." He turned to a tall fae courtier wearing a masque of birch bark. "Lord Ashdown, what news?"

The man bowed. "I'm afraid we've had no word from the Tempestarii. But there are a thousand rumours and old grievances are being remembered. There is talk of another war."

Lord Vael leaned forward, shadows deepening around him. "War benefits no one."

"Yet someone was behind the theft of the amulets," Lord Ashdown replied. "Those imps are not intelligent enough to act of their own accord."

"Hans Von Winteregg," Lady Vael murmured, her fingers tapping against her goblet. I noticed it was almost empty and hastily reached for the silver pitcher. "A name long forgotten. Do we believe he has returned?"

"The Tempestarii seem to think so," Lord Ashdown replied. "Deema has sent couriers to every court, seeking information on his whereabouts."

"Von Winteregg was ambitious beyond reason," Lord Vael said. "If he has indeed returned and possesses all nine amulets, his power would be formidable."

Halfglint had been standing silently in the shadow of the throne all this time. Now he spoke. "You were there at the Riddle, were you not, Katherine?"

I froze as Lord Vael's penetrating gaze fell upon me. "Is this true?" he asked. "You witnessed the theft?"

Princess Maeryn, who'd looked bored to tears by this talk of politics, now perked up. "Tell us what happened!"

I glanced at Lady Vael. She gestured impatiently. "Answer, girl."

Halfglint watched me with amusement. I gathered my wits, determined not to appear a complete fool in front of him. "Yes, Your Majesty," I said. "I was at the Riddle when the frost imps attacked."

Every masked face turned toward me. "Well, go on," Lady

Vael prompted, her tone sharp. "Recount the tale. Every detail!"

I swallowed hard and curtseyed so I could take a moment to think. Halfglint had known I was there. He probably knew all of it already, and there was nothing to be gained by lying.

"It was during the Night Market on Feenacht," I began, injecting a breathless, frightened edge to my voice.

I told them about the ball and the Night Market and the arrival of the frost imps, how they'd put on a display that suddenly turned nasty.

"What of Lord Ravencroft's amulet?" Lady Vael inquired, leaning forward. "You saw it taken?"

I nodded. "An imp ripped it from his throat in front of me."

Princess Maeryn clapped her hands, the bells on her mask chiming merrily. "How thrilling!" she exclaimed. "Such a bold act, to steal *all* the amulets in one fell swoop. This Winteregg is intriguing."

"He's dangerous," Lord Vael corrected.

"But what could he want with all nine amulets?" a courtier in a fox mask wondered.

"If Winteregg uses the moonstone to enter our realm," Lord Vael said slowly, "I am not disposed to strike a bargain with him. I never trusted the man."

"My love," Lady Vael countered, "perhaps we should hear him out before setting our minds to one path or another. There could be advantage in this situation."

Lord Vael turned to his wife. "You would entertain bargains with a mortal wizard whose ambitions nearly brought ruin upon us all?"

"I would merely hear his offer," Lady Vael replied. "If he possesses the keys to other realms . . ."

Halfglint stepped forward. "If I may, Your Majesties," he

said, his mismatched eyes gleaming. "What if Winteregg doesn't want a bargain? What if he has nefarious plans to use the amulets for another purpose?"

This suggestion sent a ripple through the gathered courtiers. Everyone began speaking at once, their masked faces turning to each other in speculation.

"He could combine their powers—"

"Impossible, even for a wizard of his calibre—"

"The Tempestarii would never allow—"

"But if he found a way to break the ancient pacts—"

Lady Vael rose to her feet, her white hair writhing like a living thing. "Silence!" she shrieked, shearing through the cacophony like a blade of ice.

The court fell quiet.

"I am weary of this topic," Lady Vael announced. "Speculation serves no purpose when facts are scarce. For now, we will watch our borders and wait for Winteregg to reveal his intentions." She turned to her husband and extended a pale hand. "I wish to dance."

Lord Vael took her hand, his expression unreadable. At a gesture, the musicians picked up their instruments again. The frenetic melody resumed, and the royal couple moved to the centre of the clearing where other courtiers quickly made space for them.

Lady Vael's snowy hair streamed behind her like a comet's tail, Lord Vael's cloak of raven feathers whispering with each turn. The court watched for several measures before other couples joined them, the masquerade returning to its full splendour.

I realised then what a fool I'd been—so caught up in my own problems that I'd given hardly a thought to the other amulets. But if Hans Von Winteregg truly possessed all nine, the situation was far worse than I'd imagined.

I sat docilely on the cushion. No one paid me any attention. Courtiers danced and feasted and whispered to each other behind their masks. The musicians played without tiring. Only when my head began to droop despite my best efforts did I notice a faint pink glow in the sky. Halfglint materialized beside me as the first rays of dawn broke through the forest. "Your service for the night is over, Katherine," he said. "Come."

I rose stiffly, my legs numb from sitting so long. Around us, the Folk were drifting away like morning mist. The tables of food, the musicians, the torches—all vanished as daylight strengthened.

I saw with a start that Lord and Lady Vael were already gone, their thrones empty. Halfglint led me along a forest path until somehow we were back inside stone corridors that felt solid and real after the dreamlike quality of the masquerade.

By the time we reached my chamber, the night had caught up with me. My limbs felt leaden, my brain slow and stupid.

"Sleep well," Halfglint said. "You will attend Lady Vael at dusk."

He left and I entered my tiny room. Richard would be waking to find me gone. Had it only been a single night? Or was I already losing time?

I lay down fully dressed, too tired even to take off my shoes. As sleep claimed me, I clutched at one clear thought: Hans Von Winteregg had Richard's moonstone. And if he used it to come here, I would take it back from him or die trying.

26

WHAT A SILLY CREATURE!

I measured my sanity in grains of salt.

Each represented another hour of clarity in this waking dream of a castle. I ate and drank little, yet I could feel the magic unraveling the edges of my memories. Like ivy slowly creeping up a wall, it found purchase in the tiniest cracks.

The nights bled into one another until I could no longer distinguish one from the next. Each evening brought a revel—sometimes masked, sometimes not. I slept once the sun rose and Lady Vael retreated to her chamber.

In those precious moments of solitude, I held to thoughts of home like a drowning woman clutches the wreck of her ship. I knew that Richard, Layla, and Briar would be searching tirelessly for a way to free me. All I needed to do was not succumb until they succeeded.

Easier said than done, of course—especially since I was running out of salt.

The other handmaiden, Joan, both fascinated and repelled me. She'd been here for an ungodly number of years, that much was obvious. Her speech was peppered with phrases like "anon" and "prithee." Joan seldom displayed emotion beyond a perfunctory smile, but I got the sense she was glad to hand the night shift over to the new girl (me). Since Lady Vael lolled about doing nothing all day, it was far easier attending her during daylight hours.

"How long have you served the Vaels, Joan?" I asked one evening at dusk, as we piled a tray with dainties for our mistress. It was the only time of day our paths crossed.

Joan's blue eyes clouded. "Since the reign of King Henry, I think."

"Er, which one?"

She frowned. "The fat one with the wives. Or was it the one who fought the French? I . . . memory fails me." She grew angry after that and called me a dull, clumsy wench when I dropped one of the spoons.

I could have left it alone, but it felt important to know who she had been and how she'd ended up here. That night, when the Vaels were dancing and Halfglint lurked in his usual place behind the throne, I contrived to ask him about Joan.

"She made her bargain during the plague years," he told me. "Couldn't bear to see her beauty fade." His face held something between amusement and contempt. "Eternal youth, eternal service. A fair exchange, wouldn't you agree, Katherine?"

I thought of Nan, with her red lipstick and finger waves, her body crooked but her spirit still burning bright. It's a terrible thing to fear death so much that you'd rather be a pretty mannequin going through the motions. That's when I stopped being afraid of Joan and pitied her instead.

As the days blurred by, I noticed a growing tension within the court. There was the possibility that Winteregg could turn up at any moment, and the Vaels argued about him constantly. Yet their opinions changed as often as Lady Vael's gowns.

One night, Lord Vael might declare, "If Winteregg appears, we should hear his offer. The wizard was clever, if nothing else. He certainly managed to outwit the others."

The next, he'd say something like, "Winteregg is a liar and a rogue. If he dares set foot in our realm, we shall strip him of his stolen power immediately."

Lady Vael was equally mercurial, sometimes backing an alliance, other times violently opposing it. Their quarrels rippled through the court, causing factions to form and dissolve with bewildering speed.

Princess Maeryn spoke of Winteregg too, but with fascination. She'd often corner me when her parents were occupied, asking questions. "They say Winteregg was handsome, with piercing blue eyes and silver hair. Is it true?"

"I do not know, my lady," I replied honestly. "There were no portraits of him at the Chalet."

Maeryn sighed. "I wish I could visit the other courts. Have you been to any?"

"Just the Vale of Cherry Blossoms," I replied.

Her eyes widened. "Did you meet Elowyn and Clove?"

I nodded.

"Poor Elowyn," she said. "I hear she is very beautiful. Yet all know of the curse that was laid upon her by her aunt Morana."

A jolt of electricity went through me at the name: *Morana.*

Perhaps it was because I was in the Otherworld, but suddenly my memories of the trip with Layla spilled forth like an onrushing tide. I remembered Hanter Noz, and Night's Labyrinth, and the horned children . . . and the black-veiled witch who called herself Mother Mora.

That's what I meant to tell Adrien! I cursed my own foolishness. I should have expected to forget and written it down. But now I had yet another reason to escape the Vaels.

"Katherine?" Maeryn pouted. "Are you listening?"

"Ah, of course, princess." I propped my chin on my hands and gazed at her adoringly, which she liked very much.

"Mother and father *never* let me travel," she confided. "They say the other courts can't be trusted, but I do wish I had more friends." Her face brightened. "When Winteregg comes, perhaps he'll take me away with him. Wouldn't that be exciting?"

"Terribly," I agreed, thinking it was that blasted wizard's fault I was trapped in this realm.

Maeryn covered a yawn. "Fetch me a honeycomb," she said.

I wound through the dancing courtiers toward a long table laden with delicacies. My empty stomach growled at the sight. I hadn't eaten a bite all day. The honeycomb looked tempting, but beside it sat a basket of soft white bread, still steaming, that made me faint with hunger.

I glanced around to ensure no one was watching. Then I broke off a small piece of bread. I furtively reached into my bodice and extracted one of the last salt packets. My fingers trembled as I dropped a pinch onto the crust before popping it into my mouth.

The bread was every bit as delicious as it looked, but the salt scourged my tongue—a sharp, clean taste that cut through the haze that had been settling over me all evening. I felt more alert immediately.

A sudden sensation of eyes made my skin crawl. Halfglint was staring at me from across the clearing. My heart raced as he threaded a path between the dancers, his strange gaze never leaving my face. I expected him to drag me to Lady Vael, but instead he held out a hand.

"Would you honor me with a dance, Katherine?"

What new mockery was this? "I . . . but Princess Maeryn wants a honeycomb," I stammered.

"The princess can wait," he replied. "Look, she has already forgotten."

Indeed, Maeryn was flirting with a tall, dark-haired man who resembled Richard—she had a type, apparently. The bells on her masque tinkled as she threw her head back and laughed.

"Very well," I said, surprising myself.

Halfglint took my hand. Despite his grotesque appearance, he danced with grace. I was just thinking he wasn't so bad after all when he bent close to my ear. His breath was hot. "I know about your little trick with the salt," he whispered. "Quite clever."

I stumbled, but his hand pressed into my back. "Don't stop," he murmured. "She's watching."

Lady Vael had paused to observe us, eyes glittering behind a white swan masque.

"Are you going to tell her?" I asked bluntly, matching his whisper.

A cunning smile curved his lips. "Your secret is safe with me. I admire resourcefulness, even—perhaps especially—when it's directed against my masters."

We spun past a group of musicians playing flutes and drums. I felt a wave of dizziness and wished the song would end.

"It's no wonder Ravencroft prizes you so highly," Halfglint said. "You have a rare strength. Most mortals succumb within hours."

It seemed an odd thing to say, and an odd way to phrase it. "Thank you," I said uncertainly.

Halfglint inclined his head. "We are not all cruel, despite what the tales claim."

The music faded. He bowed to me, then straightened and strode away, leaving me alone as the next dance began. I retrieved the honeycomb and hurried to bring it to Princess Maeryn, then took my place at her mother's feet. She made no comment about the dance.

What did Halfglint have to gain by keeping my secret? Fae never helped mortals without demanding something in return. What game was he playing?

Something else nagged me, too. When I'd seen Halfglint through the standing mirror in the secret library, before we departed for the Riddle, I'd noticed scars. Thin white lines crisscrossing his knuckles. But tonight, his hands were unblemished.

I risked a glance across the clearing where Halfglint stood in conversation with Lord Vael. He must have cast a glamour to hide the scars. But why? Vanity seemed unlikely—he made no effort to alter his bizarre appearance.

Unless the scars revealed something he wished to conceal.

I observed him discreetly throughout the rest of the evening. He did not speak to me again, or even look my way. Mostly, Halfglint kept to himself. He dwelt on the periphery of power, always watching and listening yet never the centre of attention.

The more I studied him, the more convinced I became that something was *off* about the Vaels' chamberlain. A decision crystallized in my mind. When dawn came and the court dispersed, I would slip away and seek out Halfglint's chamber. Whatever the risk, it paled in comparison to what awaited me if I did nothing.

Of course, it would be far easier to search his rooms when he wasn't in them, but I had to attend Lady Vael every evening from dusk to dawn—and so did Halfglint. There must be clues there to explain his odd behavior and, perhaps, provide leverage I could use to improve my situation.

I had a single packet of salt left. About three days' worth, if I was frugal. After that, my empty smile would no longer be feigned. The thought terrified me more than any punishment Lady Vael might devise.

LADY VAEL RAISED HER ALABASTER ARMS, ALLOWING ME TO unlace the fastenings down her back. I hung the garment in a wardrobe and helped her don her daytime gown—a whisper of black silk. Then I picked up a boar-hair brush with a handle of smooth bone and began the hundred vigorous strokes she demanded each evening—or morning, as dawn was now upon us, painting the chamber in golden light.

"Did you enjoy the revel tonight, my lady?" I asked.

"Mmm," she responded, neither agreement nor disagreement. "The music was tolerable. The wine, adequate."

I continued the rhythmic brushstrokes. Then, casually: "Your chamberlain dances well."

Lady Vael studied me in the glass, her expression unreadable. "Halfglint is an ugly creature," she said. "But he can be clever and I find him useful. Why do you care?"

I lowered my eyes. "Forgive me, my lady. I'm only curious about how long he's served the court."

I thought she might erupt in a rage at my presumption,

but Lady Vael sniffed. "You mortals and your obsession with time," she said. "Always measuring, counting, dividing moments like a sack of flour. We do not concern ourselves with such trivial matters."

I kept brushing. "I suppose he had always served you, then?"

Her brow creased, and I feared I'd pushed too far. "Not always," she allowed, her tone suggesting the conversation held little interest. "He came to us from another court."

"Which one?

Her sharp gaze pierced me. "What is this sudden interest in my chamberlain?"

I donned a cow-eyed expression. "It's just that he is kind to me, milady."

Lady Vael's laughter rang out, a sound like silver chimes. "What a silly creature you are! One dance and you're smitten. Oh, this is delicious." She chuckled. "Mooning over Halfglint, of all people."

I finished brushing her hair and arranged it in a loose plait. "Pardon my foolishness. I know he doesn't return my regard."

She patted my hand indulgently. "Mortal hearts are easily swayed, though I fear your taste is questionable. There are far more appealing courtiers than Halfglint."

I considered asking her where to find his chambers but decided that would be too forward. Better to maintain this impression of harmless infatuation and seek my answers elsewhere.

I helped Lady Vael into her massive bed, carved from a single slab of black marble, and pulled the sheets to her chin. "Will there be anything else, my lady?"

"Close the blinds. It is far too bright!"

I did so, then moved toward the door. As I passed a small

table, my eye caught on a silver snuffbox. With a quick backward glance, I slipped it into the pocket of my dress. Lady Vael's eyes were shut, her white braid spilling across the pillows.

The corridor outside was quiet, most of the court now passed out in their own chambers. Sleep tugged at me like a strong undertow, but I passed my own room and made my way to the kitchens. Joan stood near the cold ovens, methodically working her way through a platter of sweets left over from the night's revel. She ate with single-minded dedication, shoving them into her mouth with little appearance of enjoyment.

"Good morning, Joan," I said, sliding onto the bench across from her.

She looked up, a glaze of sugar coating her lips. "You should be abed."

"I know," I sighed, resting my chin in my hands with a moony look. "But I can't stop thinking about . . . someone."

A spark of life stirred in Joan's eyes. Juicy gossip, it seemed, could penetrate even centuries of faerie enchantment.

"Who doth it be, child? You can tell old Joan."

I lowered my voice to a conspiratorial whisper. "I danced with Halfglint last night."

"Did you now?" Joan chewed thoughtfully. "That's most rare. He never dances."

"Well, he did with me." I pulled the silver snuffbox from my pocket. "I noticed he dropped this afterwards. I'd like to return it, but I don't know where his chambers are."

Joan's gaze fixed on the snuffbox, a frown creasing her forehead. "That looks like one of Lady Vael's pieces."

My heart stuttered. "Does it? Well, I am certain Halfglint dropped it. Perhaps Lady Vael gave it to him as a gift?"

"Why would she do that?" Her face tightened with suspicion. I reached for a sweet and offered it to her.

The distraction worked. Joan plucked the bun from my hands and shoved it into her mouth. "Them's me favourite," she said, the words muffled by chewing. "Cook makes 'em with honey from the savage bees."

I waited for her to take another bite before pressing: "About Halfglint's chambers?"

She swallowed. "Eastern wing. Shiny black door." She reached for another dainty. "But he don't like to be disturbed during daylight hours. Particular about his rest, that one."

"I'll be quick," I promised, pocketing the snuffbox. "Thank you, Joan."

"See you at eventide," she said with one of her ghastly smiles.

I left her to feast and hurried through empty corridors to the east side of the castle. A fresh wind propelled me—the thrill of rebellion after days of passive obedience. After a few wrong turns, I found it: a smooth black door of polished jet. I pressed my ear to the door and heard faint, rhythmic snoring. Halfglint was in there, but he was sound asleep.

My hand hovered over the knob. If he woke, I could pretend Joan had sent me on some errand. It was a weak excuse. Halfglint would see right through it. But if I didn't try now, I would lose my nerve.

Part of me hoped the door would be locked. If so, I could return to my chamber and collapse until tonight's revelry. But the knob turned easily and the door swung inward, revealing darkness beyond.

27

THE STORM BREAKS

I paused inside Halfglint's chamber, letting my eyes adjust. Like Lady Vael, he'd drawn thick curtains to block out the sun. It was gloomy, but enough light filtered through the crack that I could see it was much larger than my tiny broom closet and cluttered with furnishings.

Rasping snores drifted from beyond an archway.

I waited another minute to be certain, then crossed to a stone table and rifled through the mound of papers. It was too dark to read any of them. I set the snuffbox on the table and tried to open a large metal box. *Locked.* Forcing it would make a racket, so I didn't bother.

The snores from the bedchamber hitched. I dropped to a crouch, heart in my throat. After a few seconds, their rhythm resumed.

I held still for a long minute, looking around. There was the washbasin we'd seen him viewing his reflection in. It had no mirror above to shave. Did fae even grow hair on their faces? Lady Vael had mirrors *everywhere*. Perhaps Halfglint avoided looking at himself. Except that he *had* been, hadn't he?

My thoughts were chasing each other in circles. I covered a yawn. It was starting to feel like a fool's errand. What could I possibly hope to find? Yet something about the room felt odd. I realised it was the wardrobe pushed against the far wall. Nearly everything in the Vaels' castle was made of stone, but the wardrobe gleamed like rich wood.

I snuck over to open it and found a row of soft tunics and a second pair of the knee-high boots Halfglint favoured. I was about to move on and search elsewhere when I noticed a faint pulse of light at the back of the wardrobe, like a trapped firefly.

I pushed the tunics aside, rooting about in the darkness. My fingers brushed something that gave me a static shock. I grasped it and pulled. A cloak unfurled from the recesses of the wardrobe—one I recognised with a jolt. I had seen it frozen in ice at the Tempestarii archive. Tiny forks of lightning danced along its hem.

Hans Von Winteregg's storm cloak.

I silently pumped a fist of victory. I *knew* they were working together!

The cloak felt damp, as if its owner had just come in from the rain. It stirred restlessly, sending small shocks up my arms. I rifled through its deep pockets and felt a tangled ball.

The amulets! I shook them out. All nine were there. Richard's moonstone, the Questels' sapphire and emeralds, seven others set with precious stones representing each of the Venerable Bloodlines.

I felt like a bloody legend just then. Layla would die when I told her the story. With the moonstone amulet, I could slip out and try to find my way back through the barrow. Or should I bring the loot to the Vaels and expose their chamberlain's treachery? No, they'd just take it from me. And then send me for more wine.

I quickly returned the amulets to the cloak's deep pocket and bundled the whole thing into my arms. When I clutched it to my chest, it emitted a low rumble of thunder.

"Hush!" I hissed at it. "Be quiet, damn you . . ."

That's when I realised the room was dead quiet.

I turned, dread pooling in my stomach. Halfglint stood in the archway. His mismatched eyes—one silver, one a bruised violet—fixed on me. I tried to run, but my feet wouldn't budge. They were also cold. I looked down to find them encased in ice.

Halfglint raised his hand, and the cloak tore from my grasp. It sailed across the room like a living shadow and settled around his shoulders. "How clever you are, Katherine." His voice sounded deeper. More commanding. "I knew you were special."

I stared at his hands. The thin white scars that crisscrossed his palms and fingers. Too late, I understood what they were.

Lightning scars. Storm summoner's scars.

My own hands began to shake. I was afraid, but I was also *livid.*

"You're not working with Hans Von Winteregg," I shouted dramatically. "You *are* Winteregg!"

A smile curved his wide mouth. He had pointy teeth like a shark. Then he laughed with genuine mirth. "The Folk think they're so far above us, yet you're the first to see the truth in five centuries. None of those idiots at court have any inkling."

"How did you manage to trick the Vaels into believing you were fae?" I asked. My feet were frozen, but my hands remained free. If I could reach the last packet of salt hidden in my bodice . . .

"Exile teaches one many things," Winteregg said, pacing a slow circle around me. The cloak floated behind him, lightning dancing along its edges. "When the Tempestarii stripped me of my amulet, I fled into the deepest regions of Faerie. I wandered there for an age and met many strange Folk."

"Ah. You made a bargain."

He gestured to his face—Halfglint's face, with its divided features. "I traded my fine looks for the ability to pass. A steep price, but worth it."

"But why serve the Vaels if you despise them?"

His expression darkened. "It is not the Vaels I despise, but their vassals, the Ravencrofts," he spat. "I hate them with every fiber of my being. It was a Ravencroft who exposed my plans to the Tempestarii and orchestrated my downfall. For five hundred years I have nursed that hatred, plotting my revenge."

He stepped closer, close enough that I could smell the metallic reek of ozone on his breath. "Eventually I sought out the Court of Silver Shadows and gained their trust. Richard's parents were too powerful for me to confront directly, so I found another way to destroy them."

The pieces fell into place with sickening clarity. "The plot to depose the Queen," I whispered. "*You* were behind it!"

Winteregg's smile turned smug. "I manipulated them both—the Ravencrofts and the Footes. I promised wealth and power beyond their estates if they placed a changeling on the throne. Of course *I* was to be the changeling." He laughed. "Ransom and Desdemona never knew I was pulling their strings. But then I learned that they planned to expose the plot, once they had gathered enough evidence. Self-righteous fools."

How I hated this man. "So they *were* innocent!"

Winteregg scoffed. "They were arrogant and ambitious, like all Ravencrofts. But they weren't traitors—not in the way the authorities believed. When I realised what they intended, I ensured their own incriminating letters were delivered to the queen's spymaster. The evidence condemned them, and I danced a jig as they were forced into exile!"

All these years, Richard believed his parents had abandoned him for their own selfish ambitions. The truth would change everything—if I lived to tell it.

Then another thought occurred to me—this one even more infuriating. "Did you happen to enchant a man in the Wild Wood," I said slowly, "and turn him into a cat?"

Winteregg gazed at me in puzzlement. Then memory sparked in his cold eyes. He shrugged, as if turning a man into an animal were a trivial matter. "Oh, that. He stumbled upon a meeting of our little cabal. Overheard things he shouldn't have—talk of the queen, of the changeling who would replace her. I couldn't allow him to spread such tales."

My hands fisted. Richard's very first finding spell had led us to Halfglint. We'd believed it a mistake, but the spell hadn't failed after all—or it had failed only partly. Instead of finding Mr. Deen, it had found the one who cast the enchantment on him.

I wanted to wring Winteregg's scrawny neck. "I suppose it was you who sent that storm after us, too," I said.

He nodded gruffly. "I wanted Ravencroft to attend the Riddle, of course. But it was better for him to be uncertain and afraid. Off-balance." A smirk. "I hoped the other idiots would blame him for the theft of the amulets, and I wasn't disappointed."

"What *about* the amulets?" I pressed. "What do you plan to do with them?"

His smile turned grim. "I will destroy them," he replied. "All but my own. There's a deep crevasse in the Alps, hidden by snow and ice. I shall throw them in, one by one. Let the connections between the so-called Venerable Bloodlines unravel. I alone will retain my amulet, my access to Faerie."

"So you'll have no rivals," I said. "Well, that's spiteful."

"Yes," he agreed without a hint of remorse.

I tried to keep him talking while I figured some way out of this mess. "Then why haven't you done it yet?"

Winteregg studied me, his head tilted. "I had intended to remain in the mortal world after the frost imps brought me the amulets," he said. "I had grown weary of Faerie and wished to come home. But something unexpected happened. I found myself drawn back to the Court of Silver Shadows."

"Why?"

"Because of you," he said.

I blinked, certain I had misheard. "Come again?"

"You remind me so much of my Amelie," he said, his voice softening. "My beloved, lost when the Tempestarii banished me. You are the spitting image of her."

Winteregg stepped closer. "I know a place across the Amberjack Ocean, far from any courts. A cliff overlooking the sea where I will build my palace." He hesitated. "I will free you from Lady Vael's claim if you come with me. Be mine, Katherine, and we will rule together."

Well, *that* was unexpected. I stared at him, at a loss. Winteregg winced and raised a scarred hand to his face. "I know I am an ugly man. Would it help if I showed you how I once appeared?"

His features warped and shifted. The man who stood before me now was handsome, I suppose, with a fine-boned face and silver hair that fell in waves to his shoulders. But his glacier-blue eyes held ruthless ambition. Here was the monster who had destroyed Richard's family. Who had enchanted my best friend's father and never spared him a second thought.

I wanted to spit at his feet and declare my undying hatred, but that would gain me nothing. "I must think," I said in a breathy voice. "This is all so sudden."

"Of course, my dear. But you must make your choice quickly. I mean to leave this place, and Lady Vael will soon be calling for you."

I bit my lip. "You would rescue me from eternal servitude?"

He held out a hand, triumphant. "We will rule side by side, Katherine."

I lowered my lashes. "Then . . . the answer is yes, my lord."

The ice around my feet melted all at once. Water rushed across the stone floor as Winteregg released me. I smiled at him—then aimed a kick between his legs and lunged for the door. I was almost there when his hand closed around my arm. He yanked me back, arm locking around my waist like an iron band.

"You and Ravencroft deserve each other," he growled in my ear. "If you will not come willingly, then I will leave you frozen in a block of ice for Joan to find!"

28

LARKSPUR

I twisted in Winteregg's iron grip. The air had turned bitterly cold. He was a storm summoner, of course, the strongest who had ever lived.

My body grew numb and clumsy, and I thought of the wizards on Feenacht, encased in ice. Before I met the same fate, I reached into my bodice, fumbling for the last salt packet.

"Stupid girl," Winteregg hissed. "You could have been a queen!"

My fingers found the packet. I tore it open with my teeth and flung the contents into his eyes. Winteregg howled, staggering backward. "You little viper!" he snarled, tears streaming down his cheeks.

The door was right there, promising escape from this nightmare. But then I thought of Richard, and all the other families stripped of their birthrights. I couldn't leave the amulets behind.

Instead of fleeing, I grabbed at the storm cloak billowing around Winteregg's shoulders. It writhed in my grasp, sparking electric jolts up my arms. I gritted my teeth and yanked harder.

"Get off!" Winteregg roared, half-blind but still dangerous. We reeled across the room in a parody of our earlier dance, wrestling for control of the cloak.

A muffled thump came from the wardrobe, followed by a scraping sound. I barely had time to wonder what fresh horror he had conjured when the doors burst open and a man tumbled out. My Richard, dark hair rumpled and looking as astonished to see me as I was to see him.

His face hardened as he took in the fact that Winteregg was gripping my waist. "Let her go," Richard said flatly.

Winteregg spun toward his voice. His salt-reddened eyes held pure hatred. Then he began to laugh. A terrible sound—brittle and sharp, like icicles shattering.

"Lord Ravencroft," Winteregg cried. "Come to rescue his lady love!"

He released me with a shove that sent me stumbling into the stone table. "Think you're a match for me, boy?" Winteregg's hands rose, revealing his lightning-scarred knuckles. "You might be a storm summoner like your parents, but I wield power beyond your comprehension."

The air crackled with electricity. The drapes blew open and the sky beyond darkened to unnatural twilight.

"You're nothing," Winteregg spat. The glamour fell away and he looked like Halfglint again, his divided face twisting with contempt. "A footnote to a lineage I will soon erase forever."

A squall of wind and rain roared through the chamber, tearing papers from the desk and hurling them like white birds caught in a gale. It struck Richard full-force, driving him to his knees.

My gaze fell on the silver snuffbox I'd stolen from Lady

Vael. I picked it up and threw it as hard as I could. It struck Winteregg between the eyes with a satisfying crack. He staggered, his concentration broken.

I seized the opportunity to jump on his back. We crashed to the floor, my knee slamming with a crack that hurt like hell. Ignoring the pain, I jammed my hand into the sodden pocket of his cloak. My fingers closed around the tangle of amulets.

Winteregg shouted curses and imprecations. He bucked beneath me, but I held fast. With one sharp tug, I tore the amulets free—all nine of them, their chains wound together like some strange metallic creature.

"Richard!" I called, and threw the entire messy ball across the room.

He caught them one-handed. The moment he touched the moonstone, it began to pulse with an inner light. Winteregg shoved me off with a grunt. He staggered to his feet, the storm cloak crackling around him, and redoubled his assault—wind, rain, lightning, and hail, all aimed at Richard with murderous intent.

This time, Richard was ready. Thick, woody roots erupted from the ground at his feet, branching out in all directions. Some curled around his legs, anchoring him against the onslaught. Stone cracked as the roots delved down. Richard swayed, bending but not broken.

"What is this?" Winteregg muttered. "But . . . it cannot be."

For the first time, he looked afraid. He turned to flee, but roots snaked across the floor. They coiled around him like snakes, binding him in a living cage. Winteregg cursed, straining against his prison. The wind died.

"Give me back my amulet!" he screamed.

"You've done enough harm," Richard said calmly. "It's over."

The door flew open with a crash. Lord and Lady Vael stood on the threshold, flanked by guards in enameled silver plate, arrows nocked to bowstrings. Lady Vael surveyed the room with icy astonishment. "Halfglint?" she demanded. "What is the meaning of this?"

Winteregg scowled through the bars of his cage.

"He's not Halfglint, Your Majesty," I replied. "He never was. This is Hans Von Winteregg. He's been lying to you for years, using a glamour to pass as Folk."

Lady Vael's face froze. "A mortal?" she said faintly. "In my court?"

"I'm afraid so." I darted a look at him. Winteregg glared back. "In fact, his exact words were . . ."

"Go on," Lord Vael snapped.

"He said, 'None of those idiots at court have any inkling.'"

Lady Vael's eyes could have frozen lava. She made a curt gesture. The roots slithered down into the cracks and her guards seized Winteregg, whose expression had gone as blank as Joan's. "Please, your majesties," he whispered. "I can explain . . ."

"Silence!" Lord Vael commanded.

A flush crept across Lady Vael's pale skin as she turned to her husband. "If word gets out that we harbored a mortal impostor, we'll be a laughing stock!"

"Then the other courts must never learn the truth," Richard said. "I vow not to speak a word of it." His smile was hard as frost. "If you agree to release Kitty from your service."

The royal couple exchanged a look, communicating in the wordless way of those who have spent centuries together. Lord Vael cleared his throat. "She may return with you," he said stiffly. "After you dance with our daughter, as promised."

"I would be honored," Richard said. And just like that, he managed to get what he wanted from these cunning, capricious beings.

Lady Vael studied him with a narrowed gaze. "The magic you wield is unusual for a Ravencroft."

Quiet pride lit Richard's face. "I am a tree wizard," he said. "I have found my path."

"Hmmm," she said, with a lingering, thoughtful look. "It is not what I would have expected. But perhaps it suits you after all."

The guards dragged Winteregg away, his pleas for mercy fading down the corridor. The Vaels swept after them, leaving us alone. Richard crossed to me in three swift strides. He pulled me into an embrace so tight I could barely breathe. I pressed my face against his chest, listening to the beat of his heart.

"I thought I'd lost you forever," he said roughly.

"How on earth did you find a door into Halfglint's wardrobe?" I asked, my voice muffled against his shirt.

He pulled back. "I'll explain everything. But first, let's get this dance over with. Unless you wish to stay with Lady Vael?"

I laughed. "Thank you, no. I've drunk enough salted wine to last a lifetime." We were at the door when I remembered something. "Just wait a moment . . ."

Halfglint's papers were strewn about the room. I grabbed one at random found a quill and ink pot under the stone table. I dashed off a few words, folded the paper, and stuck it in my pocket. It said:

Mother Mora and the House of Echo

The court gathered to watch as Richard led Princess Maeryn through the steps of their belated dance. I hovered at the edge of the forest glade, no longer relegated to a cushion at Lady Vael's feet—my status now murky to everyone, including myself.

Richard matched Maeryn's grace, yet his manner was distant. His eyes never left mine, not even when the princess executed an elaborate turn designed to capture his attention. She noticed, of course. Her lips pressed together in a displeased line. When the music swelled to its conclusion, Maeryn squeaked and cast him a woeful look as if he'd stepped on her slipper, though I was certain he'd done no such thing.

Richard released her waist and bowed. She did not curtsy in return. Instead, she tossed her head. "Mortals are so clumsy," she said, her voice pitched to carry across the clearing. "I find I've lost interest in Lord Ravencroft. Our bargain is fulfilled and need not be renewed next year."

I bit the inside of my cheek to keep from smiling. For all her immortal power, Maeryn was like any young woman whose pride had been wounded—determined to be the one doing the rejecting, rather than the rejected.

"As your heart desires, princess," Richard replied with perfect courtesy, though I caught the relief in his face.

Maeryn turned to her parents and launched into an impassioned argument about why they should let her visit other courts, particularly the Vale of Cherry Blossoms. "Everyone says their spring festival is magnificent. I've been cooped up here for decades. It's barbaric!"

As Richard crossed the clearing to join me, I caught sight

of Joan moving among the revelers with a tray of dainties. She gave me a vague smile. If she could have been saved, I would try to spirit her away, but she was beyond that. The Court of Silver Shadows was her home now.

I waved in farewell, but Joan had turned away.

"Ready?" Richard asked.

I nodded past the tightness in my throat.

We didn't take the path I expected—the one leading to King Arthur's barrow. Instead, he guided me along rough forest tracks until we reached an ancient yew with a trunk so wide that five people holding hands could not have encircled it.

"This way," he said, laying his palm against the papery bark. A narrow, dark crevice opened in the trunk. "Trust me."

I took his hand and together we stepped through.

For one dizzying moment, I tumbled end over end. Then my feet met solid ground. I blinked in the sudden glare of sunlight. Richard steadied me against him until my head stopped spinning. We stood in the meadow behind the inn, beside the oak Richard and I had planted together.

Except that . . .

"It's huge!" I exclaimed, craning my neck to marvel at the tree's spreading crown. "And it's still green." I frowned. "How many days have I been gone?"

"Not still green," he said gently. "Green *again*. Winter came and went. It's been more than six months."

I reeled at this news. "It seemed no more than a fortnight." I immediately thought of Nan. She *was* ninety-two. "Everyone is well in the village?"

"Perfectly, except for the fact that its heart and soul was gone."

I blushed. "Tell me what happened. All the way from the beginning."

Richard's face darkened. "I woke to find you gone. First, I tore the house apart, though I knew it was useless. I . . . will not dwell on the despair that took me. Suffice to say I decided to follow Nyx's advice and sit by the tree. There was nothing else to do."

"And?"

"The dryad did not show herself."

"What did you do then?"

"I stayed."

"For how long?"

He laid a hand on the trunk. "One hundred and fifty-eight days."

I was stunned. "You? Richard Ravencroft?"

He grinned. "Like the Buddha under his Bodhi tree."

I squinted. "Are you certain you're not a changeling?"

"Briar brought food. Layla came, too, just to quietly sit. She always believed in me."

"Did you grow a beard?"

"Down to my waist," he replied solemnly. "Sparrows built a nest in it."

"That sounds nice." I thought of the little birdhouse Mr. Deen had affixed below the eaves of the inn before he'd vanished. Every spring, the house sparrows cleaned it out and started new families. "Their babies are awfully noisy though. They must have woken you early with their cheeping to be fed."

He laughed. "I might have made up that bit. But I did sit here for nearly six months."

"Like our very own Green Man."

Richard looked pleased. "I did slip into the Dancing Toadstool for a bath every so often. I didn't want to offend the dryad."

"Well, that's a relief," I said lightly, though his sacrifice touched me. "What about your doctor duties?"

"I took a leave of absence. Dr. Harlow from Southlea Cross filled in for me." He looked thoughtful. "After a while I stopped noticing the passage of time. I only knew I had to wait. And one day, she came." His expression softened. "I offered to bind my heart and magic if she would help me. She said she didn't have that power, but the tree did, and she asked it to accept my offer."

I stared at the oak with grateful awe. "And it agreed?"

Richard nodded. "It granted me passage through wood—any wood, anywhere, living or dead. Though it's uncommon luck that the door led to Winteregg's wardrobe."

"I know why. It's the only wooden thing in the Vaels' castle. Everything else is metal and stone. Winteregg must have conjured it to hide the cloak and amulets." I shuddered, thinking how close I'd come to being his next victim. "Your timing *was* fortunate."

"Very," Richard agreed.

"There's something I need to tell you." I took a deep breath. "Winteregg confirmed that your parents were innocent of the plot to kidnap the queen. In fact, they were planning to expose it. Winteregg framed them after he learned what they intended. He'd nursed a grudge against your family that went back centuries, and your parents were just pawns in his game of revenge."

I expected the storied Ravencroft temper to erupt, but Richard looked thoughtful. "I always hoped there was more to the story," he said. "It's a relief to finally know the truth."

"You're not furious?"

He shrugged, and I saw just how much he'd changed in the time I was away. That nervous energy, that barely-contained intensity, had transformed into something steadier. "I am angry at Winteregg," he admitted. "Of course I am. But I've had enough of grudges."

I patted his hand. "Did Layla lend you that book she has by the Dalai Lama?"

Richard laughed. Then he darted a glance at the oak and leaned to my ear, his voice the barest whisper. "I know her name, Kitty. It's Larkspur."

He sat down with his back against the tree. I joined him. We listened to the wind stir the boughs. Cloud-shadows moved across the meadow. At dusk, a twiggy creature crept out, with bark-like skin and tangled hair the red of new buds. She was smaller than Nyx and far wilder. She stared at me with beetle-dark eyes.

"Thank you," I said quietly.

Larkspur fled back into the tree.

"She'll speak to you someday," Richard said, rising to his feet and offering me his hand. "Maybe in a decade or so."

I laughed. We had all the time in the world. Not the endless, meaningless stretch of eternity that Joan faced, but the finite span of mortal days to be savored and filled with meaning.

We entered the Dancing Toadstool together, following the homey scents of bread and wood smoke. The common room erupted in cheers—the entire village seemed to have gathered, waiting with stubborn hope for our return. Nan rose from her chair by the fire, her red velvet smoking jacket matching her lipstick. Dr. Singer beamed beside her. Briar and Layla rushed forward to mush me between them.

"Thank god," Layla whispered. "We were about to go commando and mount a full-scale invasion."

Mrs. Deen wiped tears on her apron. Her husband winked at me. His eyes were the mellow gold of autumn tansy, and he looked happy. Charlotte de Berry stood regally beside the hearth, wrapped in a silk shawl of rose-gold. I disengaged myself and approached her.

"You saved me, Madame," I said softly. "You above all."

She smiled. "*Marcher avec un ami dans le noir est mieux que de marcher seul dans la lumière.* It means that walking with a friend in the dark is better than walking alone in the light. Helen Keller said that. I am glad I could walk with you, Kitty, if only in spirit."

I embraced her. "Thanks to you, I was never alone."

"I knew he'd bring you back," Nan said, her voice thick. I turned and she pulled me into a fierce hug. "Boots don't stay lost for long."

Richard had his share of admirers, too. I caught his eye across the crowded room. His grin held the promise of laughter and talk and kisses and dinners, a future to be built together. One that was perfectly, wonderfully ordinary.

29

TANGLED UP WITH FAERIES

Three days of rest and Mrs. Deen's cooking did wonders for my waifish, raccoon-eyed appearance, though I still had trouble falling asleep before dawn, like a veteran nightclub promoter forced to take the day shift.

The Deens had left that morning for a holiday in Ibiza and the inn was quiet—until Adrien arrived in a thunder of hoofbeats. He left his mount in the inn's old stable, which Layla had refurbished to house Rainbow Dash, Applejack, Pip, and Twilight Sparkle. The life-sized My Little Ponies were now the pride of the village, and she delighted in riding Rainbow Dash to the Southlea Cross public library and securing her steed to the bike rack while she used their free internet.

"This little inn grows more charming every time I visit," Adrien remarked, sprawling in an armchair by the cold hearth. "Perhaps I shall buy a cottage nearby."

"I thought you hated the English gloom," Layla reminded him. She was lolling in the window seat, reading a book.

"I do," he said cheerfully. "I shall come when I am feeling blue and want to wallow in misery."

"You could rent my parents' cottage," I said. "It's in need of a tenant."

My mother and father were semi-famous artists who traveled so often I hadn't seen them in more than three years.

"Perfect!" Adrien exclaimed. "My very own pied-à-terre in Little Groating. My solicitor will make the arrangements." He turned to Richard. "Now where is it, cousin? Jean-Marie's bald spot is getting bigger every day, and he's taken up smoking again. Imagine being the first Questel in fourteen generations to lose the amulet."

Richard handed over the gorgeous sapphire surrounded by emeralds; Adrien kissed it like a holy relic and hung it around his neck. The rest of the amulets sat in one of Nan's old cigar boxes.

"The question remains," Richard said, his own moonstone gleaming at his throat, "how do we return them without Grimaldi claiming it's proof I stole them in the first place?"

I snorted. "He'd love that. Another chance to blame the Ravencrofts for everything wrong in the world."

Nan slapped her knee. "Just mail the blasted things! Pop them in the post with a nice note. 'Found this lying about, thought you might want it back. Cheers, a concerned citizen.'"

Richard barked a laugh. "We may have no other choice—"

A loud thump came from the kitchen, followed by Quince's outraged voice. "I keep telling them, but they won't listen! My sitting room is *not* a public thoroughfare!"

Richard, bless him, moved to stand in front of me. A ball of blue flame materialized in Adrien's palm, and Layla raised her heavy book. Together, we cautiously entered the kitchen.

Briar was in there making garlicky hummus. She gripped the whisk like it was a medieval mace.

"What's going on, darling?" Layla whispered.

Briar made a face and shrugged.

The pantry door stood open. I spotted two figures—one tall and human, the other small and brownie-shaped.

"Sorry about that, mate," said Charlie Maikori, brushing flour from his hoodie. "Took a wrong turn at the roundabout."

Quince bristled and jabbed a finger at Charlie's knee. "Do I barge into your home without so much as a by-your-leave? Do I traipse across your grandmother's carpet in muddy boots? This is private property, you oversized, inconsiderate—"

"I've got some jade buttons," Charlie interrupted in a placating tone, pulling a small pouch out of his satchel. "From the Shanghai market. Antiques, dead rare."

Quince's tirade halted mid-syllable. He snatched the pouch and peered inside. "Well. That's . . . an acceptable toll. But have the grace to knock next time!" With that, he stormed off to his cupboard, the pouch clutched to his chest.

Charlie gave us a wave. "Sorry to turn up like this. Kitty, Layla. Hope I'm not interrupting."

Layla lowered her book and clapped him on the shoulder. "We're glad to see you, Charlie. I suppose it's about the amulets."

He nodded. "The Vaels turned Hans Von Winteregg over to the Tempestarii. They seemed anxious to be rid of him. He's imprisoned in the cloud fortress. All very hush-hush, top secret stuff. The frost imps he bribed to do his bidding have been rounded up as well."

Winteregg/Halfglint occasionally haunted my dreams. I was glad to know he was locked up tight.

"Well, that's good news," Richard said, brightening. "Er, sorry, I'm Richard Ravencroft."

They shook. "Nice to meet youse," Charlie said. He looked at Adrien. "And you're a Questel."

Adrien smiled modestly. "Is it the hair? Or my sea-blue eyes?"

Charlie looked amused. He touched his throat. "Ah, your amulet . . ."

Adrien laughed. "Of course."

"Speaking of which," Richard said, "will Deema take the rest of them off my hands? I don't want to be the one to return them."

"Perfectly natural," Charlie said. "She hopes you'll come back with me to the Cloud Palace. She'd like to thank you herself. We'll just nip over. You'll be there and back in a blink."

Truth be told, I was getting bored. "I'll go with you," I said to Richard. "I'd like to see Deema."

"That's not all." Charlie's gaze shifted to Layla. "There's a job if you want it."

"As a courier?" Layla's face lit up with such delirious joy that I couldn't help smiling.

"Aye," Charlie said with a grin. "Welcome to the faerie version of MI6."

"Hang on, now," Briar cut in, looking anxious. "We all know what happens to people who get tangled up with the Fair Folk."

Layla moved to her side. "Most things worth doing carry risk, love," she said. "I've spent my life learning everything there is to know about the fae. All to find Dad. Now that he's back . . . I suppose I'm not sure what to do with myself."

"We run the shop together," Briar said, looking a bit hurt. "And you write books! We have a life."

"I know," Layla said. "And I love our life! If you really don't want me to, I won't. You're what I care about most in this world. But I hope you'll think about it. It would mean a lot."

Something shifted in Briar's expression—a reluctant understanding. She was terrified of losing Layla the way Sanaja had lost Arush, but she didn't want to stand in her way, either. "Dammit, you know how to get me, don't you?"

"Would you be willing to meet Deema?" Layla asked. "Learn more before we decide?"

Charlie cleared his throat. "No one said you couldn't bring guests, so it's fine by me if the lot of youse tag along."

Briar hesitated, then nodded. "Fine. But I'm reserving judgment until I know more."

As we prepared to leave, I pulled Adrien aside and told him about the woman in black we'd met at the House of Echo who called herself Mother Mora. I still had the note I'd written to myself, just in case, but I'd remembered even without it. Just as I remembered what had happened at the Court of Silver Shadows. Maybe I was getting better at resisting the dreamy magic of the Folk.

Adrien looked solemn, as if he feared getting his hopes up. But he said he would tell Elowyn the next time he went to the Vale of Cherry Blossoms—which I had a feeling would be very soon. He bid us all goodbye and collected his horse to ride back to France via the Wild Wood.

After we spoke, I caught Richard watching me. "What is it?" I asked.

"Nothing," he replied with quiet wonder. "I'm just glad to have you home."

As promised, the journey to the Cloud Palace was quicker than I expected. Charlie knocked on Quince's pantry and made a long, flowery speech begging his pardon and asking if we might pop through. With a sniff, the brownie allowed us to troop through his sitting room to the back door, which led into the Wild Wood.

Two doors later, we were at the lighthouse, and from there it was a quick stroll to the Chalet. The Tempestarii palace floated above, anchored by massive golden chains that stretched away into the azure sky. It reminded me of a great ship nearing port, the way the storm petrels swooped and dived about the battlements. Hans Von Winteregg was in there somewhere. How *awful* it must be for him to see his former Chalet just across the way. A constant reminder of all he'd lost.

I smiled.

"Impressive, aye?" Charlie said.

Briar had stopped dead, her mouth forming a perfect O of astonishment. "That's not—it can't—how is it—" She paused to draw a breath. "It's beautiful. Like a painting by Maxfield Parrish."

We coaxed her across the bridge of mist, where the kobold Nirith escorted us to the archive. Deema waited in her damp greatcoat and floppy, broad-brimmed hat. The snow leopard Ghost circled us twice, sniffing, then sat down with a chuffing sigh.

"Welcome," Deema said, "to all. A disaster has been averted, and it is thanks to you." Her gaze took in me and Richard. "Winteregg signed a confession to his numerous crimes. Copies will be sent to the authorities—mortal and wizard. I believe, Lord Ravencroft, that your parents' exile will soon be over."

Richard released an uneven breath. "That is . . . " He

cleared his throat. "Very welcome news." He stepped forward and gave Deema the cigar box. "I entrust these to your custody."

She nodded gravely. "They will be returned to their rightful owners with the simple explanation that they were recovered from Hans Von Winteregg."

Richard looked relieved. "Thank you."

Deema turned to Layla. "I assume Charlie already conveyed my offer?"

"He did." Layla stood up a little straighter. "I just have a few questions. First, can I stay in the village? I run a shop there with my wife. I won't abandon it. Or her. So I'd prefer part-time, if you've got it." She flashed a nervous grin. "I'll skip the medical and dental, paid sick leave and such, but I can't work *every* day."

Deema stared at her.

"Ah, she's pulling your leg there," Charlie said.

"I see. Mortal humour." Deema didn't smile. "You need not work every day. In fact, weeks might pass without a summons. But Charlie told me there is a faerie door at the local inn, which would make it easy for you to come and go. I will send a storm petrel if I want you. If you cannot answer the summons, you are free to decline, and I will find another courier. Let me be clear: It is *not* a binding contract."

Briar looked very glad at this, and Layla looked glad that *she* was glad.

"The courier's life is not without risk," Deema added, "but you won't travel alone, not at first. Charlie has offered to train you until you know the ways better."

Layla shot him a grateful look. "Honestly, I feel like I've spent my whole life waiting for this without even knowing it existed."

"Most of us have side jobs," Charlie put in. "I teach jujitsu classes at a dojo in Edinburgh when I'm not running messages."

"We pay our couriers well," Deema added. "In gold."

Briar turned to Layla, taking her hands. "The Deen family seems fated to live with one foot in this world and one in Faerie," she said with a wry smile. "I'm part of that family now, so standing in the way is futile. Plus, I want you to be happy. If this is what you truly want, I'll support you all the way."

Layla lit up and hugged her tight. When they finally parted, Deema presented Layla with her own Atlas, bound in red cloth with gold lettering. "Welcome to the courier corps," she said. "May your feet stay on the road—and the monsters stay in the shadows."

Briar frowned. "Monsters?" she muttered. She opened her mouth like she might object after all, but Layla already had the Atlas, and Charlie was shaking her hand. "We'll get you navigating the trickier routes in no time," he promised.

They clustered together, discussing courier protocols. Richard took my hand and led me onto a balcony overlooking a sea of clouds that stretched to the horizon.

"We've scarcely had a moment alone since you came back," he said.

I'd been either sleeping or surrounded by well-wishers since our return. Now I turned to study him. "Lady Vael was right. Tree magic suits you. I would never have guessed so, but it does."

"I still have a hundred questions," he admitted. "Adrien suggested I write to Nikos and Chara Kazan. They're both accomplished tree wizards and he says they'd be happy to help me." He tugged a hand through his dark hair. "I did some reading in the family archives. Did you know my great-great-grandmother Felicia was a tree wizard? The talent can skip many generations and suddenly pop up."

"Your affinity found its way home," I said with a smile.

"Exactly." His expression grew serious. "What about you, Kitty? Are you happy?"

"More than I can explain," I said honestly.

"I noticed you haven't restarted your walking tours," he said, watching me.

I shrugged, trying to seem casual, though I did miss them. "Well, with your estate closed, it's not quite as much of an attraction."

"What if it wasn't?" he asked. "What if we brought your tours back to Ravencroft Hall? The grounds, the house—all of it."

I blinked in surprise. "Are you sure about that? I seem to remember you saying you didn't want to be, and I quote, *gawked at*."

"By other wizards," he said. "I don't care if it's a retired couple from Sussex with sensible walking shoes and binoculars dangling around their necks. Kitty, don't you know by now that I would do anything to make you happy?"

I threw my arms around him, seized by simple happiness that made my chest hurt. Leading walking tours might not be the exciting, glamorous life of a courier, but it was mine. All I wanted was to amble the old, familiar paths, tell the old stories, and have a kind man waiting for me at the end of each day.

30

IN WHICH I AM QUITE CONTENT

Richard insisted on lifting the mild curse his ancestor had placed on the gargoyles. He meant to be helpful, but I felt nostalgic for the old watery bowels and sweaty palms. They'd been part of the vintage Ravencroft Hall experience.

On the positive side, no one peed their pants upon crossing the boundary anymore. And I didn't have to worry about clients with heart conditions and anxiety disorders.

"The gargoyles date back to the sixteenth century," I told the group as we strolled past with nary a twinge of unease. "They were enchanted by Barnabas Ravencroft to drive away unwanted visitors, but the new master of the Hall has generously made the sentinels more tour-friendly."

A girl of about ten with glasses too large for her face (she reminded me of Layla at that age) tugged on my sleeve. "Are they alive, miss?" she asked. "Do they move when no one's looking?"

I dropped my voice so her mum couldn't hear. "On moonless nights, yes. But don't worry, the master keeps them well-fed with raw meat so they won't hunt teenagers who sneak out to snog each other."

"Blimey," she said with a happy shiver.

Today's group was a typical mix: a retired gay couple from Sussex with matching Cheaney boots and high-mag Viking Peregrine binoculars (how on earth did Richard know?); a hedge fund type wearing a watch worth more than my annual income; a university student researching folklore for her thesis; and a mother with two children—the girl who'd asked about the gargoyles and her sticky-looking brother.

Rounding out the group was an athletic woman in her fifties named Linda, clad in neon yellow lycra and a spray-tan. This was her third tour with me. She was super nice and a big tipper.

"The Hall has been owned by the Ravencroft family for centuries," I said. "But the grounds have only recently been reopened to visitors, thanks to the current lord's progressive views."

We crested a low hill overlooking the manor. Phone cameras started clicking away, but they weren't pointed at the Grade II property of "special architectural and historic interest." They weren't even filming the topiary beasts, who romped off in the distance like overgrown puppies.

No, it was the two men on the lawn who were the focus of my amateur paparazzi.

I had to admit that Richard and Adrien made a striking pair—one dark and scowling, the other golden-haired and gesturing vehemently as they argued at the net.

"That's Lord Ravencroft," I said, "and his cousin, Adrien de Questel, visiting from the south of France." I chuckled. "Don't let appearances fool you, they're quite close."

Richard made a rude hand sign and threw his racket to

the ground. Adrien tossed his arms up in disgust. Then he lit a cigarette and began to gesture angrily with *that*. He wore mirrored aviator sunglasses and snug white shorts and a white polo, and looked like he'd wandered out of a Ralph Lauren photo shoot from 1986.

"Is that a tennis court?" the uni student asked. "Why are the lines moving?"

"It's wizard tennis," I explained. "A bit different from the regular kind."

The violent argument subsided. Adrien retreated to the service line, while Richard swayed like a cobra on the other side of the court, sweatband pulled low on his forehead. The ball—a poisonous green with tiny sharp teeth—let out a derisive laugh as Adrien whacked it.

"You call that a serve?" the ball screamed as it sailed across the net. "My grandmother hits harder, and she's been dead for fifty years!"

The kids tugged at their mother's hands, desperate to get closer. I led the group to a reasonably safe vantage point and hoped no one would get bitten (although I made sure they'd all signed legal waivers ahead of time).

Richard spotted me, his smile warming my chest like a sip of brandy on a winter's night. Adrien, unable to resist showing off for a crowd, executed a between-the-legs shot that sent the ball whizzing across the net.

"Mind your feet, you feckin' idiot!" the ball shrieked. "I don't need a view of yer hairy bollocks!"

Richard returned it with a powerful backhand and the cousins volleyed for a minute—until the ball's ceaseless taunts finally made him snap. He spewed back a torrent of abuse that made the young mother say, "Oh my," and vainly try to cover her children's ears.

"It's not *my* fault you hit like a first-year apprentice!" the ball whined.

Richard's expression darkened. Apparently, his newfound "tree wizard serenity" only stretched so far. His next forehand lobbed the ball high over our heads. We all craned to watch it go, a dwindling speck against the sky, still shrieking obscenities as it disappeared over the hill in the direction of the bog.

There was a distant splash.

"That's not very sporting, cousin," Adrien called, leaning on his racquet with a grin.

Richard shrugged. "Oops," he said. "I suppose that one's out."

"Don't worry, love, I'll fetch it!" Linda called over her shoulder, power-walking toward the bog. "I do triathlons, you know. I'll have it back in two ticks!"

I stared after her. Nelly, the hag who dwelt there, had promised not to eat anyone, but that was before we'd started pelting her pond with foul-mouthed tennis balls.

I glared at Richard, who had the grace to look sheepish. "Sorry," he mouthed with a wince.

Adrien didn't bother hiding his smirk, the wretched man. "Better hurry, Kitty."

I pictured Nelly rising from the depths, her long pale arms unfurling like naked branches. "Wait," I shouted. "That area isn't part of the tour!"

I sprinted pell-mell down the hill, braced for a scream of horror. But as I drew closer, I heard Linda's friendly voice. "Thanks *ever* so much," she was saying. "You're a doll!"

I breasted the hill and saw them, Linda jogging in place at the edge of the pond, Nelly floating among the rushes. Linda held up the ball.

My heart slowed its mad gallop. Nelly caught my eye,

then swam away, green hair trailing out in all directions. She wore a little smile as if to say, *See, I told you I wouldn't eat any middle-aged matrons.*

Now, if Linda had been a plump bairn . . . Well, it didn't bear thinking about.

"She's quite a lovely hag," Linda called to me as she power-walked back up the hill. The ball tried to nip her and she gave it a brisk shake. "I don't see what all the fuss is about."

"You're not in least bit bothered by . . . the arms?" I asked.

"Pshaw. I wish I had a Nelly in my local pond." She winked. "Now, there used to be a Jenny Greenteeth back in my grandfather's day. Hid under the duckweed until you came very close . . ."

She chattered away as we returned to the group, and I wondered if I ought to hire Linda as an assistant guide. She was clearly competent, and Nelly liked her. What did they call it on wilderness hikes? A sweeper. The person who hung about at the rear to make sure no one got left behind. Or eaten.

"What are you thinking, love?" Linda asked. "You looked awfully serious for a moment."

I smiled and squeezed her Lycra-clad arm. "Nothing. Just that I have the best job in England."

AFTERWORD

The Ravencroft Hall series will continue with Book #3 later this year. Join my newsletter and never miss a new release!

ABOUT THE AUTHOR

Kat Ross is an award-winning and bestselling fantasy author whose series range from the Persian-inspired Fourth Element to the cozy Ravencroft Hall books. She lives in Connecticut with her son and a gang (clowder?) of anarchist cats. When she's not writing, you can find Kat wandering in the woods or poring over maps in her cartography turret. For more info and to join her newsletter, check out Kat's author website: www.katrossbooks.com

instagram.com/katrossauthor
facebook.com/KatRossAuthor
bookbub.com/authors/kat-ross
pinterest.com/pinterest.com

ALSO BY KAT ROSS

The Fourth Element Trilogy

The Fourth Talisman Series

The Fourth Empire Series

Nightmarked Series

Lord of Everfell Series

Lingua Magika Trilogy

Gaslamp Gothic Collection

Some Fine Day (dystopian YA standalone)

www.ingramcontent.com/pod-product-compliance
Lightning Source LLC
LaVergne TN
LVHW091028080826
845145LV00002B/396

* 9 7 8 1 9 5 7 3 5 8 2 6 0 *